SCOUT AND THE LAVENDER GIRL

LOVE IN AUSTIN SERIES

K.C. LITTLETON

COPYRIGHT @ 2019 by K.C. Littleton

Cover Design: www.cateashwooddesigns.com

Copy Editing and Proofreading: oneloveediting.com

Formatting (Vellum): lescourtauthorservices.com

ALL RIGHTS RESERVED

This literary work may not be reproduced or transmitted in any form or by any means, including electronic or photographic reproduction, in whole or in part, without express written permission, except in the case of brief quotations embodied in critical articles and reviews.

This is a work of fiction and any resemblance to persons, living or dead, or business establishments, events or locales is coincidental.

The Licensed Art material is being used for illustrative purposes only.

For Amy (again), because I killed her in my first book.

1

EVIE

*S*hit.

Shitshitshitshit.

I try not to curse all that often, in deference to my late mother, but even she'd have to give me this one. Marge, my yellow ochre '84 Dodge Diplomat, looks like she tried (and failed) to have sex with the U-Haul ahead of us. I mean, my car is a piece of shit, but from what I can tell, she's now a totaled piece of shit half-buried under a U-Haul, and she's a piece of shit that I can't afford to fix or replace. And this is *so* totally my fault. I was rushing to work because I was running late because my side job for a delivery app had me up until 3:00 a.m. last night.

Dammit.

Sorry, Mom. That was the last one.

Not that the late hour made much of a difference—I was awake for the rest of the night because my ex had threatened me with a lawsuit if I didn't go back and finish overseeing the last build project I'd contracted with his family. It's a pretty worthless threat, but my brain really wanted to overthink it into absolute insomnia, finally allowing me to fall asleep at the last hour, only to ignore my alarm for thirty minutes. My brain is a jerk like that.

I pull out my phone and call my friend-boss at my day job.

"What's up, Evie? The 10:30 people are starting to line up." Her breezy tone calms me down and reminds me to breathe.

"I've been in an accident," I say as I eye the tall, lanky butch, wearing Doc Martens, black skinny jeans ripped at the knees, and a dark green hoodie, hopping down from her truck. She's Latina with medium-dark skin and a scowl that could slaughter grackles from ten paces. I look down at myself—I'm a double-digit hourglass with a femme style which borders on the performative, the kind of style a person who strides through traffic like an Aztec warrior would find wholly ridiculous.

I don't realize I've dropped the phone until I hear a voice yelling at me through the speaker. I fumble for it and pull it back to my ear. "Sorry! Kim! It's just a fender bender. I'm fine."

"Again?" she asks, concerned and mildly frustrated. "That's, like, the third fender bender in six months."

"Yep," I answer distractedly. "Hey, the person I hit is coming over, and she looks hella mad. Gotta go."

Close-up I can tell she's got a few years on me, with a razor blade for a jawline, murderous cheekbones, and dense, angled brows that sweep up and back. Her thick, black hair has one long streak of white at the part and is undercut with a long flop on top, and her tilted, almond-shaped eyes have mild, kinda sexy crinkling around them and are so dark I can't see her pupils. I check my hair in the mirror—I've been rocking the lavender pin curls for a while now, my makeup is on point, and my short, DIY manicure isn't too unfortunate. She taps on the glass with one very angry fingertip, and I notice she's got silver rings on almost all of her fingers. I let my eyes drift allll the way up her tall frame until we lock eyes. *Hello.*

I try to unroll the window, but whatever was holding Marge's aging electrical system together is no longer functioning, so I push up the automatic lock, which is A) no longer automatic, and 2) no longer working. This sucks for a number of reasons, the first of which is I've got the kind of knobs that sink flush with the door when locked. So, yeah, bit of a nightmare, and I'm trapped in my car with a scary-sexy monster dyke glowering down on me. My chest heats, then flushes as I look up at her again.

Oy. I like dykes. I really, really do.

I think.

Avoiding her eyes, I reach over to the lock / unlock flippy thing on the passenger side. I press down because without fail I will always go the wrong direction first (#storyofmylife). I press up and am rewarded with a buzzy death rattle that has me jerking back, just in case Marge has decided to electrocute me as a final "eff you" for half burying her under an unforgiving U-Haul. Thankfully I remain un-electrocuted, and though neither of the front locks budges, the driver's-side back door has popped its little head out about a quarter of an inch. I can work with that.

As I figure out the lock situation, agitation rolls like waves off the world's most annoyed lesbian. Even on the other side of the glass, her vibrating anger almost feels like warmth. "Sorry, I need to crawl through the back," I say through the glass, pointing to the back of my car as though she might have missed where that is.

Her broad, square shoulders rise and fall in a frustrated breath as she gestures impatiently for me to move it along. I shrug sheepishly, unbuckle my seat belt, and super awkwardly crawl toward the back. I have to angle to the side because my hips don't exactly fit between the seats, and have a moment of panic when I get stuck (temporarily), but then I put my feet on the dashboard and push myself through.

I finally right myself, and pinch-slip, pinch-slip, pinch-open the thin bullet-like lock in the back, and swing open the door, cracking, "I've been born again. Praise Jesus!" raising my hands in the air like I'm at a revival.

Oooh.

I maaaay have just offended a Jesus person, if her sharpening jaw is any indication. Be honest with you, I can't tell if I'm more turned on or intimidated by that. My nipples are rock hard, and I may have peed on myself a little—make of that what you will.

"I hope you fucking have insurance," she snarls, gesturing at Marge to indicate her lack of confidence. She flops her hair over to the other side as her dark eyes roam over the damaged hood. I hear a soft, annoyed *pinche madre* under her breath as the cars whizz by us.

Okay, maybe not a Jesus person.

"Um, yeah, I do. I've got my insurance card right, um..." I wrinkle my nose, thinking, then hold my finger up in the air. "I left it in my glove box. Along with my purse. Be right back." I give her a full smile, then make the awkward climb back into the front seat, grab my insurance card and purse, then immediately spill its contents all over the front seats. She leans over, her forearms resting on Marge's roof, staring down at me, tilting her jaw to indicate that her patience won't be making an appearance anytime soon. I lick my lips and force myself to focus on the problem at hand.

After taking a nervous minute to scoop up the belched innards of my purse, I rebirth myself into the back seat and swing open the door with a flourish. "That was even better the second time," I crack. "I'm for sure going to heaven now."

Zero reaction.

#awkward.

"Tough room," I mutter, *finally* netting an eyebrow raise.

The Austin traffic is starting to gather around us. The people are friendly enough, but this is a fairly popular overpass for accidents, and we've got to get out of the way.

Sorry, annoyed folks just trying to get to work. I suck. I know I do.

Gesturing in a let's-get-this-going circular motion, she asks, "Do you think you can at least move your car?"

I shake my head. "Pretty sure Marge is *dead* dead," I say, a little sadly.

Blowing out an exasperated breath, she asks, "Do you mind if I pull the truck out of the way?"

She's asking because that will definitely not make Marge any better. I nod and wait back by my car, where I decide that watching her walk away is at least as much fun as watching her walk toward me. I've mentioned the square shoulders, so you're well aware of those. Her ass is so tight it's stupid, and her legs are... oh, hey there.

"Are you coming?" she asks, staring daggers at me.

"What?" I ask, starting to wonder if I know her from somewhere.

She shakes her head. "*Oye*, I'm not going to leave you out here in the middle of traffic." Gesturing her hand like a blade, she demands, "Get in the truck."

I take in the cars zipping around us and nod. Good call. I jog over to the passenger side and hoist myself up into the orange-and-white truck, laughing to myself.

"Why are *you* laughing?" she asks sternly. I try not to imagine her using that stern voice in bed because this is a very serious situation and I am an adult who is super hosed for a car right now. But I'm also a woman in her midthirties who can't help herself.

"I was just thinking—damn, it's not even our first date and you've already brought the U-Haul. That's initiative," I say, raising my eyebrow at her.

Huh. She really does look familiar.

Scout

I. Do. Not. Like. Bisexuals. They are so *fucking* unreliable. And this pinup-wannabe with purple-yet-vintage hair has bisexual written all over her, a combination of interest and fear in equal measure. She has soft, pale skin, huge, amber eyes, gorgeous cheekbones, a generous mouth with shapely red lips, lots of eye makeup, and ridiculous, stupid curves for days. I had to tear my eyes from her ass when she crawled back into the front seat because I have literally zero time for this. Not my thing, dude.

And why is she joking? I have my entire life in the back of this damned truck—*because of a fucking bisexual*—and some of that shit in the back is precious fucking cargo. I knew I should have carried my grandmother's teacups in the front with me. Now I'm going to have to unpack to see if they made it, *and* I'm late to my appointment with my new apartment manager.

"So, have you always been bi, or was that just a phase in college?" I snap, sounding meaner than I meant to.

Except.

Okay.

Now she's laughing at me.

"Gosh, always, I suppose," she says, shrugging as she purses her full lips. "I mean, ever since I kissed the preacher's son… and then his daughter. I was what, five, maybe? So… almost thirty years?" She says the "thirty" into her palm like she's trying to hide her real age. I would not have guessed she was out of her twenties, but I turned forty-one last month, so I might not be the best judge.

"And, since we're making assumptions," she says, jutting her fist under her chin while sarcastically slow-blinking her wide, honeyed eyes at me. "Lesbian, obviously. Cis, probably. Sole wearer of the strap-on, undoubtedly."

My lip twitches, but only because she's ridiculous. Not because I used to be a god with a strap-on.

"How'd I do? Am I close?" she asks, leaning over the console with a twinkle in her eye. "Bet you like it when they call you Big Daddy."

I'm not sure why I do it—maybe it's the subtle kd lang reference—but I give her a short nod. Her laugh fills the cabin, and I shake my head as I pull the truck forward. Immediately we hear the squeal of metal on metal, then a thump as the U-Haul clears her car. That effectively, if abruptly, stops her laughter and pushes her back onto her side of the console. I do feel a little bad as I glance over and catch her putting a palm to her forehead. We turn off the bridge and park in the emergency lane.

"I'm going to check for damage," I say as I jump out of the truck. I quickly stride to the back and remove the padlock and pull up the cargo door in one swift motion. *Dammit.* I see the box with my grandmother's teacups tumpted over on its side. I scramble up on the bumper and grab the box, then hop down to shut and lock the door. A quick sweep of the back of the truck shows exactly zero damage. Meanwhile, her car looks like it was in a huge can opener accident. Sucks to be her.

Not my problem.

I jump into the front seat and gently set the precious cargo between us. "Doesn't look like you did any damage to the truck, and I don't have time to wait for the cops." I sound like a dick, I know I do. But she smells faintly of coconuts and something else, something warm and earthy to balance the sweet, and it's pissing me off. Worry stitches her thick, shapely brows together. *Do not engage, Scout. And stop looking at her lips.*

"Did whatever's in there make it out okay?" she asks, pointing at the box between us, genuine concern on her face.

I huff out an exasperated breath. "I don't know. I'll figure it out when I get my apartments."

She nods and grabs her purse, which, by the way, is absurdly huge, and removes a piece of pink paper and a turquoise pen. She writes in smooth, flowing strokes, then presses the paper to my palm. "Here's my info. If anything's broken, let me know and I'll pay for it."

"Okay," I mutter, knowing that I will *not* be calling her. Most people are intimidated by my size and my muscles, or at least they used to be. She sees my annoyance and peers up at me with curiosity.

"Don't you need to call a tow truck, maybe?" I say, sounding sharp and impatient.

She jerks at my tone. "Yeah... probably should, huh?"

I stare out the window as she calls the service, letting her voice fade in the background. As I scan the Austin skyline, I hope I've made the right choice.

I'd been working the business angle the last couple of years, ever since my WNBA team, the San Antonio Stars, moved to LA. I'd spent nine years on the court and eight on the sidelines, a good run by any measure, but I wasn't invited along for the move. My knees thanked me—most of my cohort had retired years before, and pro-athletic life was costing me more money than it made me. Throughout my career I'd dumped most of my earnings into investments, mostly with a group of retired lady players who invest in small, women-run businesses to help them get off the ground. We'd had a stroke of luck early on with a retro candy store concept that we'd been able to franchise throughout the college towns in Texas and Louisiana, and that helped us to get several other well-paying businesses off the ground.

This latest company, however, had barely made it to its first six months, and frankly, it had been a bad idea from the beginning. The owner/manager of the place, Kimberly Barnes, is a good friend of mine from college, and she'd helped me through one of the darkest periods of my life. In retrospect, convincing the board to bankroll her bucket list item of owning a restaurant wasn't the smartest move, and letting her open a gourmet pizza restaurant in a town lousy with gourmet pizza restaurants didn't make that decision any smarter. She did manage to hire a really good cook, but that only stopped the bleeding. This venture is still not making money, and Kimberly has decided that she doesn't like running a restaurant after all. She's taking her buyout and leaving the business to the board.

I know she's been feeling guilty about it, especially since everything in Austin, including my non-board business, has gone completely pear-shaped, but she's sworn up and down that the property manager she recommended to me— her father's best friend and someone she's known all of her life, apparently—will more than make up for it. Kimberly's a good egg, but in this very moment I'm not what you'd call giddy about the fact that I've turned over my dream project to someone she's recommended.

Given that both my love life and my investments were in free fall, along with the fact that I found myself rudderless for the first time in my life, I decided to make a change. That sounds better than what I've been actually doing—taking my destroyed heart, my tenuous health, and getting away from the most painful year of my life with some of my sanity intact.

Except that Austin was already proving to be a tiresome bitch.

Not sure how long we've been sitting here in silence, but I look up as lights start spinning around the cabin. The tow truck. Good. I have shit to do.

We get out of the U-Haul, and the tow guy, a tall, tanned redhead with honey-brown eyes, takes one look at me and recognition shifts over his face. I know what's coming next.

"Holy shitake mushrooms. You're Scout Martinez. Where's your braid?"

The bisexual's eyes go huge, and a blush creeps up her neck as she looks between the tow truck driver and me. I plaster on my public face and greet him with a smile. "That I am. And after decades with the same hairdo, I decided I needed a change. You a fan of the Stars?"

She makes a brief, high-pitched sound like a small woodland animal gasping for air. I glance in her direction, and she's clamped her perfectly manicured, visibly shaking hand over her velvet lips. Her eyes are round as saucers, and her entire chest, neck, and jawline are scarlet.

"Well, sure, but you were on Jody Conradt's team in the late '90s. We remember you," he says, gesturing between himself and the lavender girl, a move I thought was kind of presumptuous. "UT'd transitioned to the Big 12, and you showed up in a big way. I mean, you had some clutch games—that last game, wasn't that a triple-double for you?"

I shrug, trying to look humble. But yeah, I kicked ass that year. And man, I loved Coach Conradt. Still do. She's the reason I graduated with a business degree and that I'm at least moderately successful after basketball.

My bi nightmare looks to the tow guy. "Spence, didn't she get us into the conference finals that year? Like, didn't Dad... *cry* when she hit that last three-pointer?"

His smile broadens as he nods his head. "Dad totally cried."

I scan back and forth between the two of them, the similarities on their faces now evident. "You're brother and sister?"

"Yeah." In unison. With the same expectant smile.

"Huh."

The guy Spence starts to look like he wants to ask for something, but she intercepts and hits his arm. "Spence, you are *not* going to ask for an autograph. I just hit her U-Haul! She's probably going to sue me into the next millennium!"

I suppress an eye roll. What, exactly, could I get out of a woman who drives (well, drove) an ancient Dodge Diplomat? "I'm not going to sue you." A soft smile lights up her face, intensifying the scarlet along her jaw. "But I do need to get a move on," I say with more than a little irritation. "You good?"

She nods her head, worry again creasing her brows. I'm guessing that this isn't great for her, financially.

Look, I'm not a complete asshole. I *do* feel sorry for her. She's sassy in a way I'd probably enjoy under different circumstances and has a sweetness about her that you want to surround in bubble wrap and protect from the rest of the world. She looks tired like maybe she's been working too hard for too long.

Again, not my problem.

Spence shakes his head. "Okay, sister. Let's get this piece-of-crap car out of here." He nods to me, helps his sister into the truck, then runs around to the other side and climbs in. I get back into the U-Haul and inspect the pink paper in my hand. She's written her information in sweeping penmanship, almost like calligraphy. Evie. With a 512 area code. I lift the heavy paper to my nose and catch a muted whiff of coconuts. In my rearview Spence is hooking up her car, and Evie is sitting alone in the cab of the truck. Her eyes are downcast and her shoulders are initially slumped, but after a few seconds, she shakes her head, inhales deeply as she squares her shoulders, then looks forward, catching my stare in the side-view mirror. I give her one more nod, then look again at the fine-grain paper in my hand.

Yeah.

Not even *close* to going there.

I crumple the page and put the truck in drive.

2

EVIE

I don't know why Scout Martinez is following us in her U-Haul, but it's starting to get weird. At first, we were both just heading north on Mopac, but now she's gotten off on the same exit and turned right onto Braker and has been behind us for over a mile. Thankfully, she drives past us when we take the left into the neighborhood, but I catch her quizzical look when we turn in.

As we drive past family homes, I sit back, trying to figure out how it is that I could have spent twenty minutes with my girlhood crush and not have recognized her. I mean... Scout Martinez, y'all. Total alpha on the court, completely dominated the game, and the paparazzi pictures of her that I obsessively stalked always showed her with an arm draped possessively around a beautiful woman's waist, a study in cool, sharp-jawed confidence. She'd been out of the spotlight for a while, and looked markedly different, even beyond her (very cool, very hot) hairstyle, with its dead-sexy streak of white right at the hairline. Her frame had always had a hefty musculature to it, but now she was trim in a way that bordered on gaunt. Additionally, her eyes crinkled at the sides, and they lacked the swagger of the Scout Martinez I grew up on. And while we were waiting for Spencer, she'd had a thousand-yard stare that seemed almost... sad.

She's also one of the investors in the barely making it restaurant that I work at, but I'm hoping that won't come up.

I think we all know where my luck is going on that one.

Shaking myself from my reverie, I look up as we pull to the front of the apartment complex. I check myself in the rearview mirror, fix the smeared eyeliner, and reapply my lipstick. "I'll just be a minute. Want to see if Dad still has those muscle relaxers. You don't mind taking me to work, do you?"

"Yeah, sister," he says, gesturing kindly. "I already told you. It's fine. And we'll get you squared away with another car. Stop fretting. I'll get Danny to take this one for parts, and then I'll see if Julio can use that as a down payment on a fixer-upper, which I will then fix for you."

I cringe, picking at a hangnail. "Okay, but I can't afford a monthly payment."

He shrugs, unconcerned. "Don't worry, sis. We'll figure it out." That probably meant that he would trade Julio free tows in lieu of payment. I didn't want to accept his help, but I knew he would do it anyway, if only because I would do the same in his shoes. His kind eyes calm me, and I climb down from his tow rig.

I worked for my ex's family until he stole my college savings to cover for their seriously shady business practices. His dad ended up in jail, and all I had left from the relationship was a ton of debt from the business loans I'd cosigned.

Yeah, you don't have to tell me how stupid that was. *I know.*

My friend Kim opened a pizza shop six months ago with the help of Scout's investment group, but the business has not done as well as she'd hoped, and I have been trying to help her turn it around. The pay is crap, thus the side hustle, and while our pizza is awesome, there are plenty of awesome pizza joints in Austin, and we don't stand out in any meaningful way. At least now we are breaking even.

Thinking about the last year made the already stiffening muscles in my neck tighten even further. Yeah, I'm well aware of the fact that I should probably go to a doctor to check out my neck, and it's sweet that you think I can actually afford to do that. I tense my shoulders and let them drop. *Ouch.* I need to get one of my dad's muscle relaxers and get back to it. I walk over to the office and my dad's desk. Suzi, his "resident retention specialist," comes over.

"I heard that you were in an accident. Shouldn't you be lying down?" she asks, concern on her face. Suzi is a really sweet lady, who has a super big crush on her new boss. I know that she has an angle, but the niceness is genuine, so I toss her a bone.

I rub my tender neck and shoulders. "Probably, but I don't have time for that. Do you know where my dad is?"

"He's prepping for a business meeting. Only here a month, and he's already got the big boss down to listen to his ideas. Pretty impressive, really," she says appreciatively. Her previous boss was a real #TimesUp dick, if you catch my drift, and a terrible property manager to boot. They'd lost a few residents, and the two-story complex, a beautiful oasis in the heart of Austin's tech district, was starting to look a little worse for wear. Between us, we'll get this place back on its feet. At least there's that.

"Okay. I really need to get back to work, but my neck is killing me. I think he has some muscle relaxers in his desk. Do you mind if I go grab one?"

She nods her head toward his office. "Not at all, honey. I'll let him know you were here and that you're okay. You know he worries about you."

I rub my forehead, guilt sneaking up on me. "I know, I know. Life's been a little messy, and I'm not exactly winning any daughter-of-the-year awards."

Suzi shakes her head, her mane of silver-white hair shimmering to her shoulders. "I dunno about that, Ms. Evie. He seems pretty proud of how you're handling things. Taking those extension classes for business at UT? Your side jobs? Sure, he'll worry. But I think he's happy that you're taking a chance."

I smile. She is just the sweetest. I take one of the complimentary bottles of water from the office fridge and grab a dark yellow pill from the pill box in my father's desk. I pause at the old photos on the desk. My mom really was a beauty. "Thanks, Suzi. Tell him I'm okay and not to worry."

"Will do."

Scout

Fuck, I'm lost. Got distracted following Evie's car. Not great that she lives or maybe works in the same neighborhood, but I'm sure I can avoid her. After passing I-35, turning around, waiting for my GPS to recalibrate, and finally finding the right street, I'm sitting at a four-way stop, removing my hoodie, when I see a familiar tow truck and crumpled car pass in front of me.

Great.

Evie sees me and is grinning and waving, her purple hair bouncing. I chuck the hoodie into the passenger seat, then smile-grimace and give a curt wave back, taking a right.

Thank god I've made it. I take in the series of buildings, an apartment property I named the Levee. *What a joke*, I think to myself, noticing everything that is wrong with what used to be my passion project. I own it separate from my business group, and to be honest, I hadn't been paying much attention to the place, letting the previous property management people take the wheel. This was a tactical error, as noted by the peeling paint on the cracking sign in the front of what used to be a gorgeous property.

"The Evee," I say out loud, phonetically pronouncing the sign with the missing *L*. Ironic. And fitting.

The palm trees that line the central courtyard are severely overdue for a trim, and the pool is an uninviting green. It's not quite time for swimming, but a pool should never be green. I'm already not impressed with this new manager. Goddammit, Kimberly.

Speaking of which, a large, smiling man in his sixties is making his way toward my U-Haul. He's wearing slacks and a UT polo, sharply tucked in over a slight gut. He has thick, fading red hair and seems strong for his age.

"Hi! Scout! Adam Koenig. I can't believe I'm meeting you in person," he says, grabbing my hand and pumping it up and down for all it's worth. "Thank you so much for taking the time to meet with me. Come up to the office and let's talk about plans for the place!"

"Can we start with the sign?" I grumble, gesturing at the peeling mess.

He holds out his hands in an assuring gesture. "Order is already being processed by the sign people. Your office didn't get us the approval until last week, but I know a guy, and he's going to try and have that up for us by next week."

I'm behind on my paperwork, so that's on me. "And the pool? What's going on with that?"

His smile is broad and genuine. "Yesterday was St. Patrick's Day. Figured we'd be draining it tomorrow with the pool service folks finally able to come in, so we had a barbeque down at the pool for the residents. That was Suzi's idea. I'm glad we kept her on; I think she'll work out great for resident retention."

"Okay," I say, my shoulders relaxing slightly. "The trees?"

Again, a reassuring nod. "One of my friends will take care of them for half the usual cost, and she knows what she's doing with palms. But she's busy this time of year and won't be able to help us for another two weeks. Do you want me to find a faster vendor?"

I shrug, not happy with the timeline, but glad he's on it. "No, if you have a specialist that'll give you a discount, let's stick with that timeline. I just don't like those dead palm fronds."

Grimacing, he says, "Yeah, and they tend to let roaches and termites thrive, which was the first thing we tackled when I got here."

I shake my head. "The Levee is supposed to be a boutique, luxury property, literally a breakwall from the stresses of life. And those pictures you sent me were a nightmare."

"My construction and repair guy said that we got lucky. It's limited to the one unit, and the damage has so far been cosmetic, not structural, so we caught it in time." He pauses, scratching his stubbly jaw. "May I speak freely?"

"I'd appreciate it."

"That management company you had working here was complete crap. You should sue them for the amount of the contract plus damages. The residents here said that they hadn't seen a maintenance truck out here for months. Frankly, we're about to get into the hot part of the year, and I'm glad you didn't go through AC repair season with those folks. If people don't have AC, they're going to move."

My shoulders started bunching up again. "This year has been... I was depending on someone in San Antonio to manage these details for me, and let's just say that you're part of a larger reorganization."

Adam observes me, kind honey-brown eyes squinting into a smile. "Hey, don't you worry. You've got me now. And it's just a few buildings and a pool. By the summer, everything will be fixed, and you'll be pulling in the dough. I guarantee it."

I nod again, hoping he's right. He seems trustworthy, and it sounds like he's got the town wired. "All right, so what's the first thing we need to do? Are there any requests outstanding? Anything we haven't responded to?"

"Glad you asked. I've requested accommodations for a staff maintenance person. I'm pretty handy, but we need a professional onsite to manage the ins and outs. That management company let the previous guy go and never replaced him."

"And pocketed the extra cash."

"I'm guessing."

I sigh and then look at his expectant smile. "Don't tell me—you know a guy."

He beams, glad I'd picked up on his networking ability. "I do. My son, Jake. And I'm already paying for the headcount, so it makes sense to go ahead and get the position filled right away."

"All right, fine. We'll give him a go. And since I'm your newest resident, I'll know pretty quickly if he's any good at all."

"Yes, you will. Speaking of which, he helped me get your apartment ready for move-in, and I had him stick around to help you unload your truck," he says, pointing at a familiar-looking man sauntering in our direction.

I look around, wondering if I'd somehow wandered into the twilight zone.

The man walking toward us looks exactly like the Evie's tow truck driver, with inverted coloring. I check myself in the side mirror of the U-Haul, just to make sure someone hasn't accidentally turned the contrast way up. "Adam, do you maybe have another son? Gotta be this guy's fraternal twin or something—goes by the name Spence?"

Adam's eyes widen. "Yes," he says, his mouth slack. "How do you know Spencer?"

Seriously, fuck my life.

"Your daughter rear-ended me this morning, and Spencer picked her up with his tow truck."

"Really? You're the one she hit?" he said, worry lines popping up on his forehead. "Did she seem okay to you? Suzi mentioned she needed a muscle relaxer before going into work."

I knit my brows together. Had she been hurt in the accident? How did I not see that? And why didn't she say anything? "She went into work after that?" Also, why was she taking her dad's muscle relaxers and not going to the doctor?

"I'm guessing so," he answers, shaking his head.

Jake joins us and quietly hands me the keys to my Jeep, trading them for the keys to the U-Haul. "Did y'all say something about Evie?"

While he and the tow truck driver look shockingly alike, his redheaded twin is more filled out and has a healthy-looking tan. Jake has a lean build and is pale, almost pallid, with thick, dark hair and bluish circles under his eyes, and he's wearing about as much black as I am. I look down and notice the remnants of dark purple nail polish removed too quickly.

Tilting my head at him, I explain, "She and I had a minor fender bender, and she seems to have hurt her neck and isn't getting proper medical care." My eyes fall again to his nails, and the shake of his head is subtle. God, we are all so good at being subtle. Even when you're not the one in it, the closet demands subtlety above all else.

Squaring up his shoulders, he gestures to his father. "Not surprising. Evie's kind of hardheaded anyway. She'll take care of everyone else, never stops, and can't really be told no." He pins me with a look. "But I'll keep an eye out."

Jesus.

I do not need this right now.

3

EVIE

*M*an, do I love a muscle relaxer. Let me tell you. Nothing hurts, nothing sucks, my shameful financial situation is only temporary, and everything is an illusion. Except the phone—that's really ringing. I pick up my cell and hit the button. "What's up, Pops?"

"The apartment owner agreed to let Jake manage the maintenance and keep using the staff apartment, so he moved your stuff over today. You'll be able to sleep there tonight."

"Thank him for me, will you, Pops?"

"Will do, Sugar Plum."

Playing with the ring on the back of the cell case, I ask, "You think that he'll be able to manage it?"

"I do. He put back on some muscle during his time in rehab, and she's willing to give him a try. I think having you there will be real good for him."

"Okay, cool. Even cooler that you've got a ladyboss. Think she'll be okay with me staying with him?" I keep my voice light, but this is a big one. My lease had ended, and I can't afford the jump in rent. Actually, I can't afford rent, period.

"Um. She doesn't exactly know."

"Well, she doesn't have to know. I mean, she's like, in San Antonio, right?"

The line goes quiet.

"Dad?"

"Well," he says, drawing it out. I can almost see him rubbing his chin, trying to figure out how to deliver the bad news. "She's moving to Austin and staying here until her house is ready. Six months."

"*Shiznit.* Do you think she'll be cool?"

"Language, Evie. And considering that you've already run into her this morning, I'm not so sure."

"*Dad*! You've got to *lead* with that. So, wait—your new overlord is Scout Martinez?"

"Yep," he says, sounding really happy.

"*Dad*," I grit through my teeth. "You know that Kim is working with Scout's investment group."

"The one that owns the restaurant? I'd forgotten about that."

"Yeah, Dad. You and I are essentially coworkers."

Half of the reason I let Kim talk me into this job was that I thought I might get to meet the famous Scout Martinez, but now I won't be able to avoid her.

"My first question is, why didn't you tell me a month ago that your new boss is Scout Martinez, and number two, how the hell did y'all figure out I was the one who hit her?"

"NDA. She likes to keep a low profile, and it was written in such a way that I had no intention of breaking it. And we figured it out after she saw Jake."

"Makes sense," I answer, sighing. Stupid twins are stupid. This is seriously putting a dent in my muscle relaxer.

The front door dings as our first customer of the day walks in, and I let Kim handle it as I say goodbye to my father.

Dangit.

I really need to bunk with my brother, but this is clearly not my morning for winning friends and influencing people. My mind is wandering, thinking about a certain jawline when Kim's voice pitches up. Like she's nervous. I hang back by the pizza oven to see what's going on.

"So... uh, how's it going, Scout?" she asks tentatively.

Shootshootshoot. Though Scout's a bit of a mumbler, I catch, "I've had better days."

"Oh no, what happened?" That is for sure Kim's fake-concerned voice.

"Some chick with a big ass ran into the back of my U-Haul. Bi, because of course. Didn't even bother with the insurance at that point."

Double heck.

This is so bad.

And seriously? Scout Martinez is my *jam*. Let's just say that there was *a lot* of sexual awakening during the Lady Horns' 1999 season. I mean, every boyfriend I ever had understood that she is forever on the laminated list, in the finger vault, charter member of my own personal rub club. I mean, I shook her hand once after a game and then immediately went home and used that hand to masturbate.

Okay, I'll be honest. That may have been a bit of an overshare.

But... I mean, the "Daddy" comment before I recognized her was directly from my favorite fantasy, the one where she pins me down, and...

Okay, I really heard it that time. Definitely TMI.

Anyway.

I am so screwed. *Some chick with a big ass.* I mean, sure, but... ouch. Kim knows about the accident, so she laughs nervously and clears her throat. "That's unfortunate. Any damage?"

"Not to the truck itself, but one of my grandmother's teacups is broken."

Oh, come *on*. Though it's mildly sweet that she has a grandma keepsake. Which I destroyed. But also, screw her. Dangit. I'm feeling way too many things right now.

"Sorry to hear that."

"It gets worse. She's related to my new apartment manager. That you recommended to me."

"Yeah, about that..." Kim turns her head and catches my eye. She bites her top lip.

"And her brother is the new onsite maintenance guy. Hopefully, her family is slightly less useless than she is. Maybe they don't get along, 'cause I'd like to keep that one out of my life."

Useless? *What a freaking jerk.* While I'm stuck back here, I start mentally updating my resume, because there's no way she's going to keep me on now.

"That's, um. Going to be a little difficult."

A heavy sigh reverberates throughout the small shop. "*Why?*"

She's just a mean-sounding butch, you know? And I don't know what Kim is going for, because I plan on avoiding the hell out of that woman. At least in real life. Her grumbly attitude just dirtied the hell out of my sex dreams.

I'm not even sorry.

"Well, as you mentioned, I *did* recommend her father, and he is doing an excellent job. And I was *going* to recommend that Evelyn take my place as manager when the buyout goes through."

Record scratch.

"What the *what?*" I say, coming out from behind the oven. "Buyout? Kim! When were you going to tell me? I thought we were in this together?"

Kim's eyes widen in apology. "Evie, I—"

I turn to Scout. Ooh, the nostril flare on that lesbian. And maybe some reddened cheeks for talking about me behind my back.

Dear Aztec Deliciousness,

Go fornicate yourself.

Sincerely yours,

A fat-assed bisexual.

Scout Martinez, ginormous lesbian, supercrush, and basketball hero of mine swings up the pass-through and walks up on me like she wants to scrap. Not gonna lie, it's a little thrilling to see that she hasn't lost all of her swagger. "What the hell are you doing here? Are you just *everywhere* now?"

She stops right inside my personal space and stares down at me, trying an intimidation move that I and my hand are all too familiar with. A small throb passes between my thighs, and I grin like a madwoman. She rocks back a few inches. "What the hell are you smiling at?"

Don't poke the bear, Evie. Don't. Poke. The. Bear.

Ah, well.

"You might be tall out here in the real world, *Sophia*, but on a WNBA team? Barely average. Y'all'd play Houston and Lindsey Taylor would pull that exact same move on you. Every. Time. I know that and I don't even like basketball," I say, closing the distance between us until my boobs are practically touching her flat belly. "So, fine. Give it your best shot, *you mediocre ball hog*."

Scout

I need her tits to not be touching my body right now.

"*Ball hog? Mediocre?* Do you even know what a triple-double is? Do you know how many of those I got in my career? I've broken every fucking triple-double record on every fucking team I've ever been on." I catch something sparkly in the corner of my eye and notice that she has wording across her tight shirt in gold glitter.

Fuck squared, pretty sure she caught me eyeballing her cleavage.

She arches one perfectly shaped eyebrow and quirks up her red lips like she got one over on me. Okay, fine. Let's play that game. I run my hand through my hair, flopping it over to one side, letting her see the guns and the cut waist. I mean, I'm not back up to fighting weight, but I've been putting my time in at the gym.

Oh, shit. Tactical error. Eject. Eject.

What I get back from that lavender-haired pain in my ass are the hottest fuck-me eyes I have ever seen. For the space of two blinks, the air crackles electric and those eyes tell me exactly what she wants, and they're saying she likes it rough. By the third blink she's hardened her expression again, like maybe she's already started to hate me, and that's… shit, that's even sexier.

Yeah, I have no time for that. I need to get this complication out of my restaurant.

Kimberly physically shoves us apart, her huge eyes ping-ponging back and forth between us. "Now, I think we got off on the wrong foot this morning. I think we need to step back," she says, pushing us farther apart, "and take a deep breath."

"Fuck a deep breath," I say, and pivot to my friend. "Kimberly, if this *girl* is who you have running the show, *no wonder* this place is tanking."

The human equivalent of Twilight Sparkle Pony makes a small *hmph* sound. "What did you say?" I ask, glowering down at my lavender nightmare.

"I didn't *say* anything. I made a *sound*, you ginormous jerk." She says this while managing to stare me down, even though she has to look up to do it.

"Ginormous? Have you *seen* the size of your ass? Girl, you know you're supposed to sell the pizza, *not eat it.*"

While I'd never admit it, I'm enjoying the hell out of this argument, which, bonus, is having its intended effect. Even the most confident woman is vulnerable about her body, and I've scored a direct hit. Evie is ripping off her apron and dusting the flour out of her hair.

Thank god, because I was alarmingly close to putting my hands on her.

Turning to Kim, she jabs her finger in her chest. "If *you're* not going to be here, then there is no way in hell that *this fatass*," she says, pointing to herself, "is going to stay here with *that one* breathing down my neck."

She grabs her purse and stomps out the door, swinging the bell off its hook.

My sense of victory is short-lived because Kimberly turns on me, her eyes blazing. "You *idiot*! You have to go after her!"

I shake my head. "No way. There's one thing I learned from this whole experience with Carla is that you let crazy walk out the door. You do *not* chase it!"

"You don't understand, Sophia," Kimberly says, her voice shaking. "Not only could she sue you, she's the reason why anyone comes here at all. She abuses our customers, and they love it. They lap it up. She flirts with the guys, she flirts with the girls, she listens to every sob story, she gives them free pizza when she thinks I'm not paying attention, but most importantly, and this is critical: she's the cook and the brains behind this operation. We're still in business because of her—*I'm* the shit businessperson. So, you can let her walk out the door, but your money is walking out the door with her."

Wait, what? *"That's* the broad who did that amazing, buttery Napolitano slice?"

Kimberly nods her head up and down vigorously. "Yes. *You idiot.* Now go after her!"

Son of a bitch. She couldn't have gotten that far. "I'm on it."

We are in a subsection of a mixed-use condo and shopping development, and she doesn't exactly blend in. I go around our little hamlet of shops, peering in every window, but she's not there. After ten minutes of searching, I still can't see her anywhere. I take off jogging, ignoring the breathlessness and knee pain that is a near-constant in my life. I hit the main road that runs through the place and see her about three blocks up.

A few minutes later, I tap her on the shoulder, sweat on my face from the muggy run. "Hey."

She ignores me with another prissy *hmph* and continues walking.

"Hey, slow down," I say, trying to catch my breath. "We need to talk."

She turns around on me and I bump into her, a charge shooting up my spine. She pushes me away, hard, and anger fires up in her eyes. Damn. Woman is solid.

"Holy shit, I think you bruised my ribs," I growl, annoyed at the intensity of the contact.

"You sound surprised, number 19," she tosses over her shoulder as she continues her stride. "Didn't think a fat-ass *girl* could get one over on you?"

"Hey," I say again, gruff as I put my large hand on her shoulder. "Stop. Listen to me. I was just fucking with you. Your ass isn't *that* big."

She turns on me with those murderous fuck-me eyes of hers and grabs my wrist, then locks it in the wrong direction, pulling me downward with the sheer force of her weight. My knee hits the ground right on one of my many surgery incisions and I yelp, then lean over and fall on my side. The pain jars my bones, and I can barely breathe.

She leans down and gets into my face, her honeyed amber eyes dark with spite. The subtle scent of coconut filters through the pain as she snarls, "Look, I know that I'm supposed to feel bad because clearly you're in a lot of pain. But I've had a shit day, and you're a big part of that, so I don't really care at this point. I don't have a car, I don't have a place to stay, I don't have a job, and now my neck is *freaking* killing me. So, unless you want me to break your wrist and stomp on your stupid knee, I need you to let me walk away. *Please and thank you.*" That last part sounded a lot like *go fuck yourself*.

My knee is throbbing, and I am in no shape to go after her. I hit the ground with my palm, frustrated and—annoyingly—turned on. I'm also really worried about her neck.

4

EVIE

Thirty minutes later, I knock on Spence's door, barely holding back tears, my neck and my back on fire after walking two miles in crappy tennis shoes. His wife, Annie, opens the door, takes one glance at me and wordlessly ushers me in. Their adorable cottage house is a typical Austin special—small, cramped, and overpriced. See also: overflowing with kids' toys. It's the middle of the school day, and I flop on the couch, grateful for the quiet space.

She approaches me with kind eyes and a glass of water. "Do you want to talk about it?"

My eyes redden and swell, and a few tears escape. "Not really," I respond, my voice rough.

She sits next to me and puts her arm around me. "I'm so sorry about Marge. She was an ugly car, but she took care of you."

I rub my eyes and chuckle sarcastically. "I also lost-slash-quit my job, I'm homeless, I won't be able to take care of Jake, and my life is officially a joke." Yeah, the tears are really falling now.

"Oh," she says, eyeing the breakfast table. Where a very tall ex-WNBA player sits, wearing all black, like her mood.

Motherfudger.

Like, even the way she sits is kind of gruff and demanding. I wonder what she's like in bed.

No, no I do *not* wonder that. As of this morning. Because she is a world-class jackass.

Starting *now*.

Okay, starting *now*.

I dip my head to wipe my eyes using the fabric on my shoulder before impaling her with a glare. "You know what, Martinez? If you think that I won't drag myself up off this couch and proceed to break every last freaking one of your ribs, you don't know me that well. I need you to get the hell out of this house."

Shiznit. It occurs to me, belatedly, that I could ruin things for a lot of people.

"Scratch that. I don't want you taking this out on my pops. Or my brother. What do you need?"

She snorts and stands up from the table, then ambles over and plops down on the couch next to me. She leans forward, propping her forearms on her thighs. "Well, this is one hell of a day, isn't it?"

I stare straight ahead, ignoring her hulking presence, the electricity on my skin, and the pounding in my head. "One hundred percent accurate."

"I apologize for the ass remarks. Those were hurtful and uncalled for."

I close one eye while rolling the other. "Scout, do you think that you actually hurt my feelings?" I glance over and uncertainty crosses her features. Pretty sure I've never seen that look on her face in the nearly twenty years I've been following her.

"Um, yes?" she says, shaking her head as though she knows that's the wrong answer.

"Scout, sweetie, you can't hurt my feelings by saying that my fat ass is a fat ass. It's cute that you think you can."

"Then...?" she starts, letting the question finish itself.

I pause, thinking about how I want to say this, and to whom I am saying it. Honestly, I can't believe I'm about to do this with my hero-crush. I lean in, our noses nearly touching, forcing her to look into my eyes. "You were dismissive of me from the get," I say, tugging on my hair, pointing at my face full of makeup, and gesturing to my general 'ness. "And you were willing to use what you perceived as a weakness—a vulnerability—against me. You weren't even particularly imaginative about it. And I no longer do business with unimaginative, emotionally poisonous people."

Her rich mocha eyes widen in surprise. I'm not sure what surprises her more, that someone dared call her on her bull, or the fact that she was guilty of it to begin with. Seriously, screw that. The absolute foolishness of this past year has given me a spine, and by dog, I'm going to use it. I tear my gaze away from her and look down at my manicure, picking at an imaginary hangnail.

She takes a couple of deep breaths, seeming to mull over what I'd said. After a few moments she says a soft *well, shit* under her breath and shakes her head. "You're right. I apologize. It won't happen again."

I look over and see the resolve in the set of her jaw and actually believe that she is telling the truth. "Thank you. Apology accepted."

Scout scrubs her hand over her face and turns to me. "If it's all the same to you, I'd like to start over." I pause a beat, then nod. "My name is Sophia Martinez, and I'm a property owner and wannabe venture capitalist. Most people call me Scout." She holds out her enormous hand, which I consider leaving in the air, but decorum dictates that I shake it. Her fingertips brush the inside of my wrist and I stifle a shudder. I mean, she's still Scout Martinez, y'all.

My dirty fantasies just got upgraded because I now know what she smells like (clean laundry) and what her hands feel like (strong, sensual).

Okay, *now*.

"Hi, Scout. My name is Evelyn Koenig. I'm kind of a professional screwup right now. Most people call me Evie."

"Hi, Evelyn," she says, disconnecting our grip to once again face the floor. My sister-in-law has disappeared, and it's just the two of us in the living room, surrounded by Duplos and Paw Patrol toys and Jake the Pirate paraphernalia.

Rolling my eyes, I guess out loud, "Kim told you that the recipes were mine, didn't she?"

"Yeah."

I shake my head, aggravating the muscles in my neck. *Ouch.* "Take the recipes. They're not that difficult to follow. You don't need me."

Scout tilts her head side to side. "That isn't what Kimberly said. First, you haven't signed—and shouldn't sign—them over. She says you have a way with the customers. She called me an idiot."

I chance a look at her profile and see the beginnings of a smile. I bite my lip, then snark, "She's not wrong."

Scout puts her hands out in front of her like she's holding my neck, and she squeezes. Hard. Not gonna lie, my breath caught in my throat at the gesture. Mentally I may or may not have clicked a huge Add button on my jill till visuals. We sit in silence for a few moments, letting the tension drain out. Finally, in a tone that indicates she'd rather do anything but, she asks, "What will it take to get you to come back to the store and manage it for me?"

"You won't like it," I say, wincing.

She turns fully toward me now, and our eyes latch onto one another. "Why not?"

Sitting up a little straighter and squaring my shoulders, I say, "I need to stay with Jake while I get back on my feet. And I want autonomy. And I need insurance. And a raise."

And a car. But I don't want to push it.

She repositions herself on the couch as before, leaning forward as she bobs her head up and down a couple of times. "One condition." She steeples her fingers in front of her and bunches her jaw, waiting for me to respond.

"What?" I ask, suspicious.

She shoots me a heated gaze. "We are going to go this afternoon to my orthopedist and get your neck looked at."

I roll my eyes. "Whatever. I don't really nee—"

"I'm going to stop you right there," she interrupts. "Jake mentioned that you would try to power through this. Not going to happen. It's easier if you accept that now."

Sigh. Fine.

I nod and wince.

Scout

I'm standing behind Evelyn as she climbs into my black Jeep. I'd tricked it out with emerald racing stripes, black rims, black leather, and, unfortunately for her, the biggest tires I could find. I support her arm as she blanches from the pain in her neck. Focusing on the task at hand, I'm having a harder time avoiding the fact that everything about this woman is... *too fucking much*. Red, pouty lips, dramatic eyeliner, cuffed jeans that are basically painted over a Kim Kardashian ass, and a white tee stretched across Jessica Rabbit tits. The damned shirt has "la femme" printed across it in gold letters, as if I didn't get the point the first time.

I roll up my favorite green hoodie and place it behind her neck. Her hair is in a ponytail, revealing a tattoo that curls up from her back into her hairline. I quietly inhale her coconut and earthen scent, a fact I'm not terribly proud of.

"Look," she says, nervous as I drive through a familiar neighborhood, "I don't have any money for this. I don't... I don't even know how much this is going to cost."

I shake my head. "Think of it as an insurance payout, don't make a big deal out of it."

Her pouty mouth opens in a perfect o and then barrels right along. "I'm not making a big deal out of it. I pay my way, and I don't like to take help. I'm not your charity case."

I glare at her, my eyes narrowed and my jaw hardened. She meets my stubborn look with one of her own, jutting out her chin—even though it hurts her—daring me to fight her on this. Her eyes keep scanning my features.

Letting out a huff of breath, I argue, "You're not a charity case. You're my employee. A critical employee who I need to have back in fighting shape so that I can put out about fifteen other fires. This is me being selfish and capitalistic—not charitable."

She raises her eyebrow as if to say, "Do you really expect me to believe that?" but then goes quiet. After another moment, she throws up her hands. "Fine."

I take her to my sports doc, an old guy in his sixties whose salt-and-pepper hair looks like marble against his dark skin. Jonathan, my buddy, thinks he's funny. "So, how exactly did this happen?" he asks, delicately palpating the musculature along her neck. He catches my eye, and I shift my gaze down before I can see his grin.

Evelyn twists her lips. "I ran into the back of this one," she says, gesturing to me. "Thirty-five to zero in no seconds flat."

He nods, his eyes sparkling. "Yep, that'll do it. I'm assuming you at least did so in a car?" Evelyn nods her head, and Jonathan smiles even more broadly than before. "A number of the players who ran into her on the court didn't fare any better."

"I know," she says, glancing at me, then down to the floor.

Placing a gentle hand on her shoulder, his response is kind. "Look, you've got a bad muscle strain, but no structural damage. If this soft brace feels good, wear it for a couple of days and let's see where we are. You are probably going to hurt all over. Do you have access to a pool?"

"Yep," I answer. Capturing her gaze, I say, "Once your dad gets it in working order, you're welcome to use it before and after hours, too, if that's more convenient."

She stiffens, ready to fight even that courtesy, but thinks the better of it and nods quietly.

Scrutinizing me, Jonathan continues. "And you're going to have to let her have a few days off of work—she should really rest. She's going to be in a fair amount of pain for the next day or so."

I nod and shoot a quick text to Kimberly, who agrees to keep the lights on while Evelyn recovers. Jonathan has his nurse call into the pharmacy for the pain meds. Evelyn tries to protest, but I'm not hearing it.

Why does she have to be so obstinate?

Turning to me, Jonathan's eyebrow raises. "What's happening with that knee of yours?" he says, pointing at the purpling skin around my scar, visible through my ripped jeans. "What are you doing to all of my good work? Have you taken up rugby?"

I look over at Evelyn and shake my head. She smirks and replies, "Scout was acting like a jerk, so I put her on the ground."

Jonathan studies the two of us for a few seconds longer than is comfortable, then starts laughing, deep and low. "I don't think I've ever seen anyone put you in your place, let alone take your feet out from under you."

"Bull," Evelyn coughs. "Mystics number 73"—cough—"in the paint"—cough—"every time."

I glare at her like I might just murder her. "You know, for someone who doesn't like basketball all that much, you seem to know a helluva lot about my career."

Her eyes darken momentarily, and her neck flushes. "Hey, Carla Forrester was one of the best-looking players in the league. Guess you couldn't help getting a little flustered."

Carla.

Carla who broke my heart and cheated on me with *a man*. We'd kept our relationship out of the public eye, so I'm pretty sure Evelyn doesn't know that she's barreled headlong into yet another roped-off area, but here we are. I'd spent years pining after Carla, and when we'd gotten together, we were pure, rocket-fueled chemistry—in the beginning. Five years later, and Carla is the reason I have my shit in a U-Haul and a new phone number that I haven't yet memorized. I cannot fucking deal with this shitty Venn diagram that my life has become.

"Damn." Jonathan smiles, knowing. "She's got your number."

Not if I can help it.

5

SCOUT

I drive us directly to the pharmacy, and Evelyn stiffens. "I-I can get these later."

I roll my eyes and stare at the ceiling, asking for patience. My response is quick and sharp. "I'm taking you here because I'm going to pay for your meds. We've already had this argument. Save it for when you're running my shop."

The pharmacist pushes a button on the drive-through vestibule, and I take the white paper bag, handing it Evelyn. She clearly wants to protest, then changes her mind. Bringing her eyes to mine, she mutters a soft *thank you*.

"You're welcome," I retort, my stomach twisting into a knot at the dejected look on her face and the way her shoulders slump as she eases back into the seat. I resituate the rolled hoodie, and she sighs, then leans into the support.

We get back to the apartments by early evening, and I walk her to her door. "Is your brother here?" She tries to shake her head no, but the pain stops her movement. "Don't! Move. Your. Neck. Use your words—we both know that you're more than capable of that."

She inhales deeply, clearly uncomfortable. "He made a Home Depot run, then has a thing with some friends, so not for a while." Her jaw tightens again with pain, and I put my hand on her lower back, guiding her into the apartment.

To the left are flattened moving boxes stacked neatly on a dinged-but-still-cool art deco coffee table in front of a navy blue chenille couch, with a modest flat-screen TV bolted into the wall to complete the tiny living area. Green plants liven up the space, and there are small gold details throughout. To the right is a sparse kitchen, and I note that it's not updated like the rest of the units. Instead of cool gray cabinets, snow-white countertops, and retro-modern lights, they still have the honey-oak wood, dreary Formica, and harsh overhead lighting. The carpeting and tile throughout are equally beige and overdue for an update. Yet another thing my previous management agency fucked up or, more likely, didn't do and pocketed the difference.

There's a small sturdy iron-and-wood dining table in the microscopic dining area, and papers are scattered and neatly stacked all over it. I recognize work orders in the orderly piles, and what look to be bills and junk mail in the scattered bits. A collage fills the wall above the table, a jarring and engaging mix of pop art prints, photography, and real paintings. There's a black-and-white picture of Evelyn, sitting around what looks to be a campfire, head thrown back in a full-bodied laugh, her hair in one long braid like I used to wear. She's not wearing any makeup, and her skin is porcelain.

"Here, you need to take those with food," I say, inclining my head toward the paper bag filled with prescriptions as I wander into the aged kitchen. "You hungry?"

"Starving," she says quietly as she pushes the bills back from the edge of the table and sits down.

I open the fridge, and it's practically barren. "Does he have anything to eat?" I ask, unimpressed by the desiccated broccoli.

"Ravioli. He always has the canned ravioli. Check the cupboard."

I saunter over to the cupboard and open the cheaply veneered door. Sure enough, there are a handful of the Chef Boyardee ravioli tins. I grab one and start searching for a bowl and a spoon.

"Don't bother with the bowl," she says, sighing in pain. "I just wanna go to bed. The can and a utensil are all I need."

"Are you sure?" I ask, not in love with the fact that she's going to be eating hobo-style.

She nods, wincing again.

I let out a frustrated groan. "Would you please fucking stop that?"

She jumps a little at the harshness in my voice, the pain sending a shiver down her neck. I adjust my tone and say more softly, "I'm sorry. Please don't move your neck like that."

She goes to nod but thinks better of it. "Really, I'm going to try to remember."

I sit down at the small table, my knees barely clearing the edge, and hand her the water and the pills, watching as she swallows them. I hate pain. I don't like seeing it in others, and I'm agitated seeing it on her. I peel back the lid on the ravioli and hand her the can and a spoon.

"Well, considering the fact that I put you on your bad knee, we're probably even by now," she says to herself, a small grin on her face. She slowly pulls out her ponytail, and her lavender hair hypnotically spills over her distracting tits as she spoons ravioli after ravioli into her mouth.

Within a few minutes, she scrapes out the last of the can and then eyes me quizzically. "Okay, I'm done eating. You can go."

"Is your bed set up?" I ask, knowing that it couldn't possibly be. There's no way that she can set up the bed on her own, and she shouldn't be sleeping on the floor.

"I think so."

I extend my hand to help her up. "Well, here. Let's go check."

She looks like she wants to protest, but the medication is starting to relax her shoulders. She nods quietly and takes my hand, her short nails painted in a Hello Kitty theme. Clenching my jaw, I walk her to her room, noticing that the ceiling is still popcorned and that the lighting is inadequate to actually illuminate the small hallway, though the walls have been treated with more of the bright pop art/photography/painting collaging. In between a mixed-media piece of a man in a spacesuit and an ethereal black-and-white print is a small framed photograph of Evelyn sitting next to a hospital bed, leaning over to kiss the cheek of a fragile-looking woman with a colorful headscarf. I recognize the gray pallor of chemo life and the soft beanie meant to cover and warm a sensitive bald head.

I straighten the small frame before entering Evelyn's room.

Evie

My bed is put together (thanks, Jake!), but the sheets and duvet are neatly folded to the side. I try to flip open the fitted sheet, but Scout walks past me and takes the sheet from my hand. "What the hell are you thinking?"

I raise my eyebrow, practically the only thing that doesn't hurt right now. "I'm thinking that I'd like to go to bed and that I'd like for this angry tree to get out of my room."

Her eyes narrow and she shakes her head. "Not happening, Evelyn."

"You know, my friends call me Evie," I say, hand on my hip.

"I'm not your friend, *Evelyn*," she says dryly, raising a sharp eyebrow when I make a face. Unable to hold eye contact, which I find hilarious and annoyingly endearing, her eyes fall to my hips. After a few lingering seconds, Scout refocuses and makes quick work of setting the bed. While she's much thinner now, she's no less physically impressive, and it's impossible not to watch her. Her enormous hands, used to hours of handling basketballs, are strong and deft, and her broad wingspan means that she can actually reach those blasted corners. She puts the downy comforter in the duvet cover in less than five minutes with no wrangling or sweating or cursing whatsoever.

"Are your pain meds kicking in?" she asks, watching me as I watch her.

I smile, a little dazed. "Yyyyepp."

"He didn't give you that much," she says. I'm sure the trace of concern in her voice is short-lived.

I let my head loll a bit and angle my thumbs to my chest. "Cheap drunk."

She reaches out to correct the bend in my neck, her hands warm and strong, her fierce gaze unyielding. "Don't do that. Just because it doesn't hurt doesn't mean you're not doing damage." She grabs the soft neck brace. "I think you should wear this." I nod, and she efficiently pulls my hair to the side, then fastens the brace in the back. My breath catches when she pushes me into her muscular chest, angling her face around mine to see the fastener. We lock eyes for a beat, and then I look down. Except I kind of can't because the brace prevents the movement.

She grasps my shoulders, kneading them with her large, angular hands, her eyes... worried? Maybe? "You are going to be in pain when you wake up. Can you go for a massage tomorrow?"

I roll my eyes at her. No. No, I can't afford a massage.

She huffs out an annoyed sound, then puts her finger in my face. "Don't complain. I'm going to call my sports masseuse. She'll get you squared away."

I press my lips together and put my hands on my hips. "Stop coddling me."

"You have obviously never worked for me before. I don't coddle." Giving me a once-over, she says, "Now, come on. Let's get you into bed."

Too loopy to protest or make the obvious joke, I slide under the cool, fresh sheets and my head finds the pillow. My neck is still quite sore, but I'm so happy to be in my own bed.

Fussing with the angle of my pillow, Scout doesn't look at me as she asks, "How is your neck? Pain scale of one to ten?"

Watching her hands run along the duvet, I answer, "It hurts like a mother flip, but I don't care as much, so... five?"

Her jaw tenses again. She's uncomfortable that I'm in pain, and her dark, hard eyes search my body for other issues. "Should we get you into your pjs? Would that make you more comfortable?"

Imitating my favorite anime character, I slur, "Stop trying to get me out of my clothes, you dirty lesbian."

She thins her lips, her face sharp and formidable. At least I'm pretty sure it is. I lost the ability to focus a while ago.

"I'm kidding," I say, holding out my hands. "Really. And Scout?"

"Yes?" she answers, finally turning to meet my eyes.

"Thanks. For taking care of me."

Her eyes narrow, then scan my body once more before walking out of my room.

"I'll let myself out."

6

SCOUT

*L*ook... fuck off.

I don't feel sorry for her, or whatever. She has to take her meds with food, and there's no food in the house. Besides, I'm not being that nice. I'm waking her up at 7:30.

I'll admit that her "emotionally poisonous" comment had teeth to it, and I want to prove to her that I'm normally not like that. To secure a good business partnership.

After a few minutes of knocking, I hear shuffling, and Evelyn opens the door. She's still in her "la femme" T-shirt and jeans, her eyes are dark, and her hair... ah, Jesus. It's cotton candy sex hair. She ruffles it, making it worse—or better, depending on your point of view—and winces.

"Where's your brother?" I ask, wondering why she looks so rough. How is this guy supposed to take care of my apartments if he can't even take care of his sister?

"He had an early call from 1A. Something about flooding coming down from 2A," she says, her voice scratchy.

"Why didn't they call me?" I ask, getting heated. "It's my place. I should know when things like this go wrong."

She opens one eye and scrunches her face. "No. Not in real time, at least. He let my dad know, and now he's probably either fixing whatever is causing the leak, or he's already at Home Depot picking up drywall and insulation and whatever else needs to be replaced."

"Really? Already?"

She does this weird, cute twitchy thing with her nose. "Yeah. They'll always prefer to tell you what happened after they've already taken care of it. And if he hasn't called you, whatever it was didn't cost more than $500."

"How's that possible?" I ask, worried that this sounds more like a $5,000 problem, not a $500 problem. Evelyn winces again at my question, and I realize that I've been interrogating her. "Sorry... I know you don't handle that part of it. It's just that my Austin investments seem to have more than their fair share of issues."

"That's because you hired terrible people and didn't have proper oversight. You have good people now. And you're here. It'll get better. Be patient," she answers, shifting uncomfortably. She peers at the bag in my hand. "Did you bring that for me, or did you wake me up to play twenty questions?"

"You didn't have anything for breakfast, and you need your meds," I say, holding up the groceries. Her eyes narrow and she bites her lip, making my stomach tense. Nodding to herself, she steps back and lets me enter her apartment. At my insistence she sits down at the table, which has been cleared off, and I head off to the kitchen, placing the bags on the counter and making myself at home. After rummaging through the cabinets, I find a cast iron skillet and set about cooking bacon, eggs, and toast with my mom's homemade jam.

I set the food down in front of her, and a low groan escapes her pinky-peach lips.

"Are you okay?" I ask, worried that she's in too much pain to eat.

Keeping her neck still for once in her goddamned life, she flicks those big eyes up at me. "I was so hungry. Thanks, Scout."

I shrug. All in a day's work.

She wolfs down the food in silence and takes the pills from my hand, adjusting painfully in her seat.

"Is there anything I can do to make you more comfortable?"

Her neck reddens, but she shakes her head no. And winces because she can't stop herself. She continues to eat and to shift uncomfortably in her chair.

"*Evelyn.*"

She ignores me, using the last bit of crust on her bread to sop up the remaining egg yolk. I frown, realizing that I probably should have cooked her a third egg.

"Evelyn," I say again, my voice lower than usual. She runs her napkin through her fingers, avoiding my gaze, instead pretending to scratch at a piece of food stuck to the table. "Look, I've spent plenty of time in the hospital having to depend on others to help me with intimate stuff. And you're obviously uncomfortable. What do you need?"

She goes even brighter but says nothing. Shit. This is probably my fault, and now she won't let me help her. "Please don't let what I said yesterday keep you from accepting help. I really didn't mean it. You were right, I was saying it to be a jerk. I promise I'm not judging you."

Certainly not with the state of my body.

Looking miserable, she fumbles her words a little. "I'm, uh. I... left my bra on last night. It's digging into my skin, and I don't know that I can get it, um, off."

I rub my jaw, annoyed at myself. "Shoulda let me help you in to your pajamas last night."

"Probably," she mumbles.

"Will you let me help you now?" I ask, getting up from the table.

One side of her mouth lifts. "Still trying to get me naked?"

I harden my expression, ignoring the fact that a part of my body that has been dormant for the better part of a year just fired to life. "It's not like that at all. You could clearly use a hand."

She pauses for a moment, then nods her head, and my asshole heart starts thudding in my chest.

I ignore what my body is saying—the various treatments over the last couple of years have affected my hormones. Usually in the other direction, but my body is still adjusting. I'm not some kind of pervert trying to get off on seeing her naked. I'm just not a fan of her discomfort.

We head back to her room, and I note that, while it's as unupdated as the rest of the place, her personal style infuses the space with a warm, feminine ambiance. Her antique dresser is art deco like the coffee table in the living room, and her white rug has that kind of fuzzy high pile that you can sink your feet into. Her bed is a heady mix of pearl-gray covers, crisp white linens, and soft blush accents. It's so damned inviting in the morning light, and I have to physically restrain myself from putting her on the bed and wrapping myself around her soft warmth.

Woah. Where the hell did that come from?

I school my face and wrangle my attention to the present, where I find myself having to stop her from opening an enormous busted-up suitcase on the floor.

"Why do you have to make everything so hard?" I ask, removing, I shit you not, the *duct tape* holding it together, and flipping it open with a loud thump. "Why can't you let me help you?"

Her beautiful eyes do a thing, but she shakes her head and smooths her features. "I have learned to rely on myself."

If the duct tape is any indication, someone in her life was really unfuckingreliable. Grinding my jaw, I rifle through her lacy bras and hair products and tampons and makeup and amber- and coconut-scented lotion (that I briefly consider stealing for no particular reason). It takes a minute to find a clean pair of underwear that doesn't make my face heat up, and I settle on a set of pajama shorts with poodles all over them, including a matching T-shirt featuring a poodle with a beret on her head, smoking a cigarette through a long, thin black cylinder. Shaking my head, I hold up the outfit. "Poodles? Really?"

She grins and takes them from me. "Poodles and oodles are smart. And sweet."

Like you.

Shut. Up.

"Oodles?"

"Poodle-mixes. Little bit of poodle makes everything better."

I scrunch my nose. Even her taste in dogs is girly. "So, do you have a dog?" I ask, looking around.

"No," she says, her eyes on the ground. I tilt my head at her, and she continues. "Um, I did, but I couldn't keep her with me while I was trying to figure out my living situation, so I had to leave her with my ex."

"We allow dogs here, Evelyn. You can bring your dog home now."

"I'm... thank you, Scout. Really. I just... I've got too many things going on right now. And I don't have the money, really. But, thank you."

I help her stand up and notice her eyes all shiny and sad, which twists my insides. Looking to change the subject, I ask, "Can I take off your bra?"

Evelyn's neck pinks and she draws her teeth across her lower lip.

Shit. That did sound... sexual.

"I mean, um, do you give me permission to help you with... it?" I say, thinning my mouth into a serious line.

Her mouth quirks up and she turns around, her back facing me. "Yes, Scout. You have my permission to take off my bra. I promise not to sue."

Nodding to myself, I reach for the hem of her shirt. Pale, tattooed skin peaks out at her waistband, and I drop the fabric like it's on fire. I shake out my hands, discharging the electricity.

C'mon, Scout. You've been around gorgeous women your entire adult life. Get your shit together.

Scrubbing my face with one hand, I close my eyes to snake the other hand up the back of her shirt and deftly unhook her bra, counting four hooks before the unforgiving material finally releases. A breathy, satisfied sound escapes her pretty lips, and I resist the groan in the back of my throat. I briefly graze my fingers over the newly freed skin, drawing a subtle inhale from Evelyn. My lip curls into a snarl when my fingertips drift into the heated indentations left behind by the bra's unforgiving bands.

Dammit.

I should have insisted on helping her with this last night.

Taking in a ragged breath, I reach up one sleeve, skimming her soft skin as I pull the strap down her arm, past her hands, first on one side, then the other. Her shoulders visibly relax, but a blotchy red color moves up her neck, where a vein is drawn up to the surface of the skin, pulsing. I want to reach out my finger to touch it, but instead ratchet down on my self-control.

"That was... efficient," she says softly.

"Not my first time doing that," I say brusquely. "Do you want me to take off your shirt?"

The blotching moves up into her face and around the helix of her ear, and for the briefest moment I want to put my lips on her reddened jaw. The moment passes.

"Um. Maybe," she says, her voice slightly distorted. I grab the hem and start to pull up, but she reaches back and snatches my wrist, the one she nearly broke yesterday. "Um. On second thought, I think I've got it."

She stills, the breath caught in her lungs as she faces away from me. "Tell you what," I say evenly, "I'll wait in the living room and can come back if you need help."

She nods and I leave this treacherous fucking room.

About five minutes later, she walks into the living room wearing her poodle pajamas, looking more like herself and smelling... sigh. Delicious.

Face washed.

Hair brushed.

Sans bra.

My eyes rove her body—her round, ungoverned breasts, her ridiculous hips, her thick, shapely legs, and her pedicured feet. There's nothing on her that isn't girly or primped or voluptuous. Her thighs are soft and inviting, her skin decadently plush. The air-conditioning clicks on, and I avert my eyes when her nipples peak beneath the thin fabric. I try to avoid imagining how she tastes. Everywhere. To be honest, I'm not entirely successful. My long fingers dance around my thighs, zinging with a desire to palm and squeeze and roll. While I'm glad to see that my libido has returned, I make a mental note to find a more appropriate outlet.

She slow-shifts her trajectory, wobbly from the meds, and goes in for a huge hug. "Thanks for helping me." Her voice is muffled because she's speaking into my shirt and... *snuggling* in against my body. Every sense is online. She smells amazing, like coconuts, but not too sweet. Her skin is unbelievably soft, and her hair is a flame of lavender down her back. Worst of all, she's moaning. My arms fall slowly around her, and I make a deal with myself. Just one squeeze. One long-ass squeeze.

"Mmmm," she moans again. "You're such a good hugger." She pulls away and ruffles her fingers through my hair. "I like this," she says, separating out the white streak and twirling it around her finger.

"Yeah?" I ask, caught between reveling in her touch and blushing at the compliment. I looked younger when I covered it up, but this last year had me deciding that people could just deal with the fact that I am now a woman in my forties. Truth be told, it makes me feel a little badass.

A smile curls up on her lips as she continues to absentmindedly twirl the strands around her finger. "Yeah," she responds softly. Her eyes go out of focus, then resharpen. She brushes the streak back into the rest of my hairdo, and a bit of color comes up on her cheeks. "Okay, well... see you tomorrow."

"Uh, what?" I ask, slightly dazed. I shake my head to clear the cobwebs. "You are not coming in tomorrow," I respond, drawing myself up to my full height, fixing her with a rigid glare.

She bites her lip and adjusts my collar. "Try and stop me."

Yeah, I'm going to need to find some adult company and quick.

Evie

I might be high on muscle relaxers, but I'm pretty sure Scout Martinez just put me in her own personal spank bank.

I guess that makes us even.

I wake up the next morning in rough condition, but way better than the day before. I take naproxen instead of the heavy stuff and give it a while to kick in. The sharp edge of pain is dulled, and while I can't exactly roll my neck, I can slowly turn and nod. I'll take that as a win.

I get to the shop around 8:00 and start up the wood-fired pizza oven, then get the dough in the industrial mixer. By 8:30 the dough is rolled into balls and set in the proofing cabinet. I dust myself off and remove my flour-splashed apron and check on the emails for the day, as well as the online preorders that have come in overnight. I print everything out and look through the orders for inspiration for today's "pizza of the day." Somebody added jalapeños to a Hawaiian pizza, so I switch out a few ingredients and by 10:00 I have the coffee percolating and I'm rolling out a fresh large pizza with my killer marinara, far too much freshly shredded buttery mozzarella, pepperoni, pepperoncinis, small pineapple cubes, and a quick drizzle of my secret ingredient. By the time my service industry folks walk in the door, the pie is ready, the pepperoni is perfectly crisped, and the pineapple is caramelized. Smells like heaven.

Raymond walks in, his usual flirty self. "Hey, hot stuff. What is that decadent smell in there?" He's in his midforties, a really terrible dresser, and a little too honest about his various drug habits. He asked me out a few weeks ago but was gracious when I said no.

"I call it my Spicy Hawaiian," I say with a smile and a raised eyebrow. I toss a slice onto a paper plate and slide it over to him. "Tell me what you think."

He blows on the fresh pie for a moment, then gingerly picks it up and folds it in half, taking an enormous, mouth-searing bite. A deep, orgasmic groan rumbles from within his chest. "Lady, what the hell are you doing to me? The edges on the pepperoni are fantastic, and the pineapple... I've never had pineapple on a pizza before, and I am totally hooked. This is going to go in the permanent rotation, you mark my words."

He says that almost every morning, but I kinda like it. As he's mimicking Meg Ryan, Terry walks in. Terry's a chef in his sixties and is a huge, huge flirt. "Looks like you got Ray going again, this morning

—can't wait to try it out. Say, where were you the last coupla days? It's not the same without you, you know?"

"Ah, thanks, sweetie," I say, sliding him a slice. "I was in a minor fender bender and had mild whiplash."

Terry grabs me by the hand and looks deeply into my eyes. Unlike Ray, Terry will continue to ask me out till the cows come home, but I don't think he's serious about it. "Oh no! Are you okay? Should you even be working right now?"

"No. She should not be working right now," says a dark voice from the back of the shop, sending a thrill up my spine. Scout steps out from behind the pizza oven, her huge hands on her narrow hips, her cheekbones especially sharp. "She should stop flirting with our customers and go to bed."

"Hey!" I say, brightening. "Good morning."

Scout sidles up next to me, her arms grazing mine, the sensation like brushing velvet against the pile. Peering down at me, she taps impatiently on the counter, and asks in a gruff voice, "Why are you here?"

"I've got my 10:30 crew—I can't let them go hungry. I'm already off the heavy stuff. I'll be fine," I say, slowly stretching my sore neck as I sneak a glance up at her. Her face is stern, but her scary hawk eyes are... worried. It's kinda sweet. Two more of my regulars, Lizbeth and Catherine from the hot dog place across the way, show up and ask Ray and Terry about the morning special. They nod and I slide in front of the hulking lesbian to pass them their slices. She doesn't move, and my ass brushes her upper thighs. She grunts at the contact but doesn't step back. I can feel my neck begin to heat up, but time's a tickin'.

Ray signals for another slice, and so does Terry. I still have four to five more people coming in the next few minutes, most of them coming in hungry from an overnight shift, so I brush past her again and move to the prep station to spin up another special. "Hey," I toss over my shoulder, "I've only got two more slices on this pizza, but more will be up in five. Make yourself useful—my 10:30 folks get either coffee or a small drink with their slice. Cost is five flat, cash."

Within minutes, the counter is crowded with service industry folks in their various branded tees and polos, either coming or going from work, shouldering in to get a slice. Many grab the slice, help themselves to their drink of choice, toss the bill on the counter, and are out the door seconds later, hurrying to make their own lunch rush. Ray sees that we're already out of coffee and goes about brewing another gallon. I've brushed past Scout about twenty times, and each time she stands her ground, not giving me the right of way. Since she is fully capable of moving out of the way, I can only assume that she's not bothered by the hip checks and booty brushes. Either that, or she's enjoying them, nevermind the scowl on her face.

By 10:55, the place is empty, and I flip over the "We're Open!" sign. My neck is starting to fatigue, but it'll be less busy through the rest of the day. Scout finally comes from behind the counter, taking the large percolator out of my grasp. "You should not be carrying this," she says as she efficiently strides to the back of the shop. She's wearing this black leather cuff thing on her wrist that accentuates her cabled arms, and it makes me wonder if she's into a little light BDSM, maybe some power dynamics...

Seem to have drifted there for a second.

Suffice to say, I'm not exactly turned off by the thought of it, but I more or less successfully push that out of my mind and go to the back to complete the prep for the rest of the day.

As I'm chopping up the vegetables, her looming presence prickles the skin on my neck. She huffs when I ignore her, and then starts. "So... this is the 1030 entry I see on the ledger every day."

"Yep," I say, popping the *p* for emphasis as I slice through some fresh radishes.

"Whose idea was that, to open early for the service folks?"

"Mine," I say, not looking up from deveining a bell pepper.

She blows out another breath. "Are you aware that your little 10:30 special is the only reason why this store breaks even every month?"

"Not the only reason." I move on to mushrooms as she shifts closer.

"That's right. You also set up the preorder system. We'd been running almost $5,000 in the red every month for the first three months," Scout says, her voice husky. "Those two changes put us at even." She's close enough for me to smell her soap and feel her heat.

"Yep," I say again, stopping to stretch my neck. "Guess Kim knew what she was doing when she—" I lose my line of conversation when she puts her large warm hands on my shoulders. Her thumbs dig into my traps to release the tension, and when she moves up to the sensitive skin on my neck, I practically whimper. She moves her hands down to my shoulders and spins me around. Her tough, angled eyes worry as she runs her thumbs along my clavicles, pushing in on painful trigger points. I square my jaw and lock my face, trying not to moan.

Avoiding my eyes, she asks, "Does your neck hurt? Scale of one to ten?"

"Five," I lie.

"Bullshit."

"Six or seven."

"So, eight," she says, her smoldering black eyes finally finding mine. She moves her thumbs lightly up the front of my neck and I inhale sharply, then wince. I grab the edge of the butcher block behind me, trying to root myself somehow. I bite my lip and her eyes sweep down to the movement, then flick to the door as the bell rings in Kim. Scout curses under her breath, quickly removing her hands and their attendant heat from my person.

"You called Kim?" I say, taking in her softened expression, which she immediately hardens.

"Yeah. Can't have my money maker in pain all day, now can I?" she says, studying my body in a way that heats my neck. "You're off duty till next week, and don't give me any shit—you're not losing any pay. I need you to come into work ready to go. Can you manage that?" she asks, her voice low and rough.

I nod and go to take off my apron, but she's there, untying the string that holds it in place, her sharp, black eyes locked with mine. "I'll check on you later tonight," she says and turns to Kim to continue the day without me.

7

SCOUT

*L*et me preface this by stating unequivocally that I am extremely fit, especially at this point of my recovery. I maintain the workout I had at the peak of my career—with a few modifications for my knee, of course—and I can keep up with the best of them. But this day behind the counter at the pizza shop has me spent. My feet hurt, my back hurts, and my knee is way unhappy with me. We closed at 9:00 and didn't leave until almost 10:00. Definitely need more employees, but that is subject to board approval. More to figure out later. Right now, I just want to make sure that Evelyn's all right, and then I want to fall into bed and sleep for a million years.

Technically, her apartment is right next to mine, though the two could not be more different from one another. While hers is a cramped and outdated two-bedroom, mine is a fully updated townhouse with an open floor plan and open wood and wrought iron staircase that cuts through the middle of the space, leading up to three spacious bedrooms.

I knock lightly on the door to avoid waking her if she is already asleep. Jake, her brother and twin of the tow truck driver, opens the door.

I haven't said anything yet, so Jake clears his throat and greets me.

"Hi, Scout. Is anything wrong with your apartment?" he asks sincerely.

He's an inch or so taller than me, and this evening he's shirtless—clearly a fan of the gym and probably a runner. His eyes, however, are still black with lack of sleep. Pretty sure there's more to his story, but I'm too tired to suss it out now.

I scan past him into the living room. I notice the duvet folded up on the couch behind him and remember that he's in the middle of patching up the drywall after getting the infestation under control. "No, I was checking on Evelyn. Making sure she actually rested today." His eyebrow raises a little, but he doesn't pursue it.

"She's finally taking the recommend dose of pain meds, so she's in bed—" His explanation is interrupted by what can only be described as caterwauling. "But it sounds like she's up if you want to check in on her."

I laugh and make my way toward her bedroom door, steeling myself to enter my own private hell.

Evelyn is wearing a flimsy romper with no bra, her hair is loose and sexy, and she's dancing (a little stiffly), singing along (sort of) to that Katy Perry song about kissing girls, and wearing her soft neck brace as a hairband. My belly tightens.

"Pretty sure that's supposed to go around your neck," I say wryly, catching a peek of the soft swell of her exposed side boob. She turns off the music and quickly spins to face me, her honeyed eyes wide, her pouty mouth perfectly round. This vulnerable look of hers sends bolts of desire through my belly and destinations farther south. The slight clothing reveals more tattooing along her ribs. When she shifts again, a pale pink nipple slips out, then back under the practically see-through material, and my muscles—fuck, the whole room—tenses at the sight of it.

"What, exactly, are you wearing?" I ask, gesturing at the soft, thin, body-draping onesie, dragging my eyes to hers.

"It's my sleep sack," she says, her neck reddening as she pulls it up.

"My old dog had a sleep sack. This… doesn't look like that."

"And this is why you'll never design for a sleepwear line," she jokes, trying to rib me.

"And you listening to that song is why lesbians don't like bisexuals," I say harshly.

The redness creeps up along her jawline, but she stands her ground. "You're telling me that you don't like kissing girls?"

"Oh, I love kissing girls," I say as I saunter over and pull her neck brace off her head. I'm too close to her, and I know it. I take in her beautiful face, unable—or unwilling—to look away. "But then again, so do you."

The blush creeps up to her cheeks and ears, but she holds my gaze, her eyes fierce. "I'm pretty sure I would."

Her wording knocks me back. "Wait, you've never actually kissed a girl before?"

She runs her teeth along her lower lip and shakes her head.

"Like, *never*?"

Fuck. Me.

"Unless you're counting my five-year-old kiss, which, by the way, got me a paddling and grounded for the rest of the summer, then... no." Her cheeks flame bright red with this admission.

"Okay, now I'm really confused," I say as I stoop and snake my long arms around her neck to fasten the brace. By the way, it's easier to do this from the back, but there's a helluva lot more contact doing it this way. Don't judge me. "There's literally no way that a woman of my persuasion hasn't tried to pick you up or drunkenly kiss you in a club or, I dunno, stood outside your door until you said yes to a date," I say, naming all of the ways in which I've demonstrated my attraction to a woman. All of the things I'm actively avoiding right about now.

She stiffens beneath my touch, and a soft breath rises up from her chest. I bite my inner lip, buzzy from my effect on her. "It's not something my family would support."

Ah, *man*.

I step back and glare at her intently. "Are you telling me that I have hired a bunch of homophobes to take care of this complex?"

Her eyes fly open. "No! No, not... not exactly. It was my mom. She loved the church." She holds up her hands when she sees my anger. "But she also loved us, I think more than even church. And she died almost fifteen years ago. I really think that she would have come around. I do. And, if I'm honest," she says, pointing in the direction of the living room, dropping her voice to a whisper, "I think my brother struggles with it. But my dad and Spence have this... illogical, misguided need to uphold the things that were important to her. They go to church every Sunday, even though they hate it, and they try to be good humans. At least they try to obey the rules."

"Except for the one about love, apparently. Must be nice to be bi, then. *You* can hide." I gesture to myself. "*I* can't." Not sure why this bothers me so much, but it does. I'm used to random people shouting shit at me. I mean, I'm a six-foot-two, athletic woman with dyke hair. It happens. Just never in my inner circle. Never where it's supposed to be safe. I turn to leave, anxious to avoid the insecurity beginning to gnaw at me, but her soft hand reaches out for my wrist.

"I'm not hiding," she insists. "If they were completely irredeemable people, I wouldn't stay so close to them. But they are good people. They are really wrong about this one thing, and once my life is somewhat reordered, I'm going to tell them about me. It'll be hard, but I know that they'll come around. I *know* they will." She peeks up at me, and her eyes are warm pools pleading with me, begging me to believe her. I give a little ground with a faint nod, to which she breathes a sigh of relief and puts her head to my shoulder. That move sets my belly on fire, and whatever shampoo she's using is chipping away at my self-control.

We stay that way for a beat too long, and before I can pull away, she leans in for a hug, her softness wrapping around my hard planes and angles. The loneliness of this past year cuts in comparison to the warmth of her embrace, and I step away to avoid the emotion rising to the surface. The movement once again slips the fabric away from her nipple, which is now a darker color and beginning to peak. She captures my gaze, holding it as she slowly—too slowly—covers herself.

Jesus. Christ.

My hand reaches out to her face of its own accord, and I run a rough thumb along her beautiful cheekbone. She inhales sharply, her eyes dark, the unspoken connection thick in the air. Her lips quiver a tiny bit, and I want so much to taste them, to feel them return my pressure. I need to stop, but my body, so long without the soft lips of a beautiful woman, is on autopilot.

I gently lace my fingers over her brace, leaning in, executive function completely turned off. I press my lips to hers, and fire races through my veins. Her hands go to my waist to pull me in, and her warm fingertips brush the skin by my waistband. A heated, mewling sound escapes her throat, so I deepen the kiss and part her lips with my tongue. She opens up to me, delicately touching her tongue to mine, shooting electricity through my dusty nerve endings, lighting up my entire body. Wetness slips through my pulsing core, a nearly forgotten sensation. I once again press myself to her body as she welds to mine, both of us needy.

My internal alarm blares a warning, which I ignore for a few more precious seconds as our tongues become more insistent and my hands find their way to her ribs and the roundness of her breasts. My thumb circles that teasing nipple of hers, and her entire body jerks. Her gasp freezes our kiss, our lips still skimming one another. Her round, dark honey eyes search mine, looking for reassurance. I push softly into her lips and continue to thumb her nipple, bringing my knee between her legs. She molds herself to me and begins a slow roll of friction against my thigh. I can tell by the way the fabric slides along my thigh that she's wet and ready.

It's enough for my brain to finally surface and think about what it is that I am doing.

Shit.

Stop it, Scout. Stop.

Stop fondling your pharmacologically compromised bisexual employee.

Painfully, I wrench myself away. Her eyes show disappointment and raw want, and her swollen lips open in protest. "Fuck," I say roughly.

"Please don't stop, Scout." Her whispered words are breathy as she continues to push her hot core against my thigh. Pressing my hand to her breast, her honey-dipped eyes erode my resolve and my sanity. "You don't have to stop."

My thumb steals one last caress, and I finally pull away, regretting each retreating inch. I take another large step back, my hands in a defensive posture. "I absolutely have to stop. I'm your boss and I'm in no place to paper train a newbie. But… you deserved to be properly kissed by a woman. So at least that's squared away. I've got to go. Long day tomorrow."

Leaving her breathless, with a confused and hurt look brewing on her face, I stride out the door, trying to convince myself that I'm not running.

8

EVIE

It's the morning after my sleep sack apocalypse, and I wake in a rage.

That... *lesbian.*

She plants a top five kiss on me, hits second base like a tornado, has me practically rubbing one out on her thigh, and then scuttles off with some bullcorn excuse about not wanting to "paper train" me. *Me.*

I don't know who the heck she thinks I am.

I may be new to girls, but I am not new to sex. I'm a freaking sex goddess. I *live* to please in bed. I know for a fact that I could make that woman's eyes roll to the back of her head. I may not have ever gone down on a lady before, but I know what I like, and I have fantasized about it, plenty. The last three days especially, in technicolor, lurid detail.

Side note: I'd gone to her massage therapist yesterday, and that woman is a dang miracle worker. I'm on the mend, and ready to scrap with this gorgeous butch.

Anyway.

I can't decide if I want to deck her or sleep with her, but either way, I am going to mess with her head. I look down at the app and swipe right. A message pops up a few minutes later, and by the time I'm out the door, I've got a plan in place.

"Nope. Turn around." Scout barely looks up from the dough she's preparing when I walk into the shop.

"I have a job to do. And you're overworking the dough," I say, wresting the poor lump from her man hands, annoyed that the contact sends a wave of heat up to my jawline.

Clenching her jaw, she protests, "This recipe—*your recipe*—says to knead it for ten minutes."

I roll my perfectly lined eyes dramatically. "Yeah, in the electric mixer, not with your Gigantor mitts. You probably haven't even washed your hands properly," I say, hipping her out of the way. Without a second glance, I throw out the wad of dough and start over.

"Hey!" she shouts at me. "That's wasteful!"

I gawk at her like she's grown a third head. "That's about seventeen cents' worth of flour and ingredients. You do it wrong, you start over. Simple as that. And you weren't making enough. And don't yell at me." *It's because you're sexually frustrated, and that's on you, you giant beanpole.* I may or may not have muttered some of that under my breath.

"I'm trying to keep things in budget," she says, modulating her tone.

I turn around and glare up at her. "Is that why you let Kim buy a $20,000 wood-fired oven before I could stop her? Like, what kind of budget is that? Also, not for nothing, not only is the oven expensive, it's too small. One pie at a time. *For a pizza restaurant.* Between that and the damned wood that needs to be shoved into that thing every hour on the hour, you're paying half a salary just to keep that princess oven operational."

"The pizza out of this oven is the best pizza I've ever had. People will pay for quality pizza," she says as though that were the line she used to convince herself to buy this ridiculous setup. I roll my eyes and shake my head at her.

"That's because it's *my* pizza, you near-sighted beanstalk," I growl, annoyed that she didn't recognize my work. "Seriously, there's not a thing you've done with this place that is scalable or sustainable. I mean, you don't even have a dishwasher in here. I have to wash everything by hand at the end of the night. Sheer madness."

She throws her hands up in the air. "Those were all decisions that Kimberly..." A dark mood crosses her face. "Fuck it. Fine. What *exactly* am I supposed to do about this now?"

I reach up and tap the middle of her forehead. "You could sell this gorgeous piece of worthless and get a good used triple-decker brick oven for half the cost on eBay, and then you could take the rest of that money to get a ding dang dishwasher and hire some part-time help for us this quarter."

Scout

Fuck. Me. Squared.

I've been ripping my hair out for the last six months trying to figure out how to make this pizza shop profitable, and the damned bisexual tells me in under thirty seconds how to do it. And now she's hip-checked me out of the way while she zips around the kitchen, making the dough, chopping up the toppings, handling the 10:30 rush, and generally being a pain in my ass.

I've never felt so useless in my entire life.

We make it till about 6:00, and I can see that she's starting to hurt again. "Are you staying on top of your pain meds?" I ask after she winces for the fifteen hundredth time.

"Muscle relaxers and knives don't mix, Scout."

"Then take a break."

"No, ma'am," she says, brushing by me for the eighty-seventh time today. "I'm leaving early, and I don't want you to ruin my reputation with your dirty mitts and terrible dough skills."

I stand over her, stopping her forward progress, palming her tender shoulders. "We will probably have five customers for the rest of the night. There's plenty of stuff here. I can handle it. Go home and rest. Please."

She juts out her chin, about to protest, when the bell above the door chimes. I push her toward the door and put on my best face for my incoming guest.

Fuck. Carla.

"It's pretty dead in here, Sophia. Thought you were coming here to revitalize this place."

Carla is my height but otherwise my opposite in every way. Her hair cascades down in long, caramel curls, she has beautiful cheekbones and a gorgeous smile, and her body is feminine, all lithe curves and grace.

I'd been so broken up over her that I hadn't realized what a shitty human being she actually was. All of those passive-aggressive barbs. All of those comments about how other ex-players were doing better off financially, and that she would be driving around in a Maybach if I'd just played my cards right. All of those texts begging me come back / god ur so ugly / baby pls come home / fuck off u dyke bitch. All of the ways in which she undercut me. I ignore the ache across my chest and face her.

"Hello, Carla. Poisonous as ever, I see." Evelyn's ear tips up at my choice of words, pausing as she slings her preposterous bag over her shoulder. We exchange a look, and she briefly nods at me, as if to say that she's not going anywhere. Clearly she's picked a side, and I'm a little too happy that it's mine.

"So, what, exactly, are you doing here?" Carla asks, disdain on her shapely lips and in her tone.

I square up, hoping that she doesn't sense the vulnerability just under the surface. "That's none of your business."

Her eyebrow raises arrogantly. "It *is* my business. This week's report isn't good."

I bite the inside of my lower lip, willing myself to buck up. Pinning her with a glare, I retort, "I don't waltz into your holdings and demand an accounting."

Her lip quirks up. "That's because my holdings are profitable. The board needs an update."

God, I hope Evelyn at least waits to call me out on this one. "*Fine.*

If the board wants an update, please remind them that it's only been a few days since I've been in-house. I've already identified several inefficiencies with the way our food is processed and cooked and will be rectifying those immediately. I've retained key talent to make sure that the quality remains high, and I anticipate that we'll be expanding this operation by the end of the year."

Carla purses her lips and gives me a once-over. "Delusional as ever, I see. Good luck with that. It'd be a shame to have to shutter the entire Austin branch."

Fuck that, obviously, but I refuse to rise to the bait, especially with Evelyn here.

Carla gives me one last judgmental sweep, then turns on the $600 heels that I bought her for her birthday last year and walks out the door. Only after she's gotten into her Land Rover and driven away am I able to drop my shoulders from the vicinity of my earlobes.

I sense Evelyn behind me, hovering. "So, wow, that was Carla Forrester."

I nod, hating life, waiting for her to bust me for presenting her ideas as my own, or for being such an absolute dork around my ex. She maintains her silence.

"What?" I ask, more than a little defensive.

"She seems nice," Evelyn cracks.

I turn around and, despite the humor, note the concern in her eyes and her teeth grazing her lower lip. "She's my ex."

"That would explain the hostility."

"Probably."

She puts her hand on her hip, a high arch in her brow. "Glad to hear that I'm 'key talent.' Bet that hurt coming of your mouth."

I shake my head, grinning. "You have no idea."

9

EVIE

Look. I really feel bad about what's going to happen next. Especially since Carla Forrester came in and already kinda ruined Scout's day. But she had some bad juju from that kiss-and-run move she pulled, and that's not my fault. I jerk up when the bell on the door clangs right at 6:30. A rumpled man in his late forties, maybe early fifties, approaches the counter.

I sigh, completely deflated.

Pretty sure the picture on his profile is about fifteen years and half a head of hair ago. I'm fine with older guys. Huge fan of the very sexy, very bald Patrick Stewart. Liars? Not so much.

The cute-in-a-nerdy-way look from his pics has given way to a dark-eyed wan visage, like a before picture for a vitamin D ad. I contemplate ending the date before it begins, already uncertain about my plan to hit-it-and-quit-it with this guy, but decide to give him the benefit of the doubt. Online dating is often a cruel exercise in humiliation, and I'm not going to be a jerk to him.

I mean, I kind of am being a jerk since I'm using him to dig at Scout, but he's probably going to get laid out of the deal, so I'm not feeling overly guilty about that.

Scout approaches the counter. "How can I help you? Our special today is balsamic mushroom with fresh basil."

"Hi," he says, eyes slightly narrowed. "I'm not actually ordering anything. Is Evie here?"

From my perch, I can see her eyes darken, and she glares at him as she backs away from the counter. Searching the back of the shop, she spies me in the shadow I'd tried to disappear in and crooks her finger at me.

"What is this?" she asks, annoyed. Giving me the once-over, she angles back for a better look. "You changed?"

"*This...* is a date," I say, locking eyes with her as I put my hands on my hips, daring her to say a damned thing. She wisely keeps her mouth shut. "And I changed because I don't want to smell like pizza at a nice restaurant."

I hip-check past her, my flowery dress fluttering from the movement.

"Edward?" I ask, plastering a fake smile on my freshly glossed lips.

"Yes. You had blonde hair in the pictures," he says, tugging on the collar of his wrinkled polo.

I catch Scout's eye, responding, "Thought I'd give the blonde a break, try something new. I posted the lavender ones last night."

"Mmmm," he says as I swing up the counter to leave. Glancing back, I say, "Sophia, be a darling and close the shop, won't you? I'll be out the rest of the evening."

She gestures toward Gary, or whatever his name is, as if to say *this guy? Really?* I gesture back with a coordinated fist-and-tongue-in-cheek move. *Booyah,* you long-limbed bitch.

The date isn't completely unfortunate. Joey, or whatever, is extremely smart, and mildly humorous, even if he is a bit prickly and damp-handed.

"So... since we're done here, do you want to go back to my place?"

Honestly, I'm surprised that he liked me enough to ask. I hesitate, thinking it might be better to just end the date now, but I really do need to get laid sometime this decade. And who knows, maybe he'll be one of those quiet types who is secretly super talented in bed. I nod coyly, and he signals for the bill. We split the check, and he walks me to his Jetta. I inspect him as I let myself in on the passenger side and decide that I'm glad that he doesn't have a comb-over and that he'd probably be an okay person to go on a few dates with. I keep getting the sense that I'm being weighed and measured, but we're still on the date, so he must think I'm at least kinda okay.

We get to his apartment, which is in one of the newer, slightly generic, but well-amenitied apartment communities in Austin. The sign is new, the trees are perfectly manicured, and I'm pretty sure they don't dye the pool water green for St. Patrick's Day. He's got a first-floor apartment, which he proudly explains "cost $50 more, but is so worth it." I take his word for it and follow him into the not-too-small space with beige carpeting and black bachelor couches.

The apartment isn't dirty, exactly, but the smell of moldy... something... lingers on the air. *Middle-aged-man smell*, I think to myself as I let him lead me to one of the fake leather couches, noticing as I sit that it's too firm and slick. These are clearly not meant for comfort.

"Can I get you anything?" he asks, clearing his throat. "I have beer, water, and some white wine from last week."

I shake my head. No need to prolong the inevitable here, bud.

He gets himself a vodka soda—guess I didn't rank high enough in his opinion for liquor— and takes a few large swigs as he sits down beside me. "I don't usually have people over."

No shit.

"I like your place," I say, placating him. "This is a really nice apartment complex."

"I *know*," he says proudly. "There's *three* pools, and a slide. Plus two really great hot tubs."

I give him a once-over, seeing no evidence that the sun has *ever* grazed his face. Sigh. Let's get this show on the road. I put my hand on his knee and breathe, "Mmmm, I'd definitely like to check out the hot tubs with you."

He nods to himself and goes in for a kiss, his lips rubbery and unappealing. His hands reach for my waist in a rib-crushing grip, and I yelp. He lets go and we kiss for a bit more. I spy the boner through his chinos and begin to unbutton the front of my dress. Honestly, it'd be easier to take the thing off, but I'd rather keep it on while we do the deed, because I don't know if I can handle this man's eyes on all of my business. I suspect that he wouldn't like my body very much.

He gets bolder and begins to kiss the tops of my breasts, and I'm surprised when he unclasps the bra. The front closure opens pretty easily, but he looks unsure of how to get it all the way off. I smile, removing my bra by pulling the straps through the armholes—*like a lady*— leaving my breasts exposed through the unbuttoned fabric of my dress. I part the opening a bit more, inviting him to touch me. He grabs my breasts with too much force, scratching the skin on my rib cage with a hangnail. I yelp again and he changes tactic, scooping his hand under the unfortunate right tit, indulging in a brief and ultimately unsatisfying bout of breast-kneading. After a moment he breathes a little *huh*, and an unpleasant prickling sensation goes down the back of my neck.

"So, were you wearing a special bra?" he asks.

I sit back, puzzled by the question. His hand is still on my tit, and I'm beginning to wish it wasn't. "Uh, no. It's a regular bra. I mean, it's a good bra, but there's nothing special about it."

"But it's not like a push-up bra or a water bra or something?" he asks, his eyes flicking once again to my breast, inspecting it.

"No, why?" I ask, my heart starting to thud a bit harder. Not gonna lie, I'm completely thrown by this line of questioning.

"Because your boobs seemed so different when you were wearing it." He shrugs, flexing his gross fingers under the weight of my right breast, jiggling it as if to inspect its firmness.

Is he really...?

Son of a bitch.

Did this *deeply* mediocre dude in a wrinkled polo with a slip 'n' slide couch—who sent me a picture of himself circa his college years—complain that my DDD breasts don't hold up under... *gravity?*

Seriously?

"Sounds like you're kind of disappointed in the date. I can go," I say, reaching for my purse.

He shrugs, clearly unimpressed with my lying funbags. "Nah, it's cool. Might as well have a good time out of it, y'know?" he says before coming at me with another round of tight-gripped, vulcanized kisses.

Having literally watched cattlemen inspect a cow's udders the way he just scrutinized and commented on my breast, I don't want his goddamned hands on me anymore. What's low-level freaking me out is that, even though I've pulled back and given him an out, he's only continued to tighten his grip around my waist.

I'm frozen like a statue, and he's still putting his lips and hands on me.

The fact of the matter is that he is a lot stronger than I am, and I don't fully trust that he'll respect my desire to go. My brain fires up a solution that borders on overkill, but my mom always told me that it's okay to risk looking foolish to find my way to safety.

Thus resolved, I put my hands firmly on his shoulders and push away from his kiss. Initially he holds on tighter, but finally I wrench myself out of his grip, trying to look demure and sensual, not alarmed and grossed out. "Well then, I have to freshen up before we go any further."

"Oh," he says, licking his lips, "you can, um, use the bathroom in the hall."

"That's so *sweet*. You stay right here, darlin'. I'll be right back."

He nods and his eyes follow me as I walk to the bathroom. I close the door, count to twenty, and then silently open it again. He's on the couch, typing on his phone, so I make my way across the hall into the first bedroom with an open door. That $50 extra a month he pays for a ground-floor apartment is *so worth it*. I quickly walk over to the window while bringing up the Uber app. I quietly—so damned quietly—raise the plastic blinds, flip up the lock, and ease the window open. I see that a driver is less than a mile away and hit the button as I climb out. My foot catches the sill, and I fall out, about a foot and a half down to the soft ground. Not bad, but my neck is super aware of the jolt, and warm liquid drips down the front of my leg where my shin found a stabby rock. No big deal, just a scrape. I can fix that when I get home.

"Hey! Is everything okay back there?" he yells from the couch.

I get up and stick my head back through the window. "Oh yeah, just one more minute!"

I turn and bolt to the front of the complex, grateful that I have my purse, but pissed that I had to leave my heels and my favorite bra behind. I wave over the Uber driver, relief and judgment pouring through me.

Scout

Moving is such a pain in the ass, especially with the store hours. I was exhausted after the long shift, but seeing Evelyn leave with that loser pissed me off. I mean, what the hell was she thinking? What could she possibly see in a guy like that? It's her life, but she's going about it all wrong. She mentioned giving blonde hair a break. I bet she looks hella sexy as a blonde.

I was still so annoyed when I got home that I had to work it off by unpacking the last of my moving boxes. At least that's accomplished, and now I just need to throw out the garbage and recycling before I can call it a night.

Walking through the quiet complex in the dark, I'm reminded of why I bought this property in the first place. The group didn't want in on the investment, but I had to have it. It's in the middle of a suburban neighborhood but feels like an oasis. I gaze up at the night sky through the overgrown palms and can see the vision again. The Koenigs have done a good job putting things right, and even though I am completely impatient with the progress, they have made major improvements.

As I round the corner and crunch down the path back to my apartment, I see a car pull into the parking lot and drive in this general direction. I pause, pretty sure I know its occupant. The door opens and my uncooperative heart speeds up at the sight of lavender hair, then drops when I see her face. Unhappy. Disappointed. I'm not going to pretend I'm sorry that she didn't enjoy her date, but her sad face does things to me. I scan down her body because I enjoy torturing my — Wait.

What.

The.

Fuck.

She isn't wearing shoes, and there is... that is blood on her shin. *Blood.* And her dress looks different than it did when she left, and it takes me a moment to realize that the difference is that she's no longer wearing a bra, and my blood begins to boil.

"Evelyn!" I shout, jogging toward her. Her startled response breaks my heart. "Did that guy...?"

I don't even want to say the words.

I am already envisioning the thirty-seven ways in which I'm going to kill that *fucking* dickhole.

I watch as she spackles together her composure and holds up her hands. "No, nothing like that. I just had to eject out of the date, and we were at a point where I realized I didn't know if I could trust that it would go in a good way."

"So you fought your way out?" I ask, pointing to her bloody shins. I kneel down, inspecting them, gutted by how dirty her pretty feet are. Her face blotches red, and she bats at my hands.

"Um, excuse me. I need details. Right now," I insist, rising to my full height above her.

She shakes her head, avoiding my eyes as she worries her bottom lip with her teeth.

I put my hands on her shoulders and lean in. "I'm seriously not going anywhere until you tell me what happened."

Looking utterly mortified, she whispers, "Don't *laugh*."

God, she's killing me. "Evelyn, I'm not going to laugh at you."

She sighs heavily. "I climbed out of a window."

Okay, maybe I want to laugh a little. But then I think about the scenarios that would justify doing that, and my amusement vanishes. "What *happened*? What would make you climb out of a window?"

She sighs, looking down at her dirty feet. "I probably overreacted. He, uh," she says, shifting her eyes back up to me. "Never mind. It's too embarrassing."

I pull her in a little closer and bob my head. "You'd better tell me because I haven't ruled out homicide."

My tone has an effect on her body, causing her to sway slightly. She stares off in the distance, her neck and face a creeping red. "I, uh... I don't think he really liked me and he, uh.... " She stops, shaking her head.

"*Evelyn*," I growl, holding on to the last of my patience.

She blows out a big breath and says in one rushed-together sentence, "He indicated that he preferred the way my tits looked before I took off my bra."

My face scrunches in confusion. "What?"

"So, yeah... that was a showstopper for me."

Hold up. "He said *what*?"

"I am not going to repeat what he said. I am going to go inside right now to wash it off of me," she says, her face scarlet.

"Okay, but I'm confused. He actually said something about your tits—*your* tits—while—" I pause, not wanting to picture it. "—getting it on with you?"

"Thankfully, we were only rounding bases at that point."

Look, let's move past the fact that I'm super fucking relieved that she didn't sleep with him. "Can we focus for a second on the fact that he had a problem with *your* tits?"

She looked away, jaw clenched. "I mean, I know that a bra is essentially a lie, like, hey, my boobs really aren't up here, but... damn. I wasn't trying to be dishonest by wearing a nice bra on my date."

Like, how is it that she even took this asshat's words to heart? I am so confused.

I skim my hands up and down her soft arms. "Look at me."

She blows out a breath and peeks up at me through her thick lashes.

"I know that I'm your boss. And your father's boss, and your brother's boss. And that I crossed a line the other night, which we are going to pretend didn't happen. But I am a *connoisseur* of boobs. I'm the *shit* when it comes to tits. And I can say, unequivocally, that *you* have spectacular breasts, with or without a bra. With a bra, they are super happy and bouncy, and without they are soft and heavy and incredibly sensual. That guy? *Is a fucking idiot* and should never be allowed to put his hands on another pair of soft tits for the rest of his sad, masturbatory life."

She flushes as I describe her tits to her, and riiiight as I start to wonder if maybe I hadn't broken the law (again), her shoulders begin to shake with laughter. Still avoiding my eyes, she leans her forehead into my chest, continuing to shake. Also, maybe she's still crying a little? But mostly laughing. I think.

Her forehead is still on my chest as she admits, "I spent the entire evening going, well... so what if he no longer looks like his profile picture? So what if he can't be assed to wear a clean, unwrinkled shirt on a date? So what if he can't be bothered to open the door for me? So what if his apartment smells like mildew and serial killer? 'Cause at least he thinks my tits are saggy!" Her shoulders shake a bit more until she finally calms and leans away from my chest. She wipes away the errant mascara and fixes her eyes on me, waiting, it seems, for my judgment. "Guess I really showed you."

I bite back another smile, my ego temporarily stroked from her admission that attempting to sleep with someone to get one over on me wasn't a great idea.

She reads my expression and mutters something that sounds like *Happy?* under her breath.

"You need a better standard for yourself," I say, unable to make my voice sound soft. "Please don't bring any other losers into my pizza shop. It'll crater the business because I *will* start tossing them out on their asses."

She laughs and softly punches my arm, sending a heated rush to my chest. "Okay, welp. *That* was embarrassing. Let's just add that to the list of things we are going to pretend never happened, m'kay? And on that note… good night."

"Hey," I say, grabbing her arm again. Out of concern, not because her skin feels like satin under my fingertips. She goes stiff, and I immediately let her go, wondering exactly how bad this date might have gotten had she not ditched him. "Your shins. Do I need to take you anywhere?"

She shakes her head, her expression curious. "It's just a scrape. I'll be fine. See you in the morning."

I watch as she walks down the path to her front door and listen as her brother reacts to seeing her bloodied shins. As they close the door, I try to convince myself that I'm okay with letting someone who's not me help her.

10

EVIE

Okay, so, new plan. Head down. Get the work done, especially now that Kim has taken her payout and is living her best life in the Mayan Riviera, as evidenced by her jealousy-inducing Instagram. Stop dating crap humans, and definitely stop trying to get one over on Scout, who I've decided is a french bread kind of person. A bit crusty and abrasive on the outside, but warm and doughy on the inside. In other words, good people. Hot people. Arms cut like she's ready for battle people.

All of which is to say that she isn't getting any less sexy or frustrating. I know that it's my lack of experience, and especially my bi-ness, that scares her. Honestly, I get it. I really do. But it still kind of pisses me off. I mean, if you're attracted to someone, can you not just proceed with caution? After the concern she showed in the aftermath of that disastrous date, our mutual attraction is undeniable, and yet she denies it at every opportunity.

I've respected her wishes and kept my distance, but for the last few weeks I've felt her eyes on me when she thinks I'm not looking. Like right now. We are alone in the shop, closing up for the night, and her gaze is a slow burn on the back of my neck. I know not to turn around, lest I frighten her back into the shadows. Instead, I stay busy with my hands, letting her eyes rove over the parts of me that I prefer she would touch.

"I've got the rest of this, Evelyn. You can go home now," she says, the exhaustion from weeks of twelve- and thirteen-hour days touching her voice.

Only now can our eyes find each other, and in that brief moment the air between us is electric. Even in exhaustion, my skin nearly vibrates from need. The nipple that she caressed with her calloused thumb however many weeks ago has the memory of an elephant. It reaches out, and my eyes stroke hers, sending a silent invitation into the space between us. Her features freeze up like she's lowered a mask, and she continues counting the till as though she is not as scorched and singed as I am.

She's a dang liar, but her eyes tell me the truth, and my skin waits in nervous anticipation to get burnt by them over and over again.

Anyway.

I shake my head at her offer to let me leave early and continue to clean up.

I've quietly gone on two more dates, including one with a nice lady, making sure to keep that away from Scout. While those have gone better than that first-floor jackalope, who I blocked, I didn't want to kiss either one of them, let alone go home with them. Their eyes, while kind and smart and funny, left my skin cold and my nerve endings unaffected.

Beyond that whole pathetic mess, small but important changes are happening at the Levee. The new sign is up, and my father's friend did a fantastic job of mixing reclaimed wood with pewter letters for a retro-modern feel. The palms have been trimmed back, the pool has been cleaned and is now a gorgeous turquoise, and my father's AC guy made sure that every unit's machine was inspected, cleaned, and blowing cold for the hot summer ahead.

True to his word, Spence's buddy Julio found a car for me to drive, though he may have outdone himself. He bought an antique gold '68 Mustang Fastback from the sheriff's monthly auction in exchange for Spence running tow services during the next festival season. Spence was able to pop out the few dings and replace the cracked and faded vinyl seats, and I've named her Goldie. She'll look a little better with a fresh paint job, but that'll take some saving to accomplish. Still, she drives like a dream and, miraculously, has a functioning AC.

All in all, I'm pretty lucky, even if my heart is a bit bruised.

11

SCOUT

I should be grateful that it's time to move on to the rest of my investment portfolio, but I've already stayed a week longer than I should have at the pizza shop, and leaving isn't coming any easier.

I get in early to get the dough started, and by the time she walks through the doors, the perfectly rolled-up balls of pizza dough are on the proofing trays. She picks one up, examines it, nods her head in approval, and begins to wordlessly load them in the proofing closet.

"So, um," I start, and immediately lose the thread of what I was going to say. She's wearing the rockabilly look again today, and her shapely mouth is hella distracting.

She stops what she's doing and looks at me, her face neutral. "Yes?"

"I'm bringing in my cousin Roly to be a part-time manager to take some of the load off of you, and we can hire two part-time employees once we begin to speed up."

She smiles, but the light does not touch her eyes.

"It's time for me to start paying attention to my other investments, and I have full faith in you."

Her eyes drop to the floor, and she nods. "So, you're going, then."

"Yes. I'll still pop in from time to time, but I need to shift my focus.

I have a small firm that used to be a fairly steady grower but now seems to have stalled."

"Bluebonnet?" she asks, referring to the Bluebonnet Oil and Gas Consulting office.

"Um, yeah—you know my portfolio?"

She shrugs. "You've been trying to handle your other businesses from the desk in the back. It's a small shop. I can hear when things aren't going well."

"Huh. And what do you think?" I ask, scratching the back of my head to keep my fingers busy. Away from her.

"About the health and longevity of an oil and gas firm in the state of Texas? I have no clue. But you do have a personnel problem."

"I *know*," I groan, frustrated. "We've lost three really talented people in the last three months. Not sure I can keep up with the salaries in this area."

She rolls her eyes, her face impassive.

"What?" I shift uncomfortably, wondering what she sees.

She pulls the hem of her apron through her manicured fingers. "You lost three women in the last three months. Not just people —*women*. Lawyers."

She has been paying attention.

"And?"

Letting out a soft sigh, she hesitates, then thinks better of it. "Isn't the office manager a Forrester?"

Dammit. "Yeah. Her brother. But he hates her. Says Carla's a real cunt."

She widens her eyes. "A guy who would say that about his sister would absolutely do the same or worse with other women. When did he take over the office manager position?"

"I don't know, ten months ago, maybe." A timeline that, oh by the way, coincides with when I started losing people.

She doesn't answer the unasked question, simply raises an eyebrow.

"You don't think that..." I begin to ask, hating where this is going.

"Did he conduct exit interviews?" she asks, pinning me with a look that tells me that she doubts it.

Shit. I don't know. "I'm sure he did; that's the policy."

She scratches her chin, adopting a bored look.

I'd known that Carla's brother wasn't doing me any favors with his management of that office, but it hadn't occurred to me that he might be more than just a shitty boss. I put my head in my hands and let out a moan. "If you're right, rebuilding that office is going to take so much time. And money, neither of which the board is inclined to give me these days."

She rolls her eyes at me and starts wiping down a counter. If I want to hear what she has to say, I'm going to have to ask. Fine.

"You don't agree?"

Waving a hand at me dismissively before turning to wash her hands, she asks, "Does it matter?"

I blow out an exasperated breath. *Yes*, I say to myself, *of course it matters.* Out loud, I say, "So, what would you do?"

She dries her hands and gestures at me with her towel. "Go find the most valuable lawyer that you've lost in the last six months and find out from her why she left. And if I'm right, fire *him* and rehire *her* to take his place. With back pay. Then rehire the other two women, if they were any good."

I inhale and exhale low and slow. "They were. But it'll cost me."

She faces the wall as she hangs the hand towel to dry. "Cheaper and faster than a rebuild. I mean, it is supposed to be a woman-run business to be in your little cadre of investments, no?"

Damn. She's right. Again.

Within two weeks I'd fired Carla's brother and put Samantha Peabody in place as the manager of the Bluebonnet Oil and Gas Company office. While he hadn't physically assaulted anyone, all three of the women who'd left reported that they had the prickly sense that he was going to continue to escalate, and they were afraid to say anything since he is Carla's brother.

Samantha had been busy as a private consultant in her time away from BOGC and brought with her a top ten prospect. We were also able to hire back Lauren Christopher, a business development lawyer with an Ivy League pedigree, plus another friend of Samantha's who had a killer resume as a contract lawyer. The third lawyer liked where she'd landed but appreciated that I'd reached out to her and agreed to settle for back pay. More of my net worth out the door, though far less expensive than it could have been.

Today, I sit at the head of the conference table with the staff and begin to lay out the new HR policies within the company. When people hear that Carla's brother was not actually on vacation, but had in fact been fired for cause, applause erupts around the conference room table, and we decide to celebrate. I call Evelyn.

"Scout. Been a while," she says, sounding busy and distracted.

"What is that noise?" I ask, holding the phone away from my ear.

"That's dinner rush!" she says, and it's nice to hear the enthusiasm in her voice. We still haven't addressed that fool oven, but it looks like putting a little extra into the advertising budget is helping things along.

"Oh, I was going to put in a pizza order to celebrate turning around the Bluebonnet office. Should I get it from somewhere else?"

"Don't you dare! And besides, with the extra help we've been able to do some limited corporate delivery."

Huh. Smart.

I place the order and hear the knock on the door twenty-five minutes later. Expecting Lizbeth, who Evelyn hired from a restaurant across from ours, I step back when I see Evelyn standing there, balancing six pizzas in her hands, and a rush of warmth floods my body. She's wearing red lipstick, black eyeliner, and cuffed jeans with black, steel-toed restaurant shoes, and her white chef's coat has a smudge of marinara on the sleeve. Her lavender hair is in a floured braid down her back, and she's got a bandana headband tied at the top. My heart starts thudding, and I realize that I want to touch her so badly that I need to do something with my hands.

I take the stack of pizza boxes from her. "Do you want to join us?"

She tilts her head, uncertain.

"Come on," I say, balancing the boxes on one hand as I take hold of her arm with the other. "You should see what you've started." We walk together into the conference room, and I introduce her.

"Y'all—*this* is Evelyn."

Samantha stands up, crosses the room in a few long strides, and pulls a visibly surprised Evelyn into a hug. "Thank you. For seeing what was going on. And for saying something."

For the first time in weeks, I see her genuine smile, and it lights up the whole room. "I... it seemed weird that the only people leaving were women."

"Not so weird when you think about it," answers Lauren, her mouth full of chimichurri steak pizza.

We open the rest of the boxes, and every pizza is unique and delicious and totally her. Samantha finds a couple of six-packs in the office fridge, and we decide to make this a real celebration. I scan the room and see eight people who have more job security than they did before. It feels *good*.

I sit back and watch how the people in the room interact with Evelyn's easy, funny banter. She's lit from within, and everyone around her is charmed. She's handed out several business cards and offered to kit out Lauren's fortieth birthday party, and it's clear that she's in her element.

She looks up and sees me, arms crossed and grinning at her, and her smile falters. She re-squares her shoulders and gets back into the conversation. And it feels like someone has made a fist around my heart.

12

EVIE

This has been a weird couple of weeks. Ever since I helped out with Bluebonnet, Scout has been coming around the shop more, asking my advice on various projects, generally acting like we are friends. Which, I guess (?) we are.

I'm loathed to admit this, but when I saw her black Jeep with the green racing stripes in the parking lot this morning, I took an extra five minutes to add winged eyeliner, red lipstick, and a bandana head wrap to my look before walking in.

But that's because I'm screwing with her. To get her back.

That is a bald-faced lie.

Fine. Her eyes have been on me since I walked in the door, and it's possible that I'm trying to get her to push me against the wall and kiss me until we can't take it another minute. Happy?

Yes, that would make me very happy.

"Fuck."

It's the first thing I hear when I swing through the counter. "Morning, Scout. What's up?"

"I fucking sliced the *shit* out of my finger," she grits out, squeezing the nicked finger in pain.

I grab her by the elbow and take her to the sink, moving the biohazard away from my pristine workstation. I grimace at the sizeable cut on the tip of her finger. *Ouchouchouch.* "Oh, Scout, that's gotta hurt."

Her jaw tenses and she nods, biting her lip.

Oh, baby. I'm so, so sorry.

"You'd technically want to get stitches on a cut this bad, but fingertip stitches hurt like a motherfudger," I say, wiggling a scarred thumb at her. "If you trust me, I can take care of it with two or three Steri-Strips and some tape."

"Thought you'd enjoy seeing me in pain," she says under her breath, her eyes flitting to mine. *Bang.*

"I'd never want that," I respond, just as quietly.

Our eyes lock for a heated moment. My mouth goes dry, and the veins in my neck throb in time with the beating of my heart. I wish I could crawl into her head and figure out what is going on in there. *But not, since that sounds weird and vaguely threatening.* Needing to break the hypnosis, I clap my hands together and ask, "So! Do you want my bailing wire and duct tape method, or should we get you to the minor emergency?"

She bobs her head slightly, letting the moment go without comment. Holding out her hand, she answers, "Bailing wire and duct tape work for me."

I take her hand, cabled to my soft, and ignore the small intake of breath. After gently washing her hands with warm water and spritzing Bactine into the cut, I delicately bring the sides of the cut together and place the mini Steri-Strips using a light touch. They do a good job of holding the skin together, so I wrap two thin layers of waterproof surgical tape around the whole thing to protect it.

"Huh," she says, inspecting my work.

I grimace. "Are you okay? Did I hurt you?"

Her eyes, filled with curiosity, find mine as she shakes her head. "No. You didn't hurt me at all." Focusing back on my eyes, she continues. "I think you may have missed your calling. This is better than my courtside doctors."

Her expression reads like regret. I don't have any clue what she's reading in mine, because my mind and my heart are all over the place. I vaguely hear the bell above the door go off, wanting her to say something. I mean, I could say the obvious thing, but if she wants this, then she's going to have to go first.

My fingers are still delicately cupping hers as though they are made of porcelain and glass, and her eyes still haven't moved from mine. Her thumb softly grazes the edge of my finger, the whorls of her calloused thumbprint rough against my primped and manicured skin.

Scout looks at my lips, then back to my eyes, the air tense and sweet.

Yes, please.

"Evelyn, I—"

"Hello, Evie," says a deep, familiar voice, slaughtering the moment. I know who that low gravel tone belongs to, but turn to make sure.

Son of a motherless goat.

"Hello, Chet."

Scout

Who *the fuck* is this '50s greaser-looking white guy, and why is Evelyn suddenly standing like she's about to go into battle? I mean, I'm kind of grateful for him because I was about to do something monumentally stupid, but... damn, for a moment there I really wanted to do something monumentally stupid.

Head in the game, Martinez.

"Evelyn?" I ask, closing in on her, standing by her to scowl down at the gnat that is making every muscle in her face tense.

She holds up one finger, shaking her head. "I've got this, Scout." Pinning this unfortunate asshole with a glare, she continues. "Look, *Chet*, there is nothing here for you. At all. Get the *hell* out of this establishment."

I don't know about y'all, but I never want her to be that mad at me, ever. I mean, sure, she yelled at me that one time, but this is way, way worse. Her voice is so… even. Serene. Deadly. It's sexy as all get-out, and I think that I know exactly who this is. I mean, the only reason someone's name would sound like rotten eggs in your mouth is if you had once been married to that someone.

I look him up and down, cataloging his features. I don't find men particularly attractive, but I know enough to know that tall with a powerful, tattooed build and thick blond hair is a good look. And he's had years' worth of what I haven't had the guts to sample.

Not sure why that detail is important, since, for the moment, I've decided against monumental stupidity.

He starts to speak, but I cut him off. "Is this the four-person douche canoe who stole your college money?" Her eyes widen in surprise, not aware that I already know about her shitty ex. Kimberly gave me the high-level overview, and I'd love any excuse to take this guy to the cleaners.

"One and the same," she says, refocusing, looking through him as though he were cheap plexiglass.

I palm the pass-through counter, tempted to swing it up and then swing out. Bet if I broke his jaw, he wouldn't be so good-looking.

She holds her finger up again. "Nope. He's mine."

Turning to Dollar Store Charlie Hunnam, she continues. "I believe I asked you to leave. Do it. *Now.*" The warning in her voice is unmistakable.

He smirks, though I'm not sure what would warrant a smirk, save for the fact that he is clearly aware that he's a hot guy. Objectively. Don't worry, I'm not losing my gold star anytime soon.

"Tony said that you were working at a pizza shop and that I had to come by and see it for myself. Damn, baby. Maybe you should have stuck with me," he says, a smug smile creeping up his lips.

Excuse me? Who *the fuck* is he calling baby? And whoever that Tony asshole is, he's never stepping foot in this shop again. That's it. I'm going to jump over the damned counter. Evelyn holds up her finger one more time. "Seriously, Scout. I've got it," she says with a gleam in her eye.

The tattooed mouth-breather dully turns his ice-blue eyes to me and they widen in recognition. "Scout Martinez?"

That's right, jackass.

"Yeah, and Evelyn is the manager here, and practically a business partner."

Shit. That's probably true.

"Business partner?" he brays. "What the hell does she know about business? She never even finished school."

Evelyn cuts us both off before we get into it. "I have no need or desire to establish myself to you, *Chet*. So, if all you've come to do is gloat, you've done that, you towering douche waffle, and now you can go. Because if you don't, I'm going to let my *boss* jump over this counter and show you outside. I can promise you, it will not involve a door. Now, get out of my restaurant."

She says all of this in a low, even, biting tone. I look at her, supremely impressed. I'd be all kinds of loud by now, but she's sliced and diced him without going above the tone of voice you'd use to order an Earl Grey, hot. And she's right, I would happily throw his ass out the window.

"Careful there, *Ms.* Martinez," he says over his shoulder, as he's walking out the door. "She likes a bossy fuck, and more than that, she *really* likes to fuck the boss." He laughs at his own joke and swings through the door, jangling the bell like a dickhead. Evelyn's shoulders relax, and she takes a deep breath, like maybe she'd been siphoning off the oxygen trapped in her lungs.

"Remind me to stay on your good side," I joke. She smirks, her eyes unfocused and a little sad. I wonder if she misses her ex. Absentmindedly, she reaches for my hand, looking over her patch-up job, her soft skin a firebrand, shooting heat and desire up my arms.

She likes a bossy fuck.

Yeah, no.

Shut it down, Scout.

I don't need her touching me while thinking about loverboy's wedding tackle, or whatever it is that has her eyes turning into molten caramel. I shiver as her fingernails lightly scrape along the sensitive skin of my forearm, and I jerk back, yanking the quivering mass that used to be an arm out of her distracted hands.

Her eyes finally focus, and she faces me head-on. "Scout, I—"

I hold up a hand, turning the palm in her direction. "Thanks for the help. I'll be at Bluebonnet today. See you later."

With that, I run my hands through my hair and palm the pass-through before noticing an envelope on the counter that wasn't there before. I pick it up and hold it out to Evelyn, ignoring the look on her face, which again reads like sadness.

She grabs a butter knife and slices open the envelope, inside of which is an official-looking letter. I consider walking out the door, but whatever's in that document is causing her to lean against the counter. I go back and steady her with my hand at her waist, worried.

"Evelyn, what is this?"

13

EVIE

What is this? This is some Grade A, first-class bullcorn. Scout was totally macking on me as I bandaged her up, and then Donkey Kong came in and bro-smashed our sexy vibe. She'd looked ready to scrap with him, which had me imagining all kinds of lovely scenarios involving a little light bondage and a safe word. Honestly, I kind of zoned out for a second there, but I'm like 79 percent sure that his presence reminded Scout that I'd been in the vicinity of dick at some point in my sad, pathetic love life.

Man, if she only knew. Chet was hot and hung, to be sure, but unfortunately for me, had not one single idea what to do with the gifts he had been given. I mean, I'm a patient lover, and I don't mind showing you the ropes, but I can't make chicken salad out of chicken fertilizer, and that man couldn't buy a clue.

I bet she has a clue.

I'd clumsily tried to get us back to that hey-I'm-touching-you-and-you're-touching-me place, but then she pulled away like I'd burned her with a cigarette lighter. It looked like she was half-ready to run out the door when she spied the envelope. I recognized my name in Chet's handwriting.

I mean, Scout's hand at my waist is nice, even if worry is etching a line into her forehead. That said, the neatly folded documents that now lie on the counter can go eat a bag of dicks. The offer, or threat, depending on your point of view, is to finalize a large project for his family and get half of my money back, or be sued for breach of contract. I can't believe he actually went through with it.

"Yeah, no," states Scout, her arms crossed. "You are not going back to work with him."

"Thanks, boss. I'm aware of that. In fact, I might have already figured that out on my own."

"Okay, then why do you look so... despondent?"

"Because, now that he knows that I'm working for a rich athlete-entrepreneur who seems bound and determined to insert herself into everything, the amount of the settlement he'll accept just *doubled*."

"Settlement?" I ask, heated. "What settlement? We are going to countersue him into next week."

"We?"

"There are at least three contract lawyers who would go to bat for you in a heartbeat. That asshole won't know what hit him."

I shake my head. I didn't think he'd do this, especially since he'd taken my money, but I am on the hook for this one.

"Thing is... I did technically breach my contract with his family. This is for the Schultz contract, and I was the project manager. I left before completing the project and am therefore in breach of contract."

"Son of a bitch."

"You're tellin' me."

Scout

Fifty thousand. That's what they want for a settlement. The exact amount he stole from her, and that's his asking price. Mother. Fucker. We're sitting across from Samantha in the Bluebonnet offices, and her face is grim.

I have not told Evelyn how things are going with the rest of my operation. I am shuttering two of my offices at the end of the month—an old-fashioned hat shop that has never made money, and a travel agency made obsolete by travel websites. Even though these are good cuts that will boost my overall profitability, most of my net worth is in my properties, and my liquid cash is going to be really low until I finalize those deals.

But I can call in a favor and make it work.

I go to open my mouth, and Evelyn quickly cuts me off. "Absolutely not. You will do no such thing. Don't even suggest coming up with the money. You're working through the dissolution of The Hattery and Wings. I'm not going to be the reason you find yourself short."

How does she always just... *know*?

I shut my mouth and look at Samantha. She's a whiz with contract law, and she's reading the documents that Chet's lawyers sent over. "I'm sorry to say that they have you dead to rights, Evie. At no time did they do anything that would release you from this contract. Unless you know and have proof of fraud, tax evasion, or payment discrepancies to hold over them, you might have to pay."

"They are guilty of every single one of those things, especially on the Schultz project, but I doubt I can prove it. I'm trying to figure out why they'd come after me. It's not an idea they'd come up with on their own."

I think about it for a second. "Maybe they're being sued by a client and need you to get them back on track. I mean, you are kind of great at that, and they are probably sucking wind without you there."

Evelyn smiles and puts her forehead on my shoulder, spreading warmth through that entire side of my body. "You might be onto something. The Schultzes *definitely* have grounds to sue."

Samantha gives me a subtle look, flitting her eyes to Evelyn. Reluctantly, I sit up to break the contact, turning toward her. "Evelyn, *please* let me call in a few favors. Maybe we can get the settlement down and get the capital from my friends."

Her eyes are full of both gratitude and heartbreaking sadness. "Thank you, Scout. Really. But I can't allow you to do that."

Looking at Samantha, desperate for a better answer, I ask, "Then what *can* we do?"

Samantha scans the documents again and throws them on her desk. "I can't get her out of the contract, but there's nothing that says she can't make it worth her while."

"What are you thinking?"

"First, we should be able to get her out of those cosigned loans. I'm guessing it would be worse for them if she defaulted, so we can have them figure out the financing and get her name off of those completely. Second, if they're as crooked as she says they are, she can document any shitty behavior and maybe make a call to the IRS."

Ooooh, an audit. Yeah, that'll show them.

14

EVIE

For the next two months, I have to turn my baby over to Roly, who has taken over as the interim manager. I kind of love Roly, if only because he reminds me of a twink-sized, super-gay John Stamos. We hire Catherine, who Lizbeth recommended from her old job at the hot dog place, to help with the load. And while the restaurant is in good hands, this next step is draining my will to live.

The fastest and cheapest course of action is to go back and finalize the Schultz project, as I knew it would be. The way out is through, or some such nonsense. At least Samantha was able to negotiate the loans; turns out Chet didn't realize that they hadn't been making the payments and he was able to come up with the financing. I won't get any payback from that (because why would I), but at least I can start paying off the loans I took out to offset the Kavanaugh loan payments. Yay.

I'm still having a hard time believing that Chet would push for this. He's careless and a womanizer and a sneak, but he's not smart enough to pull off contract enforcer. I'm shocked he even knew that I was legally bound to finish the project. I plan on making him pay for that bit of previously untapped resourcefulness.

I pull into my old parking space and look down at my outfit—fitted gray slacks, a cream blouse with a pussy bow, and sensible shoes. My lips are a dreary mauve, and I've eschewed the eyeliner for a more natural look. I mean, I'm still cute, but I'm not putting any effort into it. It's 7:59 a.m. when I walk into the offices of Kavanaugh Construction. The prefab corrugated metal building has fading and peeling paint, and the limestone entryway attached to the front has grayed with dirt and rain. It's all very Texas Industrial Complex Chic.

I walk in and smell the day-old coffee and the cigars that Chet's dad, Frank, smoked after hours. Thankfully, he'll be in jail for a couple more years, so yay for small favors. Still, it smells like an '80s business office, and the interior décor hasn't been updated any time in this century. The office area, which is partitioned from the warehouse area in the back, is a small square of dingy offices with an even dingier set of tiny cubicles in the middle of the open space, offset by a receptionist desk near the entrance. The microscopic, filthy kitchen and break area are behind that. I can't believe I spent nearly five years in this place. What a waste of time.

"I didn't think you'd show up," Chet says, leaning against the doorframe so that I have to brush by him as I walk in. He's wearing a too-tight T-shirt and nut-hugger jeans, just in case anyone missed out on the fact that he works out and is packing. Subtle, he's not.

I'm carrying a large satchel purse and swing it while I walk, so it's not my fault when it grazes his junk. He backs up with an audible *oof*, and I reply breezily, "I intend to help you get the Schultz build back on track, get it completed, and then I'm on my way."

The project was supposed to be a simple cabana addition to the Schultz estate in the Rob Roy neighborhood, deep in the wealthy Austin hill country. The client was prickly from the beginning, constantly changing orders, and Chet should have never taken the job. Kavanaugh Construction has had to float the cost of the changes, and the Schultzes will not pay until everything has been settled. When a few other projects fell through and the South Austin work crew caused $100,000 in water damage during a closet installation,

Kavanaugh Construction ran short on cash. Cue the raid on my bank account.

Thing is, I'd just gotten the Schultzes to agree to a final set of drawings when I found out that Chet had stolen from me. While cheating on me.

In my absence, Chet's indelicate mother and overbearing father ruined the relationship with the quirky, indecisive family, and now they are threatening to sue.

"What do you plan on doing to get us back on track?" he asks, recovering from the run-in with my handbag.

"I'm going to give Mrs. Schultz a call and get her to agree to the original terms with a small free upgrade or two." My voice trails off at the end when I notice an older, papier-mâché-faced gentleman with a shock of white hair standing in Chet's office. He looks like money, and the kind of ass who thinks that his money gives him the right to look me up and down like a piece of meat.

Spoiler alert: It doesn't.

"Who the hell is this jackalope?" I ask, loud enough for the man to hear. He grunts appreciatively, his gaze pinned to my tits. Barf.

Chet looks over at piñata James Brolin and scowls. The man raises a questioning brow, Chet nods sharply, and the guy finger-guns him, then grabs his portfolio.

As I ponder this uncomfortable silent picture show, I realize that fascist Nick Nolte is walking in a purposeful collision course with me, hips slung forward like a heat-seeking missile, clearly not aware of my penchant for pursing a dick. I place my hands on my hips, teeth pulling at the corner of my lower lip, flirty and wide-eyed. He smirks, then bends over with a familiar *oof* as I turn and introduce his chub to the hard leather corner of my satchel.

"Oops, careful there," I say with the sweetest smile and daggers for eyes.

His face goes red with pain, but he manages to make his way out of the office without acknowledging me further.

"Seriously, who was that guy?"

Chet waves at the air, dismissing the question. "Never mind. And we can't afford upgrades," he growls.

I look at the door and look at him, and decide I don't care what business he has with evil busted Ted Danson. "You can't afford to be sued. A couple of nicer light fixtures and slightly better tile in the kitchen won't kill you."

"Fine. But the extras can't go over $2,000."

"It'll be closer to $5,000. I need to see the file and get caught up."

"$3,000, and get them to give you a firm date."

"$5,000, Chet. That's how much it will cost to get Mrs. Schultz the light fixtures she wants. It's better than being sued."

His mouth twists down, but he gives me a sharp nod.

In case you were curious, I could have gotten the Schultzes back on track with about $50 worth of Lamme's pralines and my charming personality, but I'm going to wrench every bit of cash I can from this family—legally—before I leave them in the dust.

"Maybe later. Right now, I need you to go through her emails and try to make some sense of what that damned woman wants."

Out of habit, I go to my old office, only to find that it has been filled to the absolute brim with boxes and boxes of interior flooring. Even the desk is covered in Saltillo tile.

"Oh yeah, you won't be able to use your office. You can take over one of the cubes."

The grimy cubes are the approximate color of Lady Gaga's meat dress, and at 4' x 4' barely have enough room for a monitor and a keyboard. He leans against the cube wall, the action straining the instructional integrity of his shirt, which has a rooster on it. He's got a jackass grin on his face, waiting for me to lose my temper, and I'm not even close to giving him the satisfaction.

"No problem. It'll help *you* to remember that *this*," I say, gesturing in a circle at myself, "is a temporary situation."

"Unless you decide you miss working here," he counters, crossing his arms in a way that emphasizes his physique. I know that he's doing this on purpose, because it's the same move he used to flirt with me when we were first dating. Not sure why he's trying it on me now, considering that I find him repulsive. I give him my best bored look and sit down at the desk, pulling out my laptop.

"You can't use your laptop here," he says, smugly.

All right, dillweed.

"Why? It's the same laptop I used before."

He shrugs noncommittally, kind of like our marriage. "New IT policy. Only Kavanaugh laptops can get on our network."

I know that the security measures are bullcorn because my computer had already automatically connected to their network, seeing as it is that they didn't even bother to change the damned password. But go ahead, Greaser Jesus. Tell me about the next hoop I'll need to jump through.

"Okay then, where is my Kavanaugh computer?"

He walks over to another desk and drags over an ancient laptop that weighs, I kid you not, about ten pounds. He's nearly buzzing with glee as he plunks it on the desk, emphasizing how heavy and old it is. Still maintaining a nonreactive exterior, I ask, "Will my old username and password work on this computer?"

"Yes."

Of course it will, you amateur. Why bother to archive my user account or even change a password with access to sensitive client information? I hide my grin and instead envision taking these bastards to the cleaners.

"And the VPN?"

"Nope. You can't take that home. All Kavanaugh laptops need to stay in office."

I nod. "One less thing to lug around. Can I assume that I'll be able to access my email on this thing?"

"Yeah."

I'm sure my email account has never been turned off or even forwarded.

I decide to log in to my VPN on my original computer while I'm in the office to make sure that it still works. And maybe to snoop around a bit.

Looking up at the man I used to swoon over, I say in a cool, even tone, "Looks like I have my work cut out for me. I'll get started right away."

His lips rise into another smirk, I assume thinking that he's won somehow. Using his knuckle to knock twice on the desk, he says, "It's nice to have you back, Evie. I'll let you get to it."

By 8:30, the office manager, Itsy, who I still adore, comes in and takes her place at the front desk.

"Evie? You're back?"

"For a while. I need to finalize the Schultz project."

She rolls her eyes and snorts. "Good luck with that. We call that project 'The Return of the King' because it never ends."

I laugh with her. "Oh, I'm going to get Frodo on that last boat to the Undying Lands if it kills me."

She quiets and her face turns pensive. "I've missed you. It's not the same."

"I know. You and I always managed to have a good time."

Her gaze holds mine. "It's not just that, and you know it. This whole place is falling apart. You were the only one that was stopping them from making the stupid mistakes that they insist on making. You were the only one with any vision at all for this place. It's a sinking ship."

"Abandon all hope all ye who enter here?" I say, lifting my brow.

"Basically."

"Well, let's see what I can do about that."

I spend the rest of the day catching up on emails. As I suspected, no one had bothered to monitor my account when I left, and there were several angry emails from Mrs. Schultz that went unanswered. I pick up my phone, determined to make things right for this kind-but-difficult woman.

"Mrs. Schultz. This is Evie from Kavanaugh Construction."

"Evie! Where the *hell* have you been? You abandoned me to these worthless men, and my cabana still isn't done!" Her words are harsh, but her tone is more pleading than anything else. Time to turn on the charm.

"I know, Mrs. Schultz, and I'm *so* sorry to hear it. I'm back now, and we will make sure that you get the cabana of your dreams. They've brought me back specifically to fix was has gone wrong with this project, and that starts today. Now, I know that you wanted those lovely Mantra lights in the great room, but they were out of budget. What do you say about me including those in the specs at the price of the original lights?"

Silence.

Huh. I really thought that would work.

"Squeeeeeee! Yes! I love those fixtures, but Alan wouldn't budge an inch on the budget! Evie, you're magic!"

I laugh. "I want to make sure you're happy Mrs. Schultz. This project has gone on long enough. You've already missed your Memorial Day window; let's see if we can get you into that cabana by Fourth of July."

"Yes, let's!"

I smile and place the phone back on its cradle. It was fun to get back into the client side of things, and I got her to agree to a two-month time frame. *Yes.*

I look up and Chet is leaning against the doorframe to his office, smiling his full, genuine smile. I smile back and remember what it felt like to light up at his happiness. Now, I can't wait for him to figure out that my smile will never again reach my eyes in his presence, and that forcing me to come back to this place will be the biggest mistake he's ever made.

Late in the afternoon, after making my way through several angry client emails, promising to make good on all of the things that the company legally contracted, I take my large satchel with me to the bathroom.

"That time of month, Evie?" Chet shouts from his desk, loud enough for the construction workers who've wandered over to the break area to hear.

"Yep," I say, ignoring his attempt to embarrass me. "It's a real rager this time. *Huge* clots."

He wrinkles his nose and slinks back into his office. Don't even try to play with the big girls, sonny.

I enter the small two-holer and take the larger stall, hanging my huge purse on the hook. Reaching into the purse, which Scout has on several occasions accused of having an extension charm on it, I pull out my original laptop. I boot it up silently, praying that no one else comes in and hears an errant beep.

You understand, of course, that by thinking this out loud, I've essentially jinxed myself.

Unfortunately, it's my former mother-in-law who decides to walk into the bathroom, and, even more unfortunately, she recognizes my shoes and decides to talk to me while taking the world's most disgusting dump.

I can't even make this up.

"Evie, honey. It's so good to have you back."

-ffffart-plop-

"I'm just here to finish out my contract, Mrs. Kavanaugh." I hit the mute button on my laptop, hoping that she won't hear anything else. There are, however, no mute buttons for the disaster that is coming out of her butt.

"Well, who knows will happen in the interim, dear. (*-fart-*) You should know that Chet has made a lot of changes in his life. He's not seeing that woman anymore (*-plop-*), and I know that you two could make it work again."

Nothing like getting right to it.

See also: herk.

See also also: Even my laptop has decided that it needs oxygen, and the cooling fan spins up.

"What's that sound, dear?"

-fart-

"Um, I think it might be the overhead fan," I say as I select the office VPN.

"Oh," she says. I'm hopeful that she's made her point and can leave, but we all know that I am not that lucky. "Seriously, Evie. You need to try. It is your duty as his wife. Even if you aren't his wife legally, in the eyes of the Lord, your bond is forever."

-plop-

"Well, Mrs. Kavanaugh, I don't think there's anything there for Chet and me. I'm in a relationship now and am very happy." At least I know who I'd like to be in a relationship with, and it ain't Chet.

"Oh, Evie! (-*plop-*) How could you give up on your marriage like that? (-*fart-*). A truly submissive wife would have waited (-*plop-*) patiently (-*plop-*) while her husband worked through his difficulties."

By this time, my eyes are practically watering, but at least the VPN has connected. I do a quick fist pump and jam my elbow into the partition between me and the defecating queen of construction.

"Are you okay, dear?"

"Oh, yes, Mrs. Kavanaugh. Just a bit clumsy over here."

I flush the toilet, giving me a chance to put the laptop back into my bag. "I know that you're disappointed, Mrs. Kavanaugh. But really, it's for the best."

"If you say so dear. But I hope that you'll come to change your mind."

-*plop--plop--fart--plop--plop--plop-*

Son of a bitch. I put my hands over my mouth and exit the suffocating bathroom as quickly as possible.

"Dear! Are you not going to wash your hands?"

I think about turning around and making a show of washing my hands, but my eyeballs are melting, and my nostrils would be demanding my head if I don't leave right away.

"I've got hand sanitizer," I shout as I breach the door and inhale fresh stale coffee air. God, that was close.

Darnit. Now I really do need to pee.

Scout

I'm waiting for her on the front step when she gets home from the Kavanaugh office.

"Hey there, my favorite lesbian."

I smile at her greeting and put my hands on her shoulders and look deep into her eyes. "How did the first day go? Did he try anything?"

Look, I'm not trying to act like the jealous girlfriend. It's her scuzzbag ex-hottie that I detest.

She shakes her head, her muscles starting to release under the weight of my hands. "He tried some stupid male dominance posturing when I walked in, but I crotched him with my bag and he gave me a wide berth for the rest of the day."

"Ouch."

"No doubt. What's funny is that he had this gross, overtanned guy with white hair in his office, and I knew that they were talking about me. On his way out he did that dick-first kind of walk in my direction, so I crotched him, too."

I lower my head and laugh silently. That bag is *huge*. They both probably needed bags of frozen peas on their junk after that move.

"Do you think you'll be able to get through two months at that place?" I ask, wondering if it's okay to keep my hands on her shoulders, or if that is too much touching to be considered platonic. It's a fine line.

Evelyn reaches up and rests her hands in the crooks of my elbows, making small circles on the sensitive skin with her middle fingers. "It'll be okay. And they're so lax with their network security, I'll be able to get in and poke around, see what I can find."

Anxiety knots my stomach. "That doesn't sound like the most legal thing. Please be careful, Evelyn."

She shakes her head. "It's not illegal to search for similar files to familiarize myself with the project. If I happen to find proof of illegal activity while I'm in there, then that's just tough titties. In the meantime, I'd forgotten somehow, probably a trauma response of some kind, that my ex-mother-in-law likes to have full conversations in the bathroom in the middle of her afternoon constitutional."

My face scrunches in disgust. "That sounds horrible."

She laughs, her eyes finding mine. "It's worse than you think. She believes that her son and I are still married in the eyes of the *Lord*, and therefore I should be *submissive* and *forgiving* of him." She emphasizes

Lord, submissive, and *forgiving* with a series of increasingly dramatic eyebrow arches and a heavy dose of sarcasm.

I laugh until my stomach hurts, choking out, "Never. Gonna. Happen. I can't even picture you as *submissive.*"

The heat in her eyes and the flush of her neck stops me cold. She bites her lip and looks down. Fuck. Me. I stifle a groan as my imagination takes over and sends me lurid, detailed pictures of what it would be like to yank her wrists above her head, pin her to the front door, and devour her mouth until she was begging, absolutely begging. Then I'd push her inside the apartment and... shit, I seem to have wandered a bit off the trail. Our eyes meet, and I know that she is reading my expression. The red travels up to her jawline and down to her chest, and I remove my hands from her shoulders as she turns to her door, unlocking it.

"All righty then. I've got to get inside and wash this day off of me," she says while disappearing inside before I have a chance to tell her how nice her hair looks.

15

EVIE

*A*fter Scout eye-effed me while getting the goods on my first day back with the business, we've been keeping tabs via text. *Smart.*

The biggest suck of all of this is that I'll be working four days at Kavanaugh's and three days at the shop. I won't get any money from the Kavanaughs until I complete the contract, so now I'm back to no money. I'd been considering moving out of Jake's place into a place of my own, maybe getting the last fifteen hours of my MBA, but that will have to wait. Again. Scout's allowing me to work the last three to four hours of the shift on my Kavanaugh days, but it's still not quite enough. What that means is that on my Kavanaugh days I start at the office, close the restaurant, then round it all out with a couple of hours working for a local rideshare app, Classic Rides. I was able to sign up with my car because Spence's friend did a fantastic job with the interior and Spence was able to buff out the scratches without having to do a full-on paint job, even if he did have to wire the trunk shut. It turns out that a lot of people want to ride in a classic Mustang.

I should be grateful that I'm able to meet my expenses with a few rides here and there, but after a couple of weeks, I'm tired down to my marrow. I'd better pound the caffeine because, in the words of the brilliant Robert Frost, I've got miles to go before I sleep.

In the meantime, Scout managed to tear her eyes away from my ass long enough to find a buyer for our oven, so now I have to accompany my six-foot-two teenage crush to test out whether or not a gas-fired, brick-lined oven will still result in a great-tasting pizza. Because I'm a professional or whatever.

We close the shop early and arrive before the dinner rush at Hush, her friend Patty's wildly popular locavore restaurant on Rainey Street near downtown. It's the kind of place Austin is known for, and I only ever see if I'm dropping someone off. Scout insisted on using the app to book the ride with my Goldie Mustang to the restaurant but then had to drive because I was a mess and a half. Patty James is an Austin treasure, and if she likes what you're doing, she tells her friends. This isn't only about testing out the oven. It's a way to get the shop on the map, and I have no idea how Scout pulled this off.

No pressure.

"Hey, you all right?" Scout asks as we pull into the Hush parking lot. "You haven't said a single word on the drive over."

As she asks, the app notification comes up and she's tipped double the fare, despite my vehement protests. Apparently, you can't reject a tip, but the upshot is that I won't have to go back to driving for the app after our little excursion. Still, I don't know if I can deal with Scout being nice to me in this moment, so I mutter a quick "Yep" and hop out of the car. Patty's sous chef, Reynaldo, meets us and helps us bring in the tubs carrying balls of pizza dough, toppings, and my oil.

Despite my acute anxiety and general exhaustion, I really am looking forward to feeding the restaurant staff tonight. Reynaldo takes us through the back, and I pause at the entrance, both intimidated and excited. The Hush kitchen is absolutely stunning—stainless steel everywhere, shining workstations ready for the onslaught, a huge walk-in refrigerator, a bank of spider burners as far as the eye can see, and a beautiful, old-school gas-powered pizza oven. My attitude is adjusting, y'all.

Patty is a larger woman with curly graying hair, and she comes over to usher me into the kitchen with a warm smile, setting me up at her own workstation with instructions to make myself at home. It's been a while since Scout and I have spent this much time in the same space, and I once again feel her dark eyes on me as I set up my mise en place.

I've decided to try out three types of pizza: a simple pepperoni pizza, a shrimp alfredo pizza, and a BBQ chicken pizza. After rolling out the dough, taking care with the toppings, and swirling a bit of my secret recipe oil on the pies, I put them in the oven and wait. Three minutes has never felt so long in my life, and Scout seems to shift nearer to me with each passing second.

When the timer goes off about fifty years later, I open the oven and fish out the three pies with a large, wooden paddle, unintentionally hip-checking Scout in the process. She smiles and rubs her jaw, the muscles on her forearms flexing with the movement. I'm annoyed that I notice the flexing, but my nerves are too shot to contemplate it. The bubbling creations look yummy, and I plate them on Patty's nice tabletop pizza servers. I let them cool for a few minutes (which feel like millennia), then Patty, Scout, and I each take a slice.

Patty's eyes fly open as she bites into the simple pepperoni. Just as I'm absolutely convinced that I've offended the hottest up-and-coming chef in Austin, a sound comes out of her mouth that is, dare I say, pornographic.

"Oooooooh mmmmmyyyyyy ggggggooooodddd. What the *hell* are you putting on this pizza that makes it taste so good?"

Scout is similarly entranced by her slice, the dark pleasure in her eyes sending a hot sensation down the middle of my chest. For the span of a second and a half, she looks like she wants to put me on the table and do me in front of these fine cooking professionals, but then it disappears, like clockwork. Searching for mental purchase elsewhere, I put the alfredo slice to my lips and tentatively take a bite.

Son of a biscuit, that's good.

Scout pauses an extra beat, then asks, "Is it possible that the smoky flavor was distracting from your ingredients?"

I shrug, shivering from the freeze that always comes after the burn. "Good point. Maybe?"

Eyeing the pizza like she might need some alone time with it, she proclaims in a low gravel voice, "This is better than anything you've ever cooked in the restaurant."

Patty nods in emphatic agreement, eyeing the two of us with a knowing grin. "This is the bomb, ladies." She motions to her kitchen staff, and they each take a slice. The air is soon littered with curse words and sounds of utter delight. I smile as I roll out a few more pies, a foreign sensation of accomplishment spreading through my chest.

Scout's eyes find mine again, scorching my nerve endings as she shakes her head. "Evelyn, I think that you just saved my business."

I thrill at her approval, even more than Patty's, and lock gazes with her, letting her see me enjoy it. She breathes out, the air heavy, and runs her silver-ringed thumb along her bottom lip before running her hand through that thick, black hair of her hers, pushing it to the side, highlighting both the brilliant white streak and the hard edge of her jaw. Blinking a few times, her face masks over, yet again a big *do not enter* sign.

I really am very tired of that look.

My train of thought is disrupted by the head waiter walking in our direction. "Ladies, your table is ready."

I look over at Patty, and a smile cracks my face in two. "We're eating here? Really?" I revel for a few seconds in the thought of trying Patty's famous catfish puffs and her strawberry pie, but then remember my fallow bank account and shake my head. I can't afford a $500 dinner. "That is so kind, but I can't af—"

Patty shakes her head and points to Scout. "This was her idea."

I look over at Scout, questions in my eyes. She shrugs and explains, "We can't come to this restaurant and not eat here."

I inwardly thrill but pull her over to the side. "Scout, that's really nice, but I can't afford it. I mean, maybe an appetizer, but..."

Scout cocks her head at me. "Evelyn, do you think that I would take you here and make you pay when I am fully aware of your financial situation?"

Well... not fully aware.

Dismissing before I can even protest, she continues, "And before you say anything else, you're to think of this as a bonus."

I look around at what the *Austin Chronicle* had dubbed this year's "Most Romantic Restaurant," and I wonder if she has any clue as to what she is doing. She can't bring herself to ask me out on a date, and yet... look at this place. She's arranged a tasting followed by dinner at literally the most date-y place in town. While I admire the balls on her subconscious, it'd be awesome if her conscious mind would let us have a little fun in real life.

I look lovingly over the quirky wooden tables and mismatched comfy chairs and cozy booths that dot the interior of this restaurant and sigh. I would love, love, love to eat here. Fine. I'll let my crush pay for my dinner. I press my lips together and nod.

Scout

Evelyn gives the pies over to Reynaldo to finish, and a waiter takes us to a quiet corner booth, positioned by a large pane glass window overlooking Hush's herb garden. It's still bright outside, but the interior has a romantic, moody atmosphere with dimmed candelabras and tea lights everywhere. Evelyn's lavender hair glows in the candlelight, and her beautiful face is softened, her eyes pools of solid gold.

Ah, damn.

This is not a date.

Not. A. Date.

Notadate.

And I need—desperately—to stop looking at her mouth. It helps to remember that I know that she'd secretly gone on a few more dates, but between working at her ex's place, working at the pizza shop, and spending what little was left in the day driving complete strangers around the city, she hasn't had a chance to pursue any more dating.

Thank fuck.

Not sure why that's pertinent now, since *we* are not on a date, but it's a good reminder that her past willingness to put herself in the proximity of cock is a hard pass for me. A bigger *nope* than the fact that she is my employee and practically my partner in this pizza shop.

I really do need to get laid.

And that's why I need to stop checking out her tits. She's been wearing the restaurant's T-shirts and some kind of tit-loafing sports bra to work since the night I performed a goddammed soliloquy about her breasts, but tonight she's in a soft blouse and is wearing a real bra. The neckline is practically Victorian, but there is the slightest hint of cleavage. And I would give my right eyebrow if that line were one inch lower. God, she smells so good.

Focus, Scout.

Focus.

Lock. It. Down.

Thankfully, the waiter sweeps by to take our drink order and rattles off the specials for the night. We opt for the family-style prix fixe dinner, and he rushes off to get our cocktails.

"Scout, I can't thank you enough for taking me to dinner. I really appreciate it," she says earnestly, tucking a bit of hair behind her ear.

I laugh, seeing residual pizza flour on the strands. I reach across and sweep it off her hair, and she turns her face into my grazing fingertips, the action reflexive, electric. Meaningful. I snatch my hand back and vow to keep it on my side for the rest of the evening.

"You're welcome," I say, finally. "It's well deserved."

She stiffens, a reasonable reaction since I've practically recoiled from her. An unreadable emotion crosses her face, and the air between us congeals into a silence that stretches on for far too long. She's usually the one to revive a conversation when it lags, but something like resolve darkens her eyes, and now she's sitting back, her hands folded in front of her, letting the awkwardness play out.

After a few minutes, I can't stand it anymore and plow forward into small talk. "Have you seen the new sign at the apartment complex? Feedback from the residents is that they love it, and it makes the Levee seem special."

"Mmmm," she hums. "It is nice."

"And the palms..." I say, running out of sentence. Seriously, what should have gone there? *Are particularly palmy?*

"Yes, the palms," she replies, steepling her fingertips, her pressed-lipped expression completely unreadable.

"But the pool on top of everything..."

"The best."

Shit. Is it hot in here? I adjust my collar, and nothing changes on her face.

"And Jake..."

"I've got a helpful brother," she responds, all flat affect.

"Yeah, super helpful."

She takes a sip of her water and narrows her eyes at me, a challenge. We are still waiting for the waitstaff to get into place, so for ten minutes she sips her water, looking out at the small courtyard, not saying one damned thing to me. My skin feels too tight, and I have no idea what to do next because this? This is beyond an awkward pause. *This* is a disaster. Officially, completely... off the fucking rails.

The waiter shows up, and I practically chain him to the table, asking him a million questions about Patty and the restaurant and how they source their food, and, and, and... until he finally apologizes and insists that he get back to his other guests. I slump as he walks away, toying with my Chivas on the rocks. Meanwhile, Evelyn is dipping the olives into her dirty martini, gently tonguing and sucking on the little red pimento before pushing the olive between her soft lips, her amber-honey eyes shining in amusement.

Thankfully, my brain pulls out one last detail that I knew she'd want to know. "Yeah, so I, uh, found the exact replica of Patty's oven on eBay for $7,500, and since this worked out, I'll get it ordered tonight."

"So, cheaper, then," she says, her eyes immediately shifting into boredom as they drift over the herb garden.

I gulp and nod. "Practically a steal."

"Mmm."

I am seriously sweating right now. She's out of olives and has taken to dipping her pinky into the martini and sucking on it. While looking into my eyes. By the time the meal comes, I am a pile of misery and regret. I decide it's better if I let us eat in silence.

Well, sort of.

Evelyn is softly moaning with practically every bite. And yes, the food is good, and worth every penny, but that moaning has my hips tilting toward her, a distinct pulse pounding at the apex of my thighs. My dry desert is now suddenly a lush oasis, if you catch my drift, and I shift uncomfortably in my seat, aware of the clothing touching my skin. Aware of exactly what I would do to make her moan like that. I can practically taste her sweetness on my tongue.

While waiting on the check at the end of dinner, she leans forward, crooking her finger at me, asking me to come closer. I draw a shaky breath and lean in. "Um, yes?" I ask, nervously wiping my palms on my thighs.

Her eyes flash, and she asks in a dusky voice, "Are we ever going to talk about this?"

"This?" I ask, my voice pitching up.

"Us," she says simply. Except... it's not simple at all.

"Um. In what capacity?" My voice has pitched up to preteen boy, complete with cracking in the middle of "capacity."

She smiles, annoyance touching her eyes. "In the capacity of me sitting on your face," she responds, just as our waiter arrives with the check. I blindly shove several bills in his direction, which he grabs before disappearing into the ether.

I picture my face being enveloped by her soft, velvet curves, feel the weight of her on my face, and my hands tingle, desperate to hold her. Instead, I grip the antique salt shaker, accidentally cracking the lid and spilling the contents on to the table.

"I. Uh. I..." I'm so eloquent I can't stand myself. "Could have fooled me with all the dates you've been going on."

She leans forward a bit more, stealing the ruined salt shaker from my hands. "Stop. First of all, I haven't been on a date in weeks, as I'm sure you know, and two, who cares if I go on dates? I want to be with someone, and you've given every indication that you intend to keep acting like this isn't happening, and it's starting to piss me off. We're adults, Scout. We're attracted to each other. Really attracted to each other. It's pretty simple."

I shake my head, the action reflexive, electric. Meaningful. *No, it's not simple.* At all.

The annoyed expression in her eyes bleeds out to the rest of her face, and her lips purse. Fuck, she is pure sex, even when she is angry. Especially when she is angry.

"What are you so afraid of, Scout?"

I startle, trying not to fantasize angry sex with her. "What?"

She leans forward even farther, her eyes squinting in annoyance. "Why are you so afraid?"

I don't want to be pushed on this. I have my reasons, and they are none of her business.

"Are you *always* this chicken?" she pushes. "Is the thought of a relationship with a bisexual *really* so terrifying?"

Yes.

Yes, it is.

It is terrifying because at my lowest, at my sickest, I couldn't rely on the most important person in my life.

It is terrifying because these holdings in Austin are all I have, and I'm draining my savings account faster than I can replenish it.

It is terrifying because I've already canceled my contract on the house I was building.

It is terrifying because I will do or give up almost anything to avoid experiencing that kind of pain ever again.

But I don't say any of this. Instead, I lower my voice and bite out, "You're an employee, nothing more. So, get off my back about it."

The look of hurt in her eyes, the way her mouth takes several seconds to recover means that my words had their intended effect.

I think.

She shrinks back into the soft material of the booth, practically disappearing into its shadow. Her eyes shine and wobble, a bit watery, but she bites her lip and wills the tears to not topple over the dam.

You don't have to tell me.

I'm an asshole.

I know.

But at least I'm an asshole who's learned her lesson.

It is at this precise moment that her phone dings. Not looking down, she says in a soft voice that will play in my head over and over later that night, "That'll be your Uber driver. Go screw yourself, Scout."

Like I said, way off the rails.

16

EVIE

My mind is a red abyss of anger, void of words or ideas or snappy retorts. Weeks of silent sexual torture have finally fried my brain. I pick up three rides before I can stand the thought of going home, though, gun to my head, couldn't have told you where any of those drop-offs occurred. My riders are probably lucky to be alive. I blink, and I'm pulling into the complex. I blink again, and I'm reaching for my keys to open the door. And then I find myself walking into a scene for which I am wholly unprepared.

I mean, seriously—when *is* it a good time to learn that your brother is a power bottom?

How about never. Let's go with never.

"Oh my god, Evie! Shit. No—I'm so sorry! I thought you weren't coming home till later," says my brother as he's pushed against the kitchen bar with the guy from 2C all the way up his... yeah, I'm going to need a minute. And about a gallon of eye bleach.

Not that there's anything wrong with that.

But, like, I don't ever need to see a family member like that, you feel me?

It's actually kind of cute because 2C is trying to angle things so that I can't see my brother's business. Which is sweet, but I've already superglued my eyes shut for the rest of eternity.

With my hand over my eyes, I say, "It's okay, Jake. Please don't stop, or whatever, on my account. I'm going on a walk. You do you. Or Jackson, as the case may be."

Yeah, I in no way made that way more awkward and humiliating for everyone.

I've walked around the entire complex twice and consider the pool as I make my way back to the apartment. It's such a nice night, and it would feel good to put my feet in the water. I can do that.

Opening the gate, I walk past the lush, verdant greens and bright magenta bougainvillea, and I'm glad that the lean, mean lesbian decided to spring for the nicer landscaping. I roll up my jeans and sit at the pool's edge and lean back, looking up at the stars. The cool water is nice on my hot skin, and it eases the inner boiling.

I am happy that my brother is well enough to have sex, and that he chose a nice and exceptionally good-looking man with whom to get his rocks off. I mean, *clearly*, we're going to have to have some kind of schedule or signal or sock system that will help us prevent this kind of catastrophe from ever happening ever again, but I am happy for him.

I hear Scout's door open and go still. Her stompy boots are making their way up the walk, and they pause outside of the pool area. I don't move or say anything, and after a moment, her footsteps fade toward the dumpster. The lid is opened, then closed with a sharp slam, and her boots find their way home. Directly after, another set of feet, bare and strong, make their way to the pool.

I turn toward the gate and see that my brother has let himself in with worried eyes.

"Hey, brother."

"Hey, sister."

Jake rolls up his black jeans and sits next to me. He puts his feet in the water and nudges my toes. I smile and nudge back.

"So… you're gay," I state, hopefully sounding as supportive as I feel.

"Yeah," he says, looking out over the water.

"Okay."

We sit there for a few minutes, letting this information wash over us. I reach over and grab his hand.

"I'm bi."

He turns and meets my eyes with an empathetic look. "Scout?"

I let out a heavy breath. "Yeah. Scout. Except not."

"Why?" he asks, watching his toes create ripples in the water's surface.

"She doesn't trust bisexuals. I mean, she says it's because she's my boss, but the first time we met—"

"When you ran into her," he says, cracking half a smile.

I punch his arm. "Yes, then. She didn't know I worked for her and was all *bet it was just a phase in college*. Not a fan of the bi-girls."

"Can't say I blame her."

I elbow him in the ribs.

"Jackson?"

A smile plays on his lips, one that has been elusive for many, many years. "Yeah. Jackson."

"I can't help but notice that he has locs like a certain basketball player."

He shrugs. "I like what I like."

"Is it serious?" I ask, hopeful.

He tilts his head side to side. "It could be."

"So… time to let the Christians know that there be sinners in their midst?"

He sighs, resigned. "If I want to stay sober. If I want to keep my boyfriend."

"Boyfriend?" I say, allowing hope to creep into my voice.

He smiles shyly and nods.

"Does Jackson know about…?" I ask, without asking.

Head nod. "Jackson's sober, too."

"Do you want to come out together, or should I let you have your own coming out?"

He nudges my shoulder again. "Together is better. Evens the odds."

"Tomorrow?"

"As good a day as any."

We sit in silence for a few minutes, and then he gets up to leave. "You coming with me?"

I shake my head. I want answers.

"I need to go have a talk with a lesbian."

Scout

I have well and truly fucked this up. Why would I buy her dinner at such a romantic place? I need to stop sending mixed signals.

I need to stop *feeling* mixed signals.

I just… wow. I can't believe how she came at me. Like that time she put me on the ground. She's all soft curves and round edges, but then, whammo. You run into that centerline of steel and get your bell rung. She was *never* going to let me hide behind silence. She sees through me in ways that are both terrifying and hot as fuck. I know that my secrets will spill on her soon enough. She's like a freight train, bearing down on me. I can't stop it. I should probably stop trying.

But.

Damn.

I'm sorry, I don't remember my train of thought because now I'm thinking about how her nipples would taste, and, more distractingly, how her soft pussy would taste, and… I'm drifting.

That's it, I need to get my head on right. I put on workout clothes and get on my treadmill, set the pace at ten miles per hour, and fly. And then remember.

A year ago.

I'd started throwing up in the car on the way home from chemo. It had been my last round, and by far the worst, but I wasn't sure if it was the poisons running riot over my system or the fact that my relationship would be over as soon as I was well enough to live on my own. I'd pulled over twice before getting home, cursing myself for not taking a car service to the doctor's office. I hadn't wanted to be recognized, but who the hell was going to recognize me like this? I was out of breath by the time I made it to the door and threw up again in the guest bathroom downstairs. I took off the bandana that was covering my head and wetted it, wiping the vomit off my chin and shirt. Bone-weary, I sat at the bottom of the stairs for several minutes, gathering the will to walk up to my bedroom. I'd contemplated falling asleep on the couch, but my whole body hurt from the beating that it had taken, and I wanted my bed.

Finally, I pulled myself up the curving staircase and made my way down the hallway. Only then did I hear the soft moaning. Carla. I knew those moans. I'd created many of those moans in our early years. We'd already been in a bad place when I was diagnosed, and by then it had been almost a year since we'd had any real physical contact. A long time to go without, but not enough time to forget those pleasured moans. She didn't moan like that when she masturbated; she only moaned that way when she had an audience, someone who would appreciate the rare appearance of sound from her during sex. She was a quiet lover, intense, and those low, guttural, barely audible moans meant that she was rocketing from within, on fire and on the edge.

I could have left it at that. I didn't need further proof. But I am a masochist, apparently, and I opened Pandora's box. Carla was facing away from me, straddling a... familiar-looking guy. It took me a while to put it together because I'd only met him a couple of times, but it was the group's broker. The guy whose job it was to rustle up good investments for us. Matt Something-or-other. I remembered thinking that he was a good guy because he was funny and had found a number of hidden jewels for us. Yeah, not so much.

Even in that terrible knowing, there wasn't a thing about her that wasn't absolutely gorgeous. The arch of her back. The round, strong curve of her ass pumping up and down on his dick. For a fleeting moment, I was hypnotized.

Matt is about my height and build, at least the build I'd had before chemo stripped away everything. I'd been a real bruiser on the court, six foot two and nearly 200 pounds of solid muscle. As I leaned against the doorframe, trying to catch my breath, I remembered the scale at the clinic—135 pounds, skinnier and weaker than I'd ever been. The cancer had been cut from my body; chemo had taken the rest. I was a bald wisp of what I used to be. So insignificant that they hadn't even seen me. I pulled the door shut and left quietly.

I snuck out of my own house and put the car in neutral to back out of the driveway. I called Kimberly, my oldest friend; she would know what to do.

"Get the hell out of there, recharge, and get your mind on your business."

I rearranged my portfolio, quietly untangling our joined bank accounts, abandoning the holdings that couldn't quietly be rearranged, and taking massive losses to secure a clean exit. We would still be involved in the same investment group, but she no longer oversaw anything I was a part of. I didn't have any fight left in me; I wanted to heal and be done.

I won't complain too much about going from an eight-figure net worth to a seven-figure net worth in one day, nor will I complain that my radiation and recharge strategy involved taking over my beachfront rental in Kailua for nearly eight months. By day I soaked in the sun, eating the healthy local fare, and getting stronger. At night, alone, I could see her on the bed, moaning for him. I could hear the gentle slap of her thighs against his. I could still smell her sweet scent mixed with his more acrid pheromones. I hated her. I hated men. And I really hated anyone who could give their bodies to that sour-smelling mix of smells and emissions.

When my hair began to grow in, it was thicker and blacker than before, save for a new, bold streak of white. Unlike a lot of folks who get the infamous "chemo curls," my hair was still *indio*-straight, making it stick out in all directions. On my first trip to a hair place, the barber suggested that having won my battle, I should wear my hair as a reminder. He told me about the Koa, the ancient Hawaiian military force, and showed me their helmets, which were stylized with a hooked mohawk made of metal. He suggested an undercut, and for the first few months my hair stood straight on end, and I felt like a warrior. By the time I was ready to face reality, it had begun to flop over, and I liked the style so much, I've continued to grow it out while shaving the sides.

I look at my hair in the night-mirrored window. It's a reminder, and a lesson.

Don't get hurt like that again.

17

EVIE

With one hand on my hip, the other rapping loudly on her door, I glare into the peephole. The door swings open, and for about half a beat I lose my nerve. She's wearing only basketball shorts and a workout bra, her hair messily flopped to one side and sweat running down in rivulets through the muscles on her arms, belly, and legs. She's breathing heavy like she's been running for hours.

I push into her apartment and slam the door behind me, then finally ask the question I've been wanting to ask ever since that day I hit her U-Haul. "If I'm *just an employee*, then why do you look at me the way you do?" I glower up at her for all I'm worth, and she's silent, still breathing heavy. Her predator eyes are a murderous black, and I can't tell if she wants to do me or strangle me.

My eyes rake over her body, a temple carved out of wood and wire, and her muscles tense everywhere my eyes land. Growling, I push my finger into her chest. "I asked you a question, and I deserve an answer."

Stepping back from the contact, she flushes and looks down. I stand there, waiting for a response. "I apologize, I won't do it again," she responds without denial.

I huff, looking heavenward for patience. "But what if I *like* you looking at me like that?"

Her body stiffens, sways unconsciously toward me, then becomes rigid once more. "I can't take advantage of you like that."

"In what alternate universe are you taking advantage of me?" I ask incredulously. "*I'm* coming on to *you*!"

"Uh, no. You're yelling at me," she says, rubbing her jaw, the muscles of her arms flexing. "And I don't shit where I eat."

I wince at the coarse description, then re-armor. "So, I'm confused," I say, my tone dripping with sarcasm. "Was I your employee when you kissed me that one night? And what about tonight—was that really supposed to be just a working dinner? Two colleagues celebrating a successful appliance reorganization? You might want to check your shorts."

Scout rubs her face with both palms and sighs. "That first night was inappropriate. You could probably sue me."

I stare at her, mouth agape. "Is that what you're worried about? That I'm going to sue you? I want to *fuck* you, not *sue* you." I kind of shock myself by saying it that way, but at least it's the truth.

My words have a physical effect, like I've slapped her, and she snaps her dark eyes to mine. "I don't do one-night stands."

It's my turn to look away. I've been into Scout for a lot longer than I'd like to admit. I knew a month ago, I know now, and I'll know six months from now. This isn't about wanting to bang the hot sports star. I suspect that she knows I want more, but I don't relish being the person to say it out loud. The heat licks up my neck, and I know that my cheeks are starting to turn red.

Squaring my shoulders, I return her intense stare. I know for a fact that I am not the only one out on this pier; she wants this as much as I do. "Do you really think that I'm just here for that?"

Her eyes fire, then harden, and she says through her teeth, "I. Don't. Care. Why. You. Are. Here. You are everything bad for me, everything I have sworn off because all *your kind* can do is take and take and take, and I don't have anything more to give. Now get out of my place before I fire you."

I clench my jaw, turned on and enraged and mildly triumphant. *Your kind*, indeed. I *knew* the bisexual thing was a bigger deal than she was letting on, even though it can't be the whole truth. The couch behind her is a huge, white suede thing, and I want to push her down on it, sweat stains be damned. I want desperately to know what she tastes like, and I want angry, pushy sex, each of us wrestling for control, and most of all, I want her to completely overpower me and just... take me. Then hold me.

But I need this job, and my father and brother need theirs. "Fine. But don't you try to pretend that you don't know what this is."

I leave, slamming the door behind me, and march home.

Just do the job, Evie, I say to myself.

Screw everything else.

Scout

I collapse against the door as soon as it's closed. That was hard. Harder than I thought it would be. But I'd stood my ground. I'd stood up for myself. And I hadn't let someone who would be bad for me gain a toehold into my life. Never again. Never. Again.

...

...

But.

God, why does this feel like such a terrible mistake?

I push that feeling aside because it isn't helpful right now. I have a job to do. I have several jobs to do, in fact, and I've once again gotten myself laser-focused on just the one. She's distracted me from the reality of my life, and I need to get my head in the game.

Once we get the new oven going and the pricing worked out, she and Roly can handle the store. And then I can refocus on the rest of my holdings and see if there's some way—any way—to stop the bleeding on my bank account.

I race back up the stairs and punch in the highest speed on the treadmill. Time to get busy. Time to get numb.

18

EVIE

Jake and I show up at my dad's house for Sunday dinner. We're both dressed nicely, me in a cute dress and Jake in a stylish black button-down over skinny grey wash jeans. Maybe we're trying too hard, but aside from a few comments about our attire, no one seems too put off by what we're wearing. Suzi is here, which is weird but not. While we'd have preferred fewer spectators, one look into my brother's eyes told me that this couldn't wait any longer.

My father pushes his plate away and begins talking to Spence about the Spurs' chances come fall, and the children start playing with the toys in Dad's living room. Jake and I lock eyes. It's time.

"Um," Jake hums, the one syllable ringing in the air.

My dad and Spence look up quizzically. "Yes, Jake?" My father's eyes are worried and edged with disappointment, waiting for the bad news that always seemed to come from the younger twin's direction.

"Um," he says thickly, "I need to talk to you and Spence. Alone." His eyes flick to Suzi and Annie, then back to our father and brother. Suzi immediately hops up, and Annie isn't too far behind, making sure to usher the children back into the living room.

"Actually," I say, "We both need to talk to you."

"Okay," answers Spence, tensed and waiting.

I hold Jake's hand as he inhales the courage he needs. I am so proud of him in this second. In this, the hardest part of the telling. The point where you can go back or make something up or choose to push forward. He stares at my hand, takes a breath, and chooses the way forward.

"I, um. I'm gay. And I wanted you to know because I met someone and won't be hiding that anymore."

I eye Spence, and his face is impassive. I don't think he's all that surprised, but he seems to be weighing his words. My father's neck is bright red, and his mouth is open as if to speak, but nothing comes out.

Spence turns to me. "And what is your news?"

"I'm bi. And ditto. Kinda."

I search beyond the dining room into the living room, and the two women are stock-still and dead quiet. I see Suzi first, and she has a supportive look on her face. Such a sweetie. Nervously, I scan Annie's face. She's rather religious and deeply enjoys her time in church. Our eyes meet as she holds my niece closer to her chest, and she smiles. It's a genuine, heartfelt smile, and my heart lifts a little. I realize in that moment that she reminds me of my mother.

I turn my attention back to the people at the table, and while Spence has remained neutral, my father's face has turned crimson. I take inventory of Jake, who is still fragile, and cringe at the thought of my father exploding on him. My father peers up at the picture of my mother, hanging on the wall above the banquet, and gathers a measure of control.

"Dad, I—"

"I love you," he interrupts, his voice rough. "I want you to know that. I am… hurt… by this. And I need you both to leave before I say something that your mother would not forgive me for."

I nod and stand up immediately, Jake's hand in mine, and we walk out the door.

On the ride back home we are silent, letting the confrontation settle between us like a weight. As I park, I look at my silent brother and imagine how lonely he must have felt growing up. How lonely he still feels.

"That… could have gone worse," I say wryly.

A sharp burst of air from Jake's nose and a stiff half-smile are the extent of his reaction. His face tilts down, and the sadness pours off him. He just wants things to be okay.

"Are you going to see Jackson this evening?" I ask, rubbing his shoulder.

He nods. "I'm going over right now. He wanted to know how it went."

"And how did it go, in your estimation?"

"About what I thought it would. A little better, actually," he says, smiling through a tear that has traced its way down his face. "We got an 'I love you,' which is hopeful."

I nod. "It's a start." And suddenly I'm sad that I don't have a person to repair to, to snuggle up to and to make it all better for me.

Well, no.

That's not true.

I do.

She's just not there yet. And I wish I knew the real reason why.

19

SCOUT

We've had the new pizza oven in for less than a month, and we've almost doubled our sales. Evelyn's pizza tastes even better with this oven than the one at Hush. And, as it happens, when you're able to drop the price and get people really delicious pizza in a matter of minutes, they'll keep coming back. Patty has also helped, and her social media postings have pushed us solidly into the black for the first time since we opened.

I keep my visits to the pizza shop to the times that Evelyn is working at Kavanaugh's, and I haven't seen her in days. I've been keeping tabs through Kimberly, and Evelyn already has the Schultz project back on track. I saw her leaving the other day and stayed on my front step until she got into her car and drove away.

I'm not sure what bothers me more—her office-appropriate clothing, the resigned look on her face, or the exhaustion that even makeup can't hide.

20

EVIE

I'll take Murder for $500, Alex.

I'd been dreaming about Scout, and her head was starting to dip between my thighs when raised voices woke me from my precious sleep. Jake is arguing with our father over gutter shields.

Gutter shields, y'all. In the middle of my flipping sex dream.

Our father refuses to bring up the "coming out" dinner, and we haven't, either, but all of their interactions are agitated and sharp. I'd love to move out, maybe get a different place with Jake, but I have a plan and don't want to deviate from it. I mean, it's a Saturday, and I'm picking up additional hours at the restaurant to supplement my bank account.

Enjoying my stolen coffee from the complimentary setup at the fancy hotel down the block, I pull the dough out of the proofing tray and begin experimenting with different flavor profiles to come up with something tasty. I decide on a light, fresh goat cheese, pear, walnut, and arugula mixture with an aged balsamic glaze, which comes out really well. Roly walks in, and we both enjoy a breakfast slice.

"Damn, Evie, this is delicious. I mean, we do really well with your recipes, but I came in a full hour early just to get a taste."

I smile and look up when I hear the bell above the door ring, anticipating Catherine or Lizbeth.

It's Carla Forrester.

Six foot two, mahogany hair down her back, makeup on point, clothing tailored and feminine, nails done, beautiful pouty lips, and a heart-shaped face that men and women alike have fawned over for the last twenty years. Intimidatingly beautiful. She's accompanied by an equally stunning blond man, and they look like they're ready for a photoshoot.

"Where is Scout?" she demands, her demeanor imperious.

I flub my words for a second, a little starstruck until I see the guy reach for her hand. I'm not the fastest dog in the yard, but now that I know that she and Scout used to be together, Scout's issue with bisexuals is beginning to come into focus. I'd love to give Carla a piece of my mind, but she's kind of my boss, too, since she also belongs to the same investment group as Scout. So, I pull up my phone and pretend to check Scout's calendar, as if I don't already have it memorized. "Looks like she's at the independent publisher on Fifth and Colorado. Probably won't be in all day."

She gives me the once-over and asks, "What's your name?"

"Evie."

Her eyes narrow, and the once-over becomes a double-take. "You're the one she gave that promotion to."

And you're the one who is ruining things for me and Scout, you beautiful-smelling bisexual bitch.

I nod once, slowly. "I'm the store manager."

"Hmmm. We'll see about that. What's your degree in?" she asks.

Look, I'm not about to tell her that I'm not quite there, so I lie. "MBA."

She snorts and replies, "You have an MBA and *this* is what you're doing with it?" while gesturing diminishingly at the space.

"Yes, because apparently your little basketball girls' collaborative or whatever couldn't figure out that a one-pizza-at-a-time oven wasn't going to be sustainable, or that hiring a creepy, sexual-harasser family member wasn't exactly conducive to a high-functioning office environment."

Look, things just fall out of my mouth when I'm professionally frustrated and woefully undersexed.

A shadow crosses Carla's face, and she stands over me as I've seen her do on the court a hundred times. As far as intimidation techniques go… it's pretty effective. "Do you really think that she can maintain this pace? Keep all of these locations afloat with her history?"

"What history?" I ask, immediately sorry that I did.

Carla sees my reaction and smirks. "Oh, look, Matt. She doesn't even know. Guess that means her little crush on Scout is one-sided. *Pity.*"

My stomach flips as I repeat myself. "What history, Carla? Why wouldn't she be able to maintain this pace?"

Roly stands beside me and pins Carla with a look. She shrugs him off, unconcerned. "The law is pretty clear, Evie. Scout has to want you to know, and apparently, she doesn't. Would be illegal for me to say anything else."

Remembering Jake's stint at rehab, I know that health issues can't be disclosed. I think about how much thinner Scout is now and I think about my mother, and I barely hear Roly yelling at Carla to leave.

Scout

I'm walking to the publisher's office when I see the call come in from Roly and punch the green icon. "'Sup, *primo?*"

"Hey, cousin. Carla was here. Got into it with Evie."

I clench my jaw, immediately enraged. "What *the fuck* is Carla doing at my restaurant?" Carla knows that she's not supposed to interact with my employees. Especially Evie. Especially now.

"Um. She's gone now, something about wanting to talk to you."

There's a hesitation in his voice that sets my teeth on edge. "Okay..."

"She, uh..." Fuck, he's killing me. "Spit it out, Roly-man."

"She kinda hinted about your cancer."

My feet are already turning back to my car. *"What?"* The sharp violence of that question scares the mother with her kid in the stroller beside me. I start walking faster. "Why would she say anything to her? Did you get the sense that Evie knew what she was talking about?"

"Why does that bitch do anything? And no, I don't think Evie put anything together, but she's real upset. Like, she's not crying, but it's close. I was about to tell her to go home and I'll take the rest of the day."

Dammit. I *knew* it. I'm angry as hell at Carla, but the thought of Evie near tears is ripping apart my insides.

"Roly-man, if you could do that for me, I'd really appreciate it. I'll take care of this."

I climb into the Jeep and pull out into oncoming traffic. The guy I nearly cream lays on his horn, but I can't even give a damn right now. Punching the Bluetooth on my steering wheel, I call up the board president.

"Go for Trish."

"Hey, Trish, it's Scout."

"Scout, baby! Those Austin numbers are really perking up. Too bad about the hat thing and the travel thing, but I think your portfolio should start to really move in the right direction again by the new year."

"Yeah, yeah. Which is why I'm curious about Carla deciding to show up—twice—to the pizza shop. She's harassing my employees, and it has to stop."

Tricia Louis is an old-school ballplayer, a hard-as-nails businesswoman, and someone who hates bullshit as much as I do. And she is quiet.

"Trish?" I say, swerving from behind someone who dared only go five miles over the speed limit.

She hesitates, the pause thrumming through the car stereo. "Look,

Scout, I know it's not ideal with the way your relationship turned out, but the way you tanked your own portfolio after your cancer treatments had us worried. She's in Austin at least once a month, so we asked her to quietly check in on what you're doing to make sure that you're, you know…"

"Not blowing the board's money?" I say, giving the finger to the asshole who cut me off.

"Healthy. And safe. And making sound business decisions."

I throw an annoyed gesture at the dashboard. "Which I am."

"That's true. We only asked for one more visit."

I roll my eyes while merging into traffic. "Which she happened to schedule when my shared calendar indicated I'd be gone from that place of business. While nearly divulging my personal health history to an employee. How exactly is that 'checking in on me quietly'? What the hell is this about?"

Trish inhales sharply. Yeah. HIPAA laws being what they are, if Carla had opened her mouth, the board could be in some pretty deep shit.

"I'll take care of it," she says, hanging up quickly.

I'm driving through traffic like an asshole, needing to get to Evie, to see her, to comfort her. I'd love to say that I don't know what I care so much, but even you would have to call me out on that level of intellectual dishonesty.

By the time I get to the apartments, I am turned so inside out that I nearly trip getting out of the car and practically run to her apartment. Evie opens the door before I'm even finished knocking, and the hurt look on her face makes my chest contract. She ushers me in and closes the door, then leans in to maybe hug me, but her arms stay at her side, and doubt marks her features.

"Evelyn, I'm so sorry that she came after you like that," I say, putting my arms around her, pulling her against me, cursing myself for enjoying her plush warmth. "You won't have to deal with her again. The board is going to tell her to stop it."

She puts her forehead to my chest, chuckling ruefully. "Yeah, she seems the type to listen."

I pull back, trying to look her in the eyes, but she tilts her face to the side, avoiding direct contact. "I'm so sorry that she was mean to you."

She laughs again, almost bitterly. "What does she know that I don't, Scout? Are you okay?"

The terrible sadness and wringing apprehension on her face burns me to the core. So, like an asshole, I go for a cool truth. "I am okay now, and that's all you need to know."

Her big, honey-amber eyes blink as she processes my nonanswer, and in them I see everything. The sadness, the desire, the need. My heart starts thudding in my chest. *Evie.*

Her emotions are undeniable, vulnerable, and so fucking sweet. She put her hands on my face and whispers my name through her tears. *"Scout."*

I hate that I'm the reason for her wrecked expression, and I want to give in to her right then and there, but I can't bring myself to walk across this particular set of coals.

I am such a coward.

I place my hands over hers, moving them from my face. "Please... *don't.*"

It sounds like the most pitiful begging to my own ears, but she nods in acceptance, and then, with her voice breaking, levels me once again. "The worst part of this—and I mean the absolute worst part—is that she's enjoying whatever it is she has over me."

For the briefest moment her face crumples, but she blinks away the intrusive moisture and inhales deeply, shaking it off and squaring her shoulders as I've seen her do time and time and time again. In this small moment, it finally lands that she is, along with so many varied and wonderful and aggravating things, a true and pure tenderheart. And that I've been selling her short by comparing her to Carla, who was never this broken up about anything that hurt me, much less my illness.

I am the biggest goddamned fool on the planet.

As I contemplate that obvious truth, someone begins to pound on the door, causing both of us to jerk back.

"Evie! Open up! It's about Jake!" It sounds like the guy from 2C. Jack something or other.

Evie's eyes morph from melted beeswax to sharp alarm in the space of half a second. She nods once more and sets her jaw, then opens the door. 2C is standing there, looking desperate and sad. "Jackson? What's going on? Where's Jake?"

Tears are forming at the corners of his eyes as he holds up his phone and his voice strains. "I think he went to a bar."

Evie's back stiffens. I grab her phone from the counter, catching her eye as I hand it over. *I may be an asshole, but I'm here for you.* Jackson's eyes ping back and forth between the two of us. I don't know the details, but I know that Jake has a rough history and that she thought he might be gay as well. I'd already clocked him, but Jackson and I look at each other and nod, all the confirmation I need. Evie is lost to her phone, swiping her manicured finger along the screen until she taps a button, bringing up the call.

"Jake?" she says, her voice sounding of concern edged with anger. "I'm here with Jackson. Why are you at a bar?"

I can hear him speaking loudly over the phone, and her face takes on more and more concern. She looks at me and mouths *I'm sorry*. I gesture away the apology and run my fingers through my hair, wishing I could take away whatever was making her mouth turn down like that.

"I hear you, Jake. I can't believe he did that. I'm so, so sorry. But we're in this together. He'll come around. You know he will. He's—"

From what I could see, Jake has cut her off and is speaking more frantically. The only *he* in their lives that would warrant that reaction is their father. My employee.

"No," she says solemnly. She looks at me, worried, maybe worried about my reaction. "It *is* worth it, Jake. I know you want to, but it's not going to make this any better. Eventually he'll understand that... yes, of course. No, Jake. No. I don't want you to drink tonight..."

Her eyebrows knit together as she listens intently while grabbing her purse.

"I know... but this isn't about what I want, or what he... I know...

Honey, it's about you being okay in the world as you are. And I don't give a *shit* if he's having a hard time with that. He doesn't get to... no. *No.* He doesn't get to decide your worth because of that... no, honey."

Against my better judgment, I open my arm in a half-hug gesture, and she leans into me as she listens.

"Just 'cause you ordered it doesn't mean you have to drink it. Do me a favor—I'm getting in the car right now, and you just walk outside. No. I'll go in and pay the tab. Just walk outside and I'll come get you. Do you want Jackso... okay. I'm two minutes away."

She hangs up and looks at me with fear, sadness, and frustration swimming in her beautiful eyes. I put my hands on her shoulders. "Do you want me to go with you?"

She shakes her head. "I think he'd be embarrassed to have you see him like that."

I nod, not wanting to let her go. "See you later, then?" I look deep into her eyes, wishing I could protect her from this. Wishing that I weren't so goddamned *terrified*.

She nods and lets me and Jackson out before locking the apartment. She makes plans to update Jackson as she ducks into her car, then gives me a little wave as she drives off, taking a chunk of my heart with her.

21

EVIE

*J*ake had called his AA sponsor, but she's out of town, and then Jackson hadn't picked up and then I hadn't picked up. I am so, so glad that he didn't drink last night, that he answered my call instead. We stayed up most of the night, talking through things. It seems that our father lit into him when he saw Jackson leaving our apartment yesterday morning. Come to find out, he and Suzi had started dating just before our Sunday dinner, and she told him that she would not date a homophobe, and now my father is blaming us for tanking his love life.

Welp, too damned bad.

"Hey, Pops," I say, striding into his office at 8:01 a.m.

"I'm not speaking to either of you," he says, swiveling his chair away from the door.

I mean, does he not know me at all?

"Yeah, that's not going to cut it. A) I can still see you, 2) you're being a gigantic jerk and embarrassing the memory of our mother with your terrible attitude, and third of all, the son who you love so much that you sent him to a $45,000 treatment center almost drank last night after your little stunt."

He swivels back in my direction. "It's not my attitude, it's God's. If you don't like it, take it up with Him. And... if Jake drinks that's on him."

"Yes, it *is* on him. Thing is, if you're bad for his sobriety and his overall happiness, you're not really bringing much to the table now, are you? And if you're happy to be sidelined as he walks down the extraordinarily difficult path to recover from whatever has happened to him, and especially if you are actively hurting his sobriety, then you *will* lose him forever. And me, right along with him. You could be part of the solution, help him to talk about whatever got him here, but instead you choose to pick on something that is none of your business. It's none of your business, Dad, and you've got to let it go, or you will lose both of us. And if you think that Spence won't take his twin brother's side, then you don't know Spence at all."

"The Bible says—"

"The Bible can kiss my grits, Dad, 'cause it's not helping him right now. The only big book that's been of any use to him in the last year has twelve steps and a room full of drunks to recommend itself. If you want to use your book and your faith to bludgeon my brother while he is down, then all that does is confirm my suspicions."

"How *dare* you—"

"How dare *I*? I'm not the one running around like a Pharisee," I say, using a biblical reference I know he'll get. "All pumped *up* on piety. Using a showy display of faith, rather than the humble offerings of service. God doesn't need you to treat your son like shit to show him that you love him. If you want to claim Jesus, then you'd best remember that he gave us two commandments. Two. And you are failing one of those pretty badly right now. Jake's choices are between him and God, and you have no right to say any different."

"B-but, if your mother..."

"You. Leave. Our. Mother. Out. Of. This," I say, the words seething on my tongue. "She would *never* have said the things you said to him. She would want him to be happy. And she would pray and humbly ask for understanding. That's what our mother would do. And she would grow and she would evolve and she would accept. Because she loves us more than dogma, she always did, and you *always* got that wrong about her. She loved the church because it was home, and people like you make people like us feel we don't have a home to go back to."

With that, I turn on my heel and walk out of the office, nodding to Suzi as I leave. My feet hit the path, and who the hell knows where they are taking me.

22

EVIE

*I*t's been a week since the Carla and Jake fiascos, and I am for once glad about the hellacious pace of my life. I'll be honest with y'all—after spending much of the day at the Schultzes' build site listening to all of the "small adjustments" they'd like to make, then the rest of the evening at the pizza shop, I don't have the mental energy to fully obsess over whatever it is that Scout has been through.

Usually the shop is easier than the office, but Roly called in sick, which he never does, and we didn't have Catherine or Lizbeth scheduled for tonight, since it's usually less busy in the middle of the week. There'd been some kind of event in town, and because of Patty's recent recommendation in the *Chronicle*, I got overwhelmed pretty quickly. I hadn't wanted to, but I called Scout in for backup. She showed up looking as beat down and tired as I feel, but we got into our old rhythm without preamble and quietly got through the rush.

We just closed the shop, and at this point I might be leaning on the counter more than actually wiping it down. But... if I can power through two or three rides after we close up, I can hold off a few creditors and dump a little more cash into savings.

I need a Starbucks Doubleshot, stat.

Scout steps up to me, her brow furrowed. She hasn't spoken a full sentence to me in weeks, but ugh. I love the furrow of her brow so damned much. Concerned and stern in one panty-melting expression.

Sigh.

"Go home, Evelyn. You look exhausted."

I manage a half-smirk while continuing to half-heartedly half clean the counter. "Thanks, Scout, you always know how to make a girl feel beautiful."

She puts her hands on my shoulders, and it's a touch I've been craving for far too long. "This is not a debate. Get your ass home," she orders in that astringent tone of hers. I briefly imagine her ordering me to take off my panties, and suddenly I'm not so tired.

Not helpful.

"But I thought we were waiting for Jake?" My brother has started helping Scout with other areas of her business, running errands, fixing small issues at the other offices, generally being the kind of invaluable that I always knew he would be. I'm glad he's staying busy; Jackson broke things off with him after his drinking scare, and while I understand his need to prioritize his sobriety, it's been a hit to Jake's confidence. I just wish my brother could find some solid ground and am grateful that Scout is giving him the opportunity to show what he can do.

Her furrow deepens, and my renegade nipples need to calm the hell down. "Shit, that's right," she says, rubbing her beautifully strong and slightly masculine hands over her face. Her eyes are as dark as mine. "When do you think he'll be here? I'm supposed to go out with an old friend tonight."

"Wait... you have friends?" I shoot back sarcastically, my heart clenching a little around the words "go out" and "old friend."

She starts to retort, but the bell rings and Jake is walking in with the first of many gunny sacks of flour hitched over his shoulder. Scout and I make for the door, figuring we'd help him bring in the supplies, but he holds up his hand. "You both look like you can barely stand. Finish your close-out. I've got this."

My brother's tone does not brook debate, and his eyes toggle between me and Scout, daring us to challenge him on it. Scout is the first to back down. Throwing her palms up, she says, "I'm not gonna fight you on that. Thanks, Jake." With that, I go back to wiping down the counters, and she goes back to counting the till and finalizing the books for tomorrow.

By Jake's third trip back to the car, I stop looking up when the bell above the door goes off, so it takes me a minute to realize that there is a seven-foot man in the shop. Perhaps it's the temperature change or the shift in atmospheric pressure as his enormous bulk crowds out the other molecules in the space. Either way, I eventually look up. And then keep looking up for another ten minutes until I finally find his eyes.

Holy shitake mushrooms, Batman. That's Jean-Pierre Sehene.

As in, Jean-Pierre Sehene, recently retired forward of the San Antonio Spurs. My jaw drops as my eyes linger up and down his body, which is still in pro form. Damn, he's hot. And I can't wait for Jake to see him, because if I had the hots for Scout when she was a player, that is nothing compared to Jake's crush on Sehene. It's literally the reason I knew he was gay before he told me, because my sometimes-prickly, usually stoic brother can barely contain himself whenever Sehene is on TV. And now that Jean-Pierre is the defensive coach for the UT Men's basketball team, we are going to be seeing a lot more of him.

This is gonna be *so good.*

Scout

I see Evelyn's reaction before I see Jean-Pierre. She definitely thinks he's hot, and that is just the cold bucket of reality I needed, because I may or may not have become slightly obsessed with this patch of exposed ivory skin on the back of her neck. It simply does me no good to wonder if the sheen of sweat I see on her skin is as salty-sweet as I think it is.

Tearing my eyes away from my employee, I look up at my good

buddy and say in my best announcer voice, "Well, if it isn't the NBA Player of the Year, Jean-Pierre *Seeeehhhhheeeeeennnnnneeeee*!" He laughs and pulls me up into the world's best bear hug. I don't have much of an opportunity to feel small, but everyone is small next to Jean-Pierre. We both laugh and beat each other on the back a few times, and a sense of belonging inhabits my body. Jean-Pierre and I are both coming off a difficult year, and while we'd always been buds, this last year solidified us into ride-or-die territory. Retiring had been harder on him than he'd realized it would be, and at the same time his Playboy bunny-wannabe wife decided she preferred someone still in the game. One of his teammates, to be exact, and that made everything worse. Jean-Pierre was a commanding presence on the court, but a big softie in the real world and life had taken a big bite out of both of us. I'm so happy to see him and glad that he seems to have shaken off the pall of the last year.

Evelyn's head jerks up when she hears me goof around with Jean-Pierre, and a smile creeps across her lips. I think seeing me happy makes her happy, and my stomach does a flip-flop that I'm trying to not think too much about. She's about to introduce herself when Jake bumps the door open with his hip, carrying the last sack of flour on one shoulder while cradle-balancing two bushels of peaches in his other arm, sweat dripping down his face. The front of his shirt is soaked and spackled to his lean frame, and I feel bad that we didn't help him out before.

Evelyn's eyes sparkle as they dart between her brother and Jean-Pierre, one brow hitched up in amusement. I have come to rely on Jake over the last several weeks, and I know he's embarrassed that I witnessed his near fall off the wagon, but the fact that he's trying so hard tells me everything I need to know about the guy. He definitely deserves to manage the operations side of things… once I actually have the budget for an operations team. So, if he's a fan, I'm happy to make the introductions.

"Jake! Buddy—I believe you've heard of my friend, Jean-Pierre Sehene?"

Jake's whole body, previously in focused forward motion, stills immediately. The stacked bushels of peaches almost topple, but Jean-Pierre reaches down and places his gargantuan hand on the bushel in time to prevent disaster. Not exactly sure why we have two bushels of peaches, but that mystery is shelved when I see how Jake looks down at my friend's richly pigmented skin and the size of his hands, which cover nearly the entire basket. Slowly his eyes make their way up Jean-Pierre's muscular arms and down his long, neatly layered umber locs.

I grimace a little, knowing that, while Jean-Pierre likes tall, raven-haired beauties, he's straight. Thankfully, he's a pro at handling enamored fans of all genders and gives Jake a warm, bright smile. "Here, let me take that from you," his Montreal-via-Rwanda accent smooth and kind.

It's odd to see someone change right before your eyes, and to see my focused, almost taciturn maintenance guy melt into a puddle right in front of me is a thing to behold. And kinda funny. Evelyn's eyes cut to me, her eyebrow again raised in a knowing arch, and I humor her with a slight nod. Yeah, I saw.

"Merci beaucoup," Jake says, finally looking up from his stupor.

"De rien," my friend replies silkily. "Tu parles français?" I know that means "Do you speak French" because I had to answer "non" to that question every time we played an exhibition game in Paris.

"Oui, un peu," Jake replies, still a little breathless, but a bit more sure of himself. "J'ai vécu en France pendant six mois, mais j'ai oublié plus que ce dont je me souviens."

"Eh bien, ce que vous vous rappelez semble parfait."

Evelyn and I look at each other and shrug, neither of us knowing enough French to pick out what is being said, though, from the blush on Jake's cheek, I think it's complimentary. I'm also massively impressed that Jake can speak French.

"Here," Jean-Pierre says, smoothly switching back to his beautifully accented English, "let me help you get this to the back." He grabs both bushels from Jake and follows him to the back of the shop. Jake stacks the last bag of flour with the rest, while Jean-Pierre sets the peaches on the counter and takes a moment to look around the kitchen.

"Scout, this place is amazing. It's a little old-school, a little funky, and I love the pictures you have up."

I look around and chuckle. This place reflects Kimberly's unique sense of style. She gathered candid shots of friends and family in black and white and interspersed them with local art and wall sculpture, creating an atmosphere of warm welcome. Above table three is a small photo in a mosaic of others, me and Jean-Pierre mid-fist-bump. It's my favorite picture, and I'm proud to have his likeness up in the restaurant.

"Hey, Evelyn, do we have any of today's special left over?"

I look over, and she'd already anticipated my question, having rolled out a fresh ball of dough. Jean-Pierre and I agree to stay at the shop as Evie tosses the blue cheese, bacon, and prosciutto pizza into the oven, sidelining any protest. I smile, loving her stubborn way of caring for others, even though I know she has to be dead on her feet. Within moments she's slicing up her bubbling creation and shoveling it onto paper plates for us to enjoy around the prep station.

I turn to my friend, excited for the next phase in his life. "Aren't you glad you decided to move back to Austin?"

"*Oui*," he answers, groaning as Evelyn slides another slice in his direction.

Jake and I convince his sister to leave the ridesharing for another night, and we all sit around for a little while, reliving the glory days, entertaining the two fans who've given me more in real life than I ever could give them on the basketball court.

By the end of the night, both are halfway in love with him, and that sucks.

23

EVIE

I think Scout is a little jealous of my reaction to Jean-Pierre's undeniable hotness. I'm not *at all* taking advantage of that fact by talking about him every time she unintentionally strips me naked with her eyes, which means that I've been spending an inordinate amount of time over the last few days talking about Jean-Pierre's amazing jump shot and what I think he can do while volunteering for the men's basketball team now that he's here in Austin. It's a double bonus if Jake is in the room because he gets as red and blotchy as I do. Heh.

Thing is, this do-si-do is actually starting to hurt (digs about Jean-Pierre notwithstanding), and it's not the visual undressing that's the problem. It's the wall of *nope* that falls into place afterward, because my addlepated heart gets excited, then crushed every goddamned time. And as much fun as that is, I'm about over it.

I wouldn't mind (so much) if me being bi means that she is unequivocally unattracted to me. But she isn't unattracted. That tall drink of lesbian literally can't stop looking at me, even after I busted her on it a few weeks ago. But she doesn't trust me because of that old canard about bisexuals being promiscuous, like promiscuous is both the worst thing in the world and the same as untrustworthy.

News flash: I'm not, nor have I ever been, promiscuous. Like, I'm embarrassingly *un*promiscuous. Hell, my v-card was firmly in place until I was twenty-three, and I've slept with a whopping three men, all of whom I was in a relationship with at the time. I've never, ever had a one-night stand (my one attempt having failed so miserably I won't bother with that ever again), never stepped out on anyone, and am, frankly, loyal to a fault. Literally, I've stayed way past the sell-by date on every relationship I've ever been in.

Gotta say, it sucks being dinged for something that is 1) not true and b) so beyond the realm of true that I'm still paying the price for the lack of it being true.

Just last week she made some stupid joke about the fact that I had not yet slept with a woman, and therefore was... you guessed it, unreliable. Not sure why she brought that up since she's so *disinterested*, but whatever.

This morning, I notice that Scout's car is already gone when I head out for Mordor. I think about the way the Kavanaughs have done things, and it seems that she's avoiding their stupid mistakes. If I'm being honest, I'm happy to see it.

Still, going back to that smoke-stained, soul-sucking metal box day after day has taken a toll on me. I'm dead on my feet, bone-weary, and have been amusing myself trying to find something to pin on those jackasses. VPNing to the office network has been a complete waste of my time because the only person who actually kept things on the company server was me. So glad I endured the Mrs. Kavanaugh shitstorm to get that supercritical access.

I also thought I'd be able to get into the paper files much more quickly, maybe find something for the IRS to gnaw on, but no joy. Chet won't let me near that room, and he intercepts Itsy every time I ask her to grab something for me.

Thankfully, in the biggest plot twist ever, and please excuse me as I throw some salt over my shoulder lest I jinx myself, but the Schultz project is going *well*. The cabana now has four walls, including a gorgeous wall of glass looking over the grotto'd pool, and the guys are about to start on the interior. With so many stalls and delays in the build, the Schultzes had all of the time in the world to second-guess and edit their project, but now that they can finally see what it was they'd purchased, they've nearly stopped requesting changes. And, since I'd put it in her head to have the cabana done by the end of June, Mrs. Schultz is demanding faster completion so that she can put on a big Fourth of July party.

While I'd hoped to have something a bit more substantial with which to bludgeon my captors, if nothing else, I will be free of this office within the month. I can't help but try to make things better for the clients who had unfortunately put their faith in this shite company, helping smooth things over with annoyed suppliers and anxious couples.

Go ahead, say it.

I'm a sucker.

As I'm quietly handling a last-minute catering request from one of the nearby boutique hotels for the pizza shop, Chet's mother sidles up next to me. "Evie, darling. How are you doing? Still seeing that other person who isn't your husband?"

Always right to the point. I set down my phone and face my torturer.

"I'm doing well, Mrs. Kavanaugh. And yes, I am. Still seeing her."

So sue me. I'm a lying liar who lies and I'm not sorry.

Mrs. Kavanaugh's eyes fly open. "*Her*? You're seeing a... a... a *woman?*"

Oops. See also: terminally exhausted and emotionally compromised.

Chet, overhearing his mother's obvious distress, comes out of his office. "Mom, what is going on?"

Pointing at me as though I were a pariah, she stage-whispers, "Evelyn is seeing a woman. A *woman*, Chet. Surely you can give her what a *woman* can't."

First of all, I can hear you, bitch. And b) She's saying it like it's a challenge to his masculinity. Like, I don't even factor into their conversation. Lovely human, that one.

Chet's eyes darken, and he presses his mouth into a thin line as his eyes go up and down my body. "Mom, you need to leave."

"Chet!"

"Mom. Go."

She makes a small *hmph* sound, picks up her quilted Chanel purse, and walks into her office, slamming the door.

"Evie, please come to my office," Chet orders.

I reluctantly follow him inside, not sure why he's being so pissy with me.

"Please shut the door."

I do as asked and turn around to find him standing in front of me, uncomfortably close. Stiff. Angry.

"Chet, I don't—"

"Shut up, Evie," he says, backing me up to the door, placing his hands on either side of me. Looking down at me, he snarls, "So, you wouldn't have a threesome to save our marriage, but *now* you're okay with fucking a woman? Who is it? That Olive Oyl basketball dyke?"

I snarl at his description, and he nods as though that's some kind of confirmation. "Whatever, she's *barely* a woman."

I duck out of his arm cage and push him away from me. "Are you even listening to yourself? Are you seriously trying to blame the death of our marriage on the fact that I wouldn't sleep with you and another woman?"

"If the chastity belt fits," he says, stalking me.

I put my hands out in front of me, a barrier and a warning. "Chet, you were already sleeping with her. Behind my back. So no, I didn't want to have sex with the woman who was banging my husband. Guess I was just selfish back then."

Closing his fists at his side, he glares at me. "I wanted to shake it up, add the heat back into our marriage. You were always so tired, you never had time to do the fun stuff anymore."

I tilt my head back to dramatize the roll of my eyes. What an idiot. "Why do you think that is, Chet? Have you ever considered that having to manage every project, even the ones not assigned to me, just to keep this barge afloat was sucking my will to live? Did you ever consider that going to work fifty plus hours a week, then going to school fifteen hours a semester was really, really hard? Could you not see that I was burning out and could have used some help on the business front? Or the home front? Did you not hear me when I asked to go part-time so that I could finish my degree faster? I mean, did you not care that I was trying to get my MBA so that I could make this damned business better?"

He steps back and parks his beautiful and ignorant ass on the corner of his desk. "Why did you even need an MBA? I mean, you had a set job here. You were never going to have to go on another job interview a day in your life."

It's like he doesn't hear what he's saying. "Oh, I don't know—maybe it was pretty smart of me to have a backup plan, considering that I didn't want to continue to work for the guy putting it to our nineteen-year-old next-door neighbor."

"I wouldn't have done that if you'd showed me the least bit of affection or interest or even, fuck, some leg every once in a while." My brain does the equivalent of an epic eye roll. *Yeah, baby, yeah. Give me more of an opportunity to show you exactly how bad I am at the sex.* Not.

"You wanna know what's really funny? I was killing myself to help us make a better life together, to get us on a good track so that we wouldn't have to work so hard, so that we could make smarter decisions and enjoy ourselves. I might have even enjoyed a threesome if I weren't working all day to fix your screwups and then all night to catch up on my assignments."

Chet's mouth thins as he shakes his head. "Whatever you need to tell yourself, Evie. At least I've got a dick—a real one. Why fuck a dildo when you could have the real thing?"

I mumble *screw it* and stay with the deceit, because it was mostly true, save for the actual sex. "I'm with a woman who understands what I bring to the table, and she doesn't work against me, she doesn't throw my hard work in my face. She looks after me and makes sure that I'm not overdoing it, and actually seeks out and listens to my advice. Turns out, I didn't need a penis to feel valued. *I just had to get the hell away from you."*

I push past him and slam the door. I gather my things and ignore Itsy, who is asking if I'm okay.

No, I'm not okay.

I'm stuck in this dank office, working for these useless people, and even though it's temporary, it's highlighting every messed-up thing in my life. Like the fact that I'm pretending that Scout will ever have the ovaries to love me back. And lying to my ex-husband about the nature of our relationship makes me the most pathetic person on the planet, and that pisses me smooth off. I mean, god help her if either of us accidentally demonstrates the teensiest bit of affection, 'cause then she falls off the face of the earth for weeks on end, sending word by text and freaking carrier pigeon.

I would love to get into my car and drive until something makes sense in my life, but my day isn't even close to being done *because I've still got another job to go to*. Heck, the only reason I'm not doing the rideshare thing after that is because Kim is in town and wants to go out, and I only agreed to that because she promised to buy me all of the drinks.

She might want to check her bank balance because I'm gonna get *lit*.

After I finish my shift at the pizza shop.

Cheese and rice, I am so tired.

After dealing with the drama at Kavanaugh's, I thought that a simple evening slinging pizza wouldn't be so bad. I mean, what could go wrong?

I should really be more careful about asking that question.

It started when I first walked in. Roly asked if I knew anything about a large catering order, and... son of a biscuit. I hadn't hit Send on that damned message I was composing because Mama Kavanaugh couldn't leave well enough alone. Thankfully we were able to cover the order and were only a few minutes late, but doing so meant that Roly and Lizbeth had to work the hotel event, and we were out of fresh dough, along with half of the ingredients most customers would have actually wanted on a pizza. I was able to use frozen dough while proofing fresh dough while giving out free samples of the peach pizza to sway people to buy that. Which half worked.

Probably would have worked better if I hadn't screwed up three more computer orders. Thankfully, people stopped yelling when I comped their dinners.

"What kind of a pizza place runs out of pepperoni?" was a question we heard a lot tonight.

I should be grateful that Mr. Castlebridge, neighborhood scold and wearer of the world's worst toupee, likes anchovies on his pizza, and Lord knows we had plenty of that. Everyone was a little less grateful when I burned his order, and for an hour the shop smelled like smelly, charred fish.

The absolute highlight of the day had to be when I yelled at Catherine—poor, loyal, always-on-time, cute-as-a-button Catherine —until she cried. I've actually never done that before, so then we both ended up crying, and I had her go home early so that I could close up shop. At least this interminable day is over, and I'll be bottle-deep in a lovely cabernet within the hour.

While waiting for Kim, I give myself a French bath and a makeup refresh in the bathroom, then change into a white halter number with black piping and black French poodles (complete with berets) printed on it. I take a deep, *deep* breath and exhale loudly. There's nothing to be done about the bags under my eyes, but my eyeliner is evenly winged (holler), and despite the knee-deep crappy of my current existence, I'm having an extravagantly gorgeous hair day (lavender newly refreshed and pin-curled to the gods), and I'd just shotgunned my favorite caffeinated beverage.

It's amazing what a little primping can do. I feel almost human as I slip into my red, five-inch heels.

Just as I'm about to turn off the lights, I hear the bell go off.

"Are you still open?"

Mother of pearl. I forgot to lock the door.

My shoulders dip from the weight of having to do one more damned thing. Squaring up, I turn around and… oh, *hello.* A tall, distractingly handsome blonde-and-silver lesbian in her mid to late forties is standing at the door. Stout and muscular, she is wearing the hell out of her tailored, gunmetal-gray suit. She's carrying the jacket and has rolled the sleeves of her white button-down up her tanned and toned forearms, which are…

"Oh, hai," I say like a teenager as our eyes meet.

So. Totally. Busted.

Her mouth quirks up, and I bite a nail, a slight flush heating up my neck. Pulling my red lips up into a wide smile, I allow my eyes another up-down and try again. "I'm about to close, but I can toss in one last pizza. What can I get for you tonight?"

She leans in, a devilish smile setting off the fine wrinkles around her blue eyes and the white in her perfectly coiffed, slightly wavy undercut. "Excellent question. What *can* you get for me tonight?"

Hey there, Slacks.

She looks like a lesbian who wouldn't mind a walk on the bi side.

I put my elbows on the counter and rest my chin between my knuckles, the subtle lean emphasizing the dress's décolletage. Her eyes follow the lean, and I bite my first response, which ventures into the obscene, landing on, "Oh, I don't know. I'm pretty partial to today's special: mozzarella with peach slices, drizzled with rosemary oil."

Her smirk returns. "Peaches? On a pizza?"

"Of course," I say, raising my bare shoulder into a half shrug. I hold up my finger and turn to the cutting board behind me, grabbing a thick slice of Fredericksburg peach, making a show of swirling a bit of the rosemary oil onto the juicy flesh. "They're perfectly in season," I explain, holding the slice up to her mouth.

Her grin widens into full-on wolf, and she accepts the slice, her lips brushing my fingers as she bites down. I resist a wink and instead eat the other half of the peach slice, licking my fingers.

This day has suddenly gotten about ten times better.

Her eyes widen in surprise as the taste hits her palate. "Oh, wow. That's so good it's almost sexy."

"Almost?" I ask sweetly, batting my eyelashes at her. "Pity. Would you like a slice or a whole pizza?"

She bites her lower lip. "Oh, I'm going all in on that," she answers as the bell rings behind her. I assume it's Kim and keep my eye on the prize.

"Why don't you take a seat, and I'll bring it over to you in a few minutes." I point to a darker corner of the shop, preparing to tell Kim to wait in the car. I'm going to be a minute.

"I might need help eating it," she suggests, looking at my lips as a shadow falls in behind her.

A deeper voice than I'm expecting filters through and the air crackles with familiar tension. "It's closing time. You'll need to take that to go."

The suited butch looks over her shoulder. "Excuse me?" she asks, tilting her head up. "Oh, hi, Scout."

Scout, with her hair pushed back, wearing Doc Martens, a pair of shredded black jeans, a dark green T-shirt, black leather wristbands, silver rings on most of her fingers, and her black motorcycle jacket, steps up to the counter, her almond-shaped eyes burning me where they land. "Evelyn will be happy to put that in a to-go box for you. I'm sure your wife will appreciate the pizza as much as you do."

My eyes fall to the untanned skin on the butch's left ring finger. Mnh. Why, pray tell, are all of the good-looking ones such jackasses?

"Maybe I should go somewhere else," the handsome liar says, looking at me with a sheepish grin.

"Yeah, maybe you should," Scout says, raising herself to her full height, pinning the lesbian with a glare. The clearly suicidal butch pauses to look me up and down again and throws her business card on the counter before disappearing into the warm evening.

Scout picks up the card, studies it for a moment, then rips it up before stuffing it in her back pocket.

Trying to control the red that is licking up my neck and jawline, I purse my lips. "Well, hey there, Scout. To what do I owe the pleasure?"

"So, are you aiming for jerks, or do they just sniff you out?"

I do the wide blink that I know she hates but secretly loves. "I dunno. You keep showing up, so I've got to assume that I've got a beacon or some sort of sign of the Devil on my forehead. And you didn't answer my question. Why are you here?"

"Kimberly sent me to pick you up."

"What are you, my personal Uber?"

Scout tilts her head. "I'm not a car service. We're all going out tonight."

Kim. I am going to kill that girl. She did *not* mention that Dykezilla would be joining us.

"Uh, no. Kim and I were supposed to catch up, get drunk, and dance," I say, putting one slightly oily hand on my pristine hip. I look down and bite a curse, keeping my hand where it is.

Amusement lights up Scout's eyes. "She invited me."

"Awesome," I retort, looking for a clean towel. Her lips twitch as I dab at the hopeless case near my waistline. Arching a brow in her direction, I huff, "*What?*"

She leans forward on the counter, gesturing for me to come closer. Putting my hand back on my hip, I stand there, not moving. Her amused eyes drop down to my oily hand again. *Son of a biscuit*. Fine. I lean in, and her eyes lose their humor but keep their sex appeal. "Why are you hand-feeding fruit to our customers?"

I raise my brow and execute a perfectly innocent shrug. "She didn't think that peaches could taste good on a pizza."

"And do they?" Scout asks in a deeper octave, leaning in a little more.

Huh. Is she... *no*. Is she flirting with me?

I bite the edge of my bottom lip. "They taste brilliant on a pizza," I respond, wondering if it would it be too cheesy to pull the same move on Scout as I did on the vested one. Because she's looking at me expectantly. Like maybe she'd like to taste my peaches.

The actual peaches, you perverts.

With a shy smile, I slip out of the torture traps and walk barefoot to the prep table. I score a peach along its crease and twist, teasing the halves apart as juice drips through my fingertips.

The pass-through whooshes up quietly as Scout approaches me from behind, peering over my shoulder, crowding me against the workstation. The tiny baby hairs on the back of my neck electrify and stand at attention. On a slow inhale, I wrap the stone half of the peach in parchment for later, then exhale as I slice the other half. The near heat of her body makes my skin prickle, and I grow slick with the small hope that she'll lose a bit of that hard-tack control. My heart beats wildly in my chest at the thought of what that would look like.

I will into place my very last shred of focus and swirl the rosemary oil over the slices, then set the oil mixture on the butcher block and pick up a section of peach with my fingers. Scout leans in over my shoulder as I bring the fruit up to her lips, and a bit of juice drips onto my bare skin. I shiver as her lips brush my fingertips, the sound of teeth biting through ripe fruit erotic in my ears.

"*Holy shit*," she growls, her voice low. I instantly regret/cheer not wearing a bra because the halter does jack all to hide her effect on my nipples. My hand shakes slightly as I raise my fingers again, and a few more droplets of juice and herbed oil splash across my cleavage and shoulders. Her mouth encases my fingertips as she gently tongues the rest of the fruit from their grasp, and her fisted hand slides across the work surface, knocking against my hip as she groans, swallowing the fruit.

Touch me. Please, please, please touch me.

I'm a rubber band on the edge of snapping as her ragged breath chills the droplets, pebbling the delicate skin. She inhales again with a vibrating pause, then exhales her body against mine.

No words.

Just contact and *need*.

I chance a lean into her enveloping warmth and rub my cheek against her head. Her hands tense again, and I hold my breath as her arms slowly, slowly circle my middle, sliding over each other, pressing my back against her chest, her breath now hot against my neck. I don't dare say a single syllable. She nuzzles into my neck, and I shiverinhale as her tongue finds the first sweet droplet of juice and oil. Then another. And another, her tongue lighting up my skin wherever it lands. She wordlessly starts to kiss the bare skin across my shoulders, and her grip around me tightens as her hips dip and push mine forward into the workstation. Aware that we are visible from the street, I reach over and flip off the lights, cloaking the restaurant in darkness with only a few streetlamps sending fingers of light across our faces.

In the dark her kisses become more insistent as she moves up my neck, to my jaw and earlobe. I'm still leaning against her chest as her arms separate and her hands find my ribs, moving up over my breasts, her long fingers catching on my aching nipples, sending twin arcs of electricity down my spine. Up, up, up, they find the halter straps and make quick work of the button in the back, scooping out my breasts with practiced, sure hands. In one hand she gently pinches and rolls a nipple while the other pulls the skirt up to my waist, the opposing movements messing with my worldview. Smoothing over the roundness of my belly, she dips her long, silvered fingers into the white lace panties, taking a few seconds to rake through the tight-knit thatch of curls before lifting me slightly to push my thighs apart.

Fuck, that's hot.

I'm slightly terrified that she will run the second she remembers that she's rounding bases with her employee, but this is already lighting off more rockets than any non-solo sexual encounter I've ever had. I have to clamp down on every urge to moan and call her name, and the way she is taking charge is so goddamned close to every erotic fantasy about her that, in this moment, I would willingly do anything she asked me to. This sexual dichotomy is driving me a little insane, but I couldn't tear myself away if I wanted to.

Believe me, I don't want to.

Still silent, still embracing me from behind, she leans her head past my shoulder and lifts my breast, angling the nipple up to her mouth, cupping my mound possessively with her other hand. As she sucks on the reddened bud, her middle finger slips beneath the folds. She moans as her fingers find the evidence of my arousal, but I quiet a shout, hoping in the silence that she'll continue. Her ring finger joins the middle finger, stroking up and down the length of my pussy, weakening my knees and sending me farther into her body.

Her fingers pick up speed as she increases the suction and teeth grazing on the nipple, and the pressure builds against my clit. She adds a third finger, swirling all three against my swollen and dripping sex, and I can feel the orgasm begin to build in my thighs and in my spine. She changes tack and begins kneading my thighs, and I let loose a high-pitched squeal-growl of protest.

Chuckling, she draws her hand back up to my center, this time pushing through the slick, swollen lips and slipping into me with her two middle fingers, dragging them up to paint my clit, repeating again and again until my thighs begin to clench and shake. I'm about to lean in to an honest-to-god orgasm when she abruptly moves her devil hands to my ass, squeezing and stroking while kissing the sensitive skin on my neck.

Frustrated, I make to pull away when Scout mutters something like *nuh-uh* and pulls me back against her, tight. Growling in my ear, she whispers, "I need... I need to taste you. *Please.* Evie, let me taste you."

Edging me like this is fanning my frustration to the point of homicide, but her words blaze through me, my name on her lips a fiery tongue licking through my insides. My *yes* is a broken, keening sound as she slides her large hands down to my hips and turns me so that I am smashed up against her strong chest, her features cloaked in the uneven darkness.

She buries her face into my neck, lapping at the fuck-me skin near the meeting of my neck and shoulders. She reaches under my dress like she's been there before and finds the panties already half off my ass. She tugs, pulling them down past my knees, letting gravity do the rest. I look up and her eyes glitter in the dark, a command. I quickly and gingerly step out of the lacy pile of fabric at my feet, looking to her for the next set of instructions. Silently, she leans down and snatches the delicate lingerie from the ground, bringing it to her nose and inhaling deeply. Without a word, she pierces me with her cloaked gaze while deftly tucking my underwear into a side pocket on her jeans.

My brain short-circuits at the delicious dirtiness and is still behind the curve when she again reaches under the skirt, this time picking me up by my waist and plopping me, bare-assed and speechless, on the workstation. Cooled juice from the sliced peaches tingles on my skin, one cheek on the cutting board, one off. Grunting, she pulls the cutting board from under my hip and shoves it to the side, the cool bite of stainless steel on my ass and nethers. Her hands still on my hips, she pushes back using her thumbs, gentle, but no less authoritative. The subtle command to lie back is one I happily obey.

Slowly, I lower my back to the stainless steel surface and gasp when she wrenches my legs over her shoulders, her breath hot against my core. I go slack, opening myself up to her as she smiles against my pussy.

Holy shit. This is really happening.

Eengk.

Waiting a perfect beat, she nuzzles her nose against my clit, then, with a wide, velvet tongue laps at the arousal that is there, that is always there when she's around. One hand, large enough to nearly span the arch of my back, holds me in place while the other slides down my practically inverted torso to knead my breasts and pinch at my nipples.

She cradles and supports me as her tongue swirls and sucks at my needy places. The pressure is incredible, and the fantastic high sends needlepoint pleasure through my entire body. The orgasm again starts in my spine, creeping up too fast and impossible to contain.

I break the silence with a rushed whisper, "Scout. Don't stop. Please. *Fuck.* Please don't stop. Oh god... I'm going to—" and I jerk in her arms, the orgasm rolling down through my thighs and up my belly, my core throbbing harder than I knew was possible. She stands there for a few more precious moments, her breaths in sync with mine, her tongue sliding down to lazily milk the last of my orgasm. After a moment she draws her chin up, resting on the mound of curls as she holds me up. Slowly—so slowly—she first lowers me to the workstation, then pulls me up to standing. I shake, undone by what we've just done, and her strong arms hold me upright. I snake my arms under her jacket and around the back, inhaling the cloak of worn leather and the woody musk that she sometimes wears. I press my naked breasts into her leather-clad torso and gently pull her to me and place soft kisses on her neck and collarbone as her fingers drag love trails across my hips and back.

Her arms tighten around me, and I nuzzle against her collarbone. My fingers find the back edge of her T-shirt, and I slip my warm fingers underneath, drawing circles along her lower rib cage. She pulls away and I startle when she brushes her lips against mine, my name—*Evie*—a rushed whisper on her lips, then allow myself a groan when she deepens the touch into a mind-searing kiss. I arch up against her, tasting myself on her lips, and she meets my passion, pulling me in until I'm breathless. We kiss like that in the dark, moving against each other with heat and need.

We part to catch a breath, and I nuzzle against her for a second. I kiss her chin and the outside of her lips, and she lets me with a renewed skittishness that breaks my heart. I can tell she's going to bolt at any moment, but I am greedy and want as much of her as I can get. Our lips meet again and my hands find the sides of her ribs, then skate over her impossibly muscled belly, which tenses under my fingertips.

My hand drifts upward, fingertips aching for the texture of a tight bud, but the movement startles her, and she yanks my hands away from her body.

"*Fuck*. No. Stop," she says, hugging herself in the darkness.

There it is.

I step back, the freeze a shock but not a surprise. She quickly pulls the bodice of my dress up to cover my breasts, her fingers shaking with nerves I cannot place, and failing to properly work the button, she frantically ties the halter at the base of my neck.

Her breathing is strained as she rakes both hands through her hair. "Shit. *I should not have done this*," she says in a low growl, almost a command to herself.

I float my hands just outside of her arms, not touching. "Okay, we've stopped. We can stop. Can you tell me what happened there?" *Please talk to me*, I beg silently *because you just fucked my brains out*.

She has still not looked me in the eyes and once again protectively wraps her arms around herself.

"I just don't want this."

I chance a look up into the shadow of her face. "Okay, but I don't think that's true."

She steps back again, the air so chilled between us that I can almost see my breath. "It is, and I need you to respect my decision on that."

"Of course, Scout, but—"

"I don't want to talk about it anymore, Evie," she says, stepping farther from my extended hand. "Please." Even in the dark, I can see the desperation in her eyes, a kind of sadness that is making my heart fling itself headlong at her.

Jesus, that hurts.

I learned in my Astronomy extension class that a black hole will rip you in half, and you will pass parts of yourself as your body disintegrates. My heart looks like sparkling confetti as it floats by.

After an ice age, I find my voice again. "Okay, um. Then I need to close up here and go home. Please tell Kim that I'm sorry I missed her."

Scout nods and turns away from me, quickly making her way past the counter. She doesn't look at me as she silently opens the door; even the bell is quiet as the ghost of whatever the hell just happened walks out into the night.

Scout

Fucking... *just walk, Scout*. Even though my knees are Jell-O and my balance is for shit, I just have to make it to the damned car and get through this night. I don't know what happened. I just had this... urge... I wanted to mark her as mine when that stupid office dyke Tennessee Woodley—who is totally married—tried to move in on my girl.

Wait.

No.

She's not my girl. I have no claim to her. I need to get that straight. Or gay. As gay as is humanly fucking possible.

Only... I hadn't meant to hold her—taste her—the way I did, and I know it's going to cost me.

It's just... when she took off her shoes and walked barefoot over to the counter to slice up the peach and the juice started dripping between her fingers, I couldn't help myself. In her heels, she's only a little shorter than I am. Barefoot... she's... sigh. She's adorable and almost vulnerable. By that point, the food could have tasted like shit, but when it didn't... when it was light and sweet and herbal on my tongue... I thought I was going to lose my mind.

And I kind of did. I mean, I went after her like a starving person. Like an insane, starving person. I couldn't believe how many times she nearly came on my fingers, which still glisten with her wetness. Now in the safety of my Jeep, the beautiful salted coconut-and-pussy scent that is distinctly her own is in my nose, on my chin. I kiss my fingertips and lick her from my lips.

"Evelyn's not coming," I say as I sidle up next to Kimberly at the overcrowded, far-too-full-of-happy-people bar. She's tanned and relaxed-looking. I catch the bartender's attention and point to the IPA tap while sliding onto the barstool she's saved for me. Her phone is going off with a bunch of notifications, but she's pinning me with a look, a smile slowly growing on her face.

"What?" I ask self-consciously.

"Oh, honey. I've seen that look before," she chortles.

I pull back. "What look? There's no look."

She scans my face, her eyes penetrating my very thoughts. "You've got Evie's lipstick on the corner of your mouth."

"*Fuck,*" I say, wiping furiously at my lips. I didn't see any on the ride over—can't believe I missed a spot.

A Cheshire cat grin spreads along Kimberly's fine features. "Just kidding. But now that I know that you've kissed her, is that why she's not here?"

I mouth *fuck you* under my breath and then give Kimberly a curt nod.

"Ah. You screwed it up."

Evie's perfume is on my clothes and the lingering smell of peaches still have me completely sidelined, and it takes me a moment to settle on a reply. "The only screwup was actually kissing her." And then diving head-first into her crotch. I'd wet some Starbucks napkins in the Jeep with left-over canteen water and wiped down my mouth and chin, but let the evidence of what I did dry on my fingers. I still haven't washed my hands.

"Mmmm," Kimberly says, looking down at her phone. "Yeah... you're probably right."

"Yep," I nod. Then pause and look back over at my friend of many years. "Okay, that was way too easy. What gives?"

Kimberly smirks and holds up her phone.

Evie: Sorry have to cancel

Evie: May have ruined everything w Scout

Kimberly: ??

Evie: She got spooked, can't deal w that rn

Pretty sure I'm the one who fucked it up. Two more messages come in as I'm looking at the screen.

Evie: Fuck it. You should try to get Scout laid before she self-immolates.

Evie: Remember, she hates bisexuals, so purebloods only.

Dammit, Evie. I don't hate you.

Not even close.

Kimberly reads the new texts and her eyes widen. "Scout, what did you do to her? She once told me that she only uses the, quote, 'eff word' in extreme situations. Seriously, what the hell happened?"

SCOUT AND THE LAVENDER GIRL

I think of the "fuck" that tumbled from her lips right before she came and harden my look. "I don't know what you're talking about. She's just mad because I intervened when that married business butch tried to hit on her."

"Wait—did you... *taco block* Evie so that you could lay your lips all over her?"

What the fuck? "*No*. I did *not* taco block—or whatever—her. She'd never had girltime before; she's a babe in the woods. She was in no way prepared for Tennessee Woodley and all of her drama."

I think Kimberly's mouth may seriously come unhinged. "Oh, shit —Ten Woodley went in on her?"

I snort, inordinately proud of myself. Wiggling my ring finger, I respond, "Not after I showed up and pointed out her tan line."

"Yeah, but Ten and Penny are poly or open... aren't they?"

I shake my head. "I don't think it's wise to have your first time with a woman be with some unavailable dyke in a suit."

Kimberly snorts (hey, it's how we communicate) and takes a big swig of a truly ridiculous-looking fruity concoction, which is garnished with a slice of pineapple and has, I shit you not, a mini bowler perched atop its spiny rind.

"What was that about?" I ask, grabbing the pint from bartender.

Keeping her eye on the crowded room, she asks, seemingly innocently, "So... who should her first time be with? Another bi?"

Ugh. "*No*. The bi would have brought her husband, and really, she doesn't need any more dick in her life."

Kimberly bites her lips together in a thin line, trying and failing not to laugh. I'm assuming at me.

"How about a younger? A LIT, if you will." She really does find this way too funny.

I scoff at the notion. "What good would a lesbian-in-training have done for her? Then they'd both be lost, trying to scissor each other, or something else equally porn-related and stupid."

Kimberly is still drinking, but her side-eye is in full effect. "Scout— do you really think that a woman who looks like Evie is ever truly lost in bed? I mean really—do you think she actually can't handle Ten and Penny?"

I remember how she felt under my hands, my lips, how she responded to every touch, every kiss, every suck... and my stomach lurches at the thought of Tennessee and Penelope Woodley having their way with her, tasting her. *I bet she would love it with them.*

"So tell me, Scout, who should Evie—given that you've decided that she's incapable of choosing her own sexual partners—be dining at the Y with? Hmm? Maybe someone a bit more... sporting? Perhaps a slightly older, slightly grumpier lesbian whose eyes are practically superglued to either her tits or her ass whenever she's in a room?"

Kimberly.

"Absofuckinglutely not." Kimberly is unfazed by how vehemently I'm shaking my head, lying my ass off, so I proceed to list off everything wrong with that statement using my fingers. "A) She's my employee, B) she's a bisexual, and C) she was practically a girl virgin. Those are the three strikes, and she's got all of them."

Another snort. "Come on now, Ten and Penny would have taught her some valuable lessons if you hadn't gone and clam jammed her."

I narrow my eyes, a slaughtering look that she ignores entirely. "Not on my watch." The thought continues to gall me.

"So, you kissed her instead?" she teases, gesturing dramatically.

I take long pull from the hoppy beer, determined not to answer her. Kimberly stares me down for a solid ten-count before I crack.

"Fine. Yes. I kissed her." *Then edged her to the point of begging and finally put her knees over my shoulders and buried my face in her until I was dripping with her juices.* I keep that part to myself and look to the side.

Kimberly starts to slow clap, but it ends almost as soon as it begins. I chance a look in her direction, and her eyes widen with understanding. "Waitwaitwait—*was practically* a girl virgin? Not *is actually* a girl virgin? Do you know something I don't, Scout?"

I gulp the bitter liquid quickly. "It's just a turn of phrase."

She looks me over, my thoughts practically read out in her laser eyes. "I don't buy it."

I finish off the beer and raise my hand for another, completely turning away from her. "There's nothing to buy. You're letting your imagination run wild."

She makes a scoffing sound and waits for me to turn back around. "You have a terrible poker face."

I grab the fresh pint and gulp half of it down, letting nothing else past my lips.

"I can wait here all night, Scout," she says, one hand on her hip as she swirls her girly drink with the other.

"Do what you want," I say, scratching the back of my neck where Evie's soft hands held me. We go silent for a while, but Kimberly is killing me with her eyes, her knowing, smirking, kind eyes. The longer we sit there, the more my collar pulses in time with the thudding of my heart. I think about how I pushed Evie away, and how her eyes didn't even look surprised, and a low, heavy sadness sits in my chest. I look away and up, making sure that the moisture doesn't escape my eyes.

"Tell me," she says softly, with an understanding hand whisking along the broken-in sleeve of my leather jacket.

I hide face in my hands with a groan, inhaling and exhaling sweetness before giving her what she wants—a brief, sharp nod.

The softness in her voice dies a quick, painful death.

"*I was right?*" she shouts a little too gleefully, making everyone look at us. I peer at Kimberly through my fingers and her eyes are fully half the size of her head. "*You had sex with Evie?*"

"*Kimberly!*" I bite out through my teeth. "*Shut. Up.*"

"*But did you?*"

"Yes," I whisper hoarsely, pulling my jacket around myself, the heaviness returning to my chest as I run my fingers—the ones that still smell like her—through my hair. I shove that hand in my pocket and vow to keep it there for the rest of the night... until they touch the silky fabric of Evie's panties. Just as quickly I snatch my hand out and look at Kimberly through the fringe of my eyelashes.

Kimberly's jaw unhinges entirely, half hanging off her face. She punches me in the arm. "You *dog!*"

The tortured expression that I can't hope to hide stops her, and she grabs my arm. "Scout, what is it?"

I mangle the cocktail napkin with my fingers and avoid her eyes entirely. "I haven't told her."

She presses her fingers to her lips. "*Scout.*"

I grimace, painfully stretching the muscles of my face. Kimberly's expression shifts knowingly. "So, when she wanted to reciprocate…"

"I ran," I say, watching her eyes go shiny. I can't deal with the sadness and *pity* in those eyes. "Don't look at me like that, Kimberly."

She hesitates, putting her arm on my shoulder. "I'm not looking at you like anything, doll. I just… you can trust that girl. You can trust her with your truth, you can trust her with your heart, you can trust her with everything."

Those words sit like hot lead in my guts. But I can't… I just… I can't.

"I'm not for any of that right now. I'm overwhelmed enough as is, and this is one more damned thing. And I need you, and I need my family to understand that. And stop pushing me. Please, Kimberly," I say, rubbing my face. "Please stop."

Kimberly reaches over and grabs my hand (the unsullied one), her delicate face kind. "I understand, babe. I'm sorry. I'll stop. But… she's not going to hang around trying to figure you out for that much longer. And if you didn't like what Ten and Penny had in store for her, you really won't like it when some single, fully available stud sweeps her off her feet."

I know.

I nod and swallow the rest of my beer. "I just want to drink."

24

EVIE

The three miles home are somehow both unbelievably slow and instantaneous. I pull into the complex numb and unable to remember how I got there. I'm still barefoot, I realize, and Scout has my panties tucked into her pocket. I head toward my door, then indecisively turn heel and aim blindly for the pool. I walk up to the lip, willing for the strength to be calm. Willing for the night sky to give me some sense of direction. Willing for the palms to whisper whatever truth is escaping me right now. But nothing is coming to me. It's not just Scout. It's everything, all at once. It's the money that Chet stole, it's the horrible office, the never-ending days, the sleepless nights, the weight around my heart. The world is a void, a noisy, soundless thing, and I can't stand the gravity of it anymore. I look at the water, aching to be weightless. I inhale deeply and squeeze my lids shut, stifling a sob.

I'm so tired of thinking. Of trying to do the right thing. Of trying to be brave. Of reaching for the skittering thing, only to be raked by its claws again and again.

Peering into the dark waters, I drop my heels, draw in a ragged breath, and... jump.

The water closes over me and bubbles fill the space around me, lifting my skirt in a whooshing swirl.

I scream.

And scream.

And scream.

Until my throat is raw and I am choking on chlorine and moonlight and palm trees swaying in the wind. Broken and oxygen-starved, I let myself drift to the surface, where I gasp, the sound loud in my still-submerged ears. I float there under the dark sky in my beautifully ruined dress, listening as my gasps become deep breaths become rhythmic breathing. In and out. In and out.

I let it all drain away and focus on the one thing that has my heart in turmoil. *Scout.* I'd given everything of myself before and was rewarded with an emptied bank account and an ex who'd chosen his criminal family over me. Yet here I was, trying to throw myself at this emotionally unavailable human, once again holding out my valuables like a beggar. Have I seriously learned nothing?

I keep floating and breathe in the stars.

No. I've got the lesson well and truly learned.

Slowly, I make my way to the edge of the pool and rest my head on my hands, letting my body float behind me. The hot tears trail down my skin and disappear into the molded concrete. Frankly, it doesn't matter why she can't move forward. She can't, she's allowed, and I don't have to keep hurting myself.

I stay like this for a long time, then quietly let myself into my apartment. The shower is therapeutically hot on my skin, washing away whatever the pool couldn't reach, letting this craptastic day swirl down the drain with the pretty-smelling soap bubbles.

It's 4:30 in the morning, and I'm looking down at my phone like it's some foreign object I've never seen before.

I did it. I... quit. Via text.

I didn't want to quit. I didn't want to walk away from her, not with what she'd showed me last night. I can still feel her fingers, pulsing against me, her tongue on me and inside of me, giving me more pleasure in that back-of-the-store fuck than I'd had in years. Ever, really.

Beyond her passion, though, she showed me something else there in the dark. Something far more powerful.

Her fear.

Of me.

I wish I knew what she was afraid of, I wish I knew what was wrong, but she doesn't trust me, and I can't work with that. Been down that road, got the concert poster signed by the artist, don't need to do that again.

Jake is out tonight, and my old suitcase is a bit of a Humpty Dumpty at this point, so I grab a few garbage bags and pack my things. Thankfully, the last relationship disaster left me with so little that my life now fits into three Hefty bags; two if you don't count my makeup and hair stuff. It's funny how many people don't.

I toss the bags in the back of Goldie, drop into the front seat, find the loudest playlist on my phone, crank the stereo, and start driving.

Scout

Mother Jesus.

Never tell Kimberly Barnes that you just want to drink. I wake up at 8:00 a.m., still drunk, and throw up part of my spleen. Bleary-eyed and cotton-mouthed, I blink several times before my eyes can focus on my phone, which I vaguely remember going off in the middle of the night.

It takes a moment for the text to mean anything, and when it does, I start typing furiously.

Evelyn: Sophia, Thank you for the employment opportunity, and for the promotion. Unfortunately, I do not believe that we can continue to work together, and I am hereby tendering my notice, effective immediately. I have moved out of Jake's apartment, so you don't have to worry about running into me.

Shit.

Scout: *Evie, let's talk about this.*
Evelyn: *Message did not go through. Resend?*
Scout: *Why is this not going through—where are you?*
Evelyn: *Message did not go through. Resend?*

I hurl my phone across the room and am immediately annoyed that my ruggedized case didn't fly apart into a million pieces.

Yeah, this one's on me.

"You haven't heard from her?" I ask Jake, who's wearing smudged eyeliner and looks recently fucked. At least he doesn't smell like alcohol. I hold up the phone to show him the undelivered messages. He shakes his head. "Not since she texted."

Some blond guy who I don't know comes up behind Jake and wraps his arms around his waist as we talk. Jake leans back into the guy's arms, then shows me his phone:

Evie: *So, yeah. Just quit my job at the pizza shop. Going to rough it for a few days, get my head on straight and come back with a plan. Took my stuff with me; need a new place to stay.*
Spencer: *What happened, sister?*
Jake: *Are you OK?*
Kim: *Girl, stay at my place while I'm gone.*
Evie: *Thanks, guys. I'm OK. Sorta. Anyway, Kim, I might take you up on that after I get back.*

He shrugs. "I didn't get in until an hour or two ago, so I don't know when she left."

Oh, this is *so* my fault. "She was supposed to work this weekend. I mean, does she do this often? Just… abandon her responsibilities and leave others to pick up her mess?"

I don't give a damn about the restaurant.

"Ha. Right. You only ask that because you don't know Evie that well. She'd drag herself over hot coals before letting someone down. If she's doing this, it means... I don't know, really, what it means. Maybe she's reached her limit."

Yeah. I could see that. Working next to her shitty ex-husband and then spending her remaining time at either the pizza shop or doing rideshare would test anyone. Add my stupid, stupid self into the mix and I'm sure that she is just fucking *done*.

"Do you think she'll be okay? Like, do I need to worry about her hurting herself?" I ask, running my hands through my hair.

"No, that's my bailiwick. She's probably out camping somewhere, trying to reset her head so that she can get through the rest of this shitty summer."

"Evie? Camping?" I ask, holding back a laugh. No way Ms. Primp could deal with sleeping in a tent and squatting to pee.

The twink nips at Jake's neck as he tilts his head at me. "Uh, yeah. We all love camping. It's one of our favorite things to do as a family."

I scrunch my nose, confused. "How does she do her hair, her nails?"

Jake raises his eyebrow, his eyes accusing me of being an idiot. "Um, she doesn't? She tosses her hair into a ponytail, bathes in the creek, and sleeps on the ground with the rest of us."

Wait.

What?

"Are you telling me that she might be out there without even a tent to protect her?" I ask, panic curling up into my gut.

"I didn't see a tent in any of her things when she moved in. We like to stargaze."

Fucking amateur astronomers.

"Where do y'all like to camp? Where do you think she'd go if she wanted some solitude and still had to be back by Sunday dinner?"

"Um, there's several places she could be. Let me think and I'll text you her favorites."

"Thanks, Jake," I say, heading toward my Jeep. "While I'm waiting for your text, should I head north, south, east, or west?"

"South. For now. But Scout?"

"Yes?"

"If you find her, she may not appreciate it. You might be better off waiting till Sunday. Just join us for dinner."

"I don't think your dad would like that."

"We have it at my brother's house now, and he wouldn't mind, I promise you."

"Even so, send me those locations, and I can start calling around."

"Okay, but don't say I didn't warn ya."

"Noted."

While heading south on I-35, I called around to the locations that Jake sent over, and none had checked in an Evelyn Koenig. Continuing in the direction I set for myself, I started at the Frio River and spent all day looking for her at each location. Ten hours later and all I have to show for it is a more intimate knowledge of Central Texas campsites, two fill-ups for my Jeep, and an angry fucking headache. Passing through North Austin as the sun begins to set, I punch the Bluetooth connection on my entertainment console.

"Scout, playa, have you recovered from last night?"

"Kimberly."

"Ugh. Well, *you* sound frightfully sober. Who peed in your Cheerios?"

"As you are well aware, Evie quit and has moved out. She said she was going camping, but I've been all over the place and can't find her. Do you have any clue what she's thinking? Where she might be?"

Kimberly's annoying chortle filters through my sound system. "Damn. You have her hitting the Koenig reset button. Well, at least you know she likes you enough to be driven crazy by you."

"Me? Driving *her* crazy? Whatever."

"Yes, because we didn't spend the entirety of last night discussing all of the ways in which you've rubberbanded that poor girl. Congratulations."

"*Kimberly.*"

Her sigh goes off in surround sound. "Okay, fine. I have a bad idea about where you can get one more good idea, but you're not going to like it."

"*Kim. Ber. Ly.*"

"Don't say I didn't warn you."

"*Spill.*"

"Did you check the Kavanaugh offices?"

Fuck me in half and burn the ashes. "*No.*"

"They were married for five years. He might have a better idea than we do."

The bile that I hadn't already thrown up throughout the day curdles in my stomach. I hate that someone would know her better than me.

"You might be right."

"Go get our girl, Scout."

"Roger that."

Rolling up to the gray limestone entrance in the dusky light, I curse to myself. This is the shitty warehouse-slash-office that Evie comes to four days a week. No wonder she had to get out into nature; this looks like the kind of place where ambition and sunshine come to die. I curse myself again for pushing her so far away from me. Seeing an old red pickup and a shiny new Lexus in the driveway, I park and walk in through the open front doors.

"Hello?" I ask tentatively, looking around. God, even the carpet is shitty here. My eyes land on the cubicles, a square of four, and I know immediately which one is hers. The paper pinups and Hello Kitty décor are a dead giveaway. I look around and see an office filled to the ceiling with flooring samples. *Dickheads.*

"Hi there, our offices are closed—" a familiar voice begins. Chet. "Oh, hi, Scout. Evie's not here."

There's a man sitting in Chet's office, and I'm pretty sure he's the crusty white dude who tried to grind up against Evie on her first day.

I'd shut down my reaction when she told me, but here in his presence I flay him alive with a look. His smug chuckle gets under my skin, but I raise my brow and harden my jaw until he looks away.

"I can see that. Do you know where she'd be?"

He shakes his head, a smirk appearing on his stupid lips, and turns to the guy. "Hey, Woody, give me a second." Turning to me, his eyes narrow. "You're the girlfriend, shouldn't you already know that?"

"Excuse me?" I ask, confused, and thrown by the fact that I'm pretty sure I know that Woody guy from somewhere.

"My mom got it out of her. Trying to see what she can do to maybe save my marriage, and she said she was seeing a woman. I guessing that's you," he responds, attempting for nonchalant.

"Your marriage?" I ask, trying and failing to comprehend what he's saying. I know she wouldn't have let me touch her if she actually had a girlfriend.

"Yeah, Mom's a little old-fashioned like that. She wants a barefoot and pregnant daughter-in-law."

I think of a number of retorts and decide to let him believe what he wants. I wouldn't admit this otherwise, but it's kind of nice to pretend that she's my girlfriend, even if it would clearly never work out. Deciding on a different tact, I crack my neck and stand to my full height.

"She's been unhappy here, and I don't know what you have up your sleeve, but you need to quit it."

Chet opens his mouth in protest. "I didn't do anything. Did she say something? We have one disagreement yesterday and she stormed out. I've half a mind to sue her for breach of contract anyway."

"Well," I say, crowding him up against that wall, pushing my pointer finger into his chest. "Whatever you said upset her so bad that she didn't come home last night. Just said she was going to go camping. And I have no clue where she is, so you can imagine what I'd do if something were to happen to her."

I punctuate this by eviscerating him with my eyes. God, I'm such a lying sack of shit. I look over at the Woody fellow, still unable to figure out where he's from, and it really fucking bothers me.

He holds up his hands. "Hey! I don't know where she went. I mean, maybe Krause Springs since it's close and it's still nice this time of year, but this isn't my fault."

Huh. That one wasn't on the list.

I gesture to the terrible working environment. "Are you sure about that? Look at this place, man. Look at the desk you have her sitting at. It's like you do all this shit to get her to come back and then don't even want her here. Why can't she have this office? Certainly, that's not the only space you have for those tiles?"

"Hey, she had a contract to finish. And the office wasn't part of that contract." Woody nods his head in agreement with Chet but stops when he catches me looking at him.

I lean in a bit closer, almost nose to nose with him, letting him see the murder in my eyes. "Let's just say that I'm putting it back in the contract. I'll do what I can to get her here on Monday, and when she shows up, she'd better have a damned office. Know what else I'm putting back in the contract? Her dog. Waiting for her here, in this office, on Monday."

Dickhead's Adam's apple bobs up and down a few times, and then he offers only a curt nod before going back into his office with the rich dick, leaving me to let myself out.

A quick check of the Krause Springs website tells me that I've got less than an hour to get there before the gate closes, so I set out on the darkening roads, speeding to see her. And I hope she's there alone.

25

EVIE

I really do wish I had a tent. It's fun to camp under the stars when it's sixty degrees out and you're surrounded by three strapping men and a couple of camp rifles. It's a little less fun when you're a sweaty dumbass on a nylon sleeping bag in the dirt, sharing a campground with a college youth group hell bent on destroying their livers.

Thankfully, the owners have been great about having them keep the noise down, and a nice family I'd met earlier in the day didn't object when I set up my things closer to them than camping etiquette would normally allow.

It's already dark, and the gate is closed, so I'm stuck here for the night. Given the fact that I've been hiking all day and lounging in the spring-fed pool, which stays the same temperature all year round, I'm exhausted and decide to go to sleep early.

That's the plan, at least.

As I drift off, I become aware of someone walking through the trees, just off to the side of where I've camped out. I try to imagine that it's the horny co-eds from the church group going after it, but there's just one set of steps, and the sound is getting closer and closer. I keep my eyes closed and feel around in my sleeping bag for my flashlight—a heavy-duty Maglite that my father gave me for Christmas last year. The steps pause and I wait, hoping they'll turn around. Naïve idjit that I am, I'd somehow forgotten that all of my luck in the last twenty-four hours has been horrendous.

The steps go from crunching on underbrush at the tree line to quietly and quickly walking along the soft grass.

I allow them to come a bit closer, and when the shoe hits my sleeping bag, I strike out with the flashlight, connecting solidly with something that feels like a knee.

"*Fuck!*"

My eyes fly open. I'd know that foul mouth anywhere, and I aim the flashlight to the lump on the ground next to me. "Scout?" I'm greeted with a moan. "What are you doing here?"

She doesn't answer right away; she just holds her knee up to her chest and lets out a stream of expletives until the father from the family next to me bellows for Scout to shut the hell up. "Sorry!" I yell over my shoulder, then stand and shine the light on her. She's red-faced and sweating, and there is a part of me that feels so bad right now, you have no idea. I mean… shoot. I would never hurt her like that.

On the other hand…

"If you think I'm going to feel bad for you, you've got another thing coming. I can't believe you came up on my campsite like that. *Just who do you think you are?*" I whisper-shout as I make sure she isn't bleeding.

Groaning, she looks up at me and hisses through her teeth, "I was trying to make sure that you were okay."

I start walking around the campsite, gesturing like someone with a nervous disorder and too many espressos. "I came out here to get away from you so that I could *get* okay. What about that are you having a hard time understanding? And who told you I'd be out here anyway?"

She moans, curling up into a ball. I am unmoved. *Mostly.*

"And did they think it was a good idea to come out here like some kind of stalker to scare the crap out of me while I slept?"

Scout groans again, then pulls her lips in between her teeth, biting down.

Dangit, I think I really damaged her knee. I slide over one of my sleeping bags and help Scout skootch onto it so that she isn't rolling around in the dirt. She's wearing her track shorts and a Stars T-shirt, and I can see the angry, red welt right on her surgery scar. That's twice.

"Serves you right," I say, wincing as I look at her. She's on her side, so I kneel down and run my hands along her side and back, trying to calm her while the pain subsides. After a few minutes, her body loses its painful tension and she rolls onto her back, looking up at the sky. Slowly, carefully, she moves the knee up and down, just like I saw her do with Jonathan when she first took me to see him.

"I can't believe you did this. Are you ready for an ice pack?" I ask, rooting around in my food bag for the flexi-packs I'd tossed in before leaving this morning. I hope that the weight of the pack isn't too much.

She nods, her jaw still bunched in pain. As gently as possible, I set the first pack on her knee and hold it in place, the chilly plastic sending a shiver up my arm. One handed, I root around in my purse for the leftover naproxen and hand that to her with my half bottle of Gatorade. She accepts both and drains the sweet orange liquid. We sit there for several minutes, waiting for the analgesic to take effect.

She's mad at me and avoiding my face, which I find hilarious. And so annoying that I am tempted to apply a little too much pressure to this ice pack. Funnily enough, I don't think she's mad because I knee-capped her. Again. I think she's mad because she's worried, because I left without telling someone where I was going—without telling *her*. And probably for quitting.

Maybe also for moving out.

Well, too bad. I'm furious. *And horny.* But mostly furious. And I hate that I'm glad that she's here, and I hate that seeing her silver-ringed hands makes my nipples hard. I'm not even going to acknowledge what's going on—*or not*—in my nethers right now.

"So... this is Krause Springs," I say, making sure to sound good and annoyed.

"It sucks and there's no air-conditioning," she growls, gingerly bending and straightening her knee, looking up at the heavens.

"Okay, sure," I respond, "but that's only because I took a Maglite to your knee. Don't take that out on the Springs."

Her eyes glitter with anger, and she gestures to the nature around us. "It also sucks because there are no beds, or a roof, or a bar."

"But there are stars," I say, jabbing at the sky. They really are so beautiful out here in the hill country.

"There's also a rock stabbing me in my back," she whines, shifting uncomfortably. The movement causes the ice pack to slide off to the side a little. I readjust the placement and she flinches at my touch, which I find just a hair peevish.

She reaches beneath her and pulls out the offending rock, which is about the size of a quarter. I roll my eyes. "That's why I usually double up on the sleeping bags, princess. If you think you can keep your hands to yourself, I can put it back together."

Her jaw clenches. "If *you think* that I have driven all over Central Texas to let you sleep outside without a tent, then you have lost your fucking mind."

I gesture to the emptiness around us. "Dude, we're stuck here. So unless you have a tent shoved up your ass—which would explain a lot—you'd better figure out how to get comfortable."

"I don't need a tent. I have a Jeep."

Not gonna lie. That does sound more comfortable than the ground. "Fine. Can we sleep with the top off?"

"Not on your life. That's barely different from sleeping outside."

I mop sweat off my face. "Can we at least crack the windows so that we don't bake overnight?"

"Fine."

I roll up to my knees and hold out my hand. Scout grabs it and pulls herself up on her good knee. I hook her arm over my shoulder, supporting her as we stand together. After a few wincing steps, she stretches out her leg and moves the knee around a bit more, and then we gingerly make our way to her SUV.

I climb in and flatten down the back seats on her enormous Rubicon, then lay out the two sleeping bags, with plans to share the camp blanket. I know she'll be uncomfortable with that, but it is what it is.

She hoists herself up into the back, and as her shoulders skim mine, she grouses, "My back and my knees hate you right now."

We both lie down and face each other in the intimate space. "But you don't, right?" I ask, finding her dark eyes in the moonlight. I mean, I hope she doesn't.

She blinks slowly, the pain meds finally taking effect. "I don't what?"

I shrug. "Hate me. Even though I've screwed up your knee. Again."

"You didn't screw up the knee. It's sensitive in that one area, and you have a knack for getting into my sensitive areas." She reaches out and pushes a bit of hair behind my ears.

Uh, no. You have a knack for getting into *my sensitive areas.*

I breathe into the touch and try not to think about how necessary it is. How much I ache to be touched, both in general and specifically by her. "How did you know I was here?" I hadn't given my name to the people up front.

"I, um. I went to the places your brother said you might go."

My brows knit together. "That's a lot of places, Scout. And I've never been here with my brother."

I'd really only ever been here with Chet. Did she call him?

If so, then *sure...* I'm just her *employee* whom she doesn't have *any* feelings for *whatsoever.*

"So, you went to Garner State Park, Fredericksburg, Wimberley, and Dripping Springs."

"And Kerrville."

"And here," I say softly, reaching out for her arm.

She draws the arm back, wrapping it across her chest. She's practically hugging herself to avoid touching me, and I'm starting to put together that this pushmepullyou bullshit that we've got going on really isn't about me at all. Whatever she's been through, whatever Carla did to her, left one heck of a mark.

But she drove all over creation to find me, and that's not nothing.

Our eyes brush each other for the briefest moment, and my breath catches, the intensity rocketing through the small space. My body sways forward, and there, in the dark, I see it again. The fear behind her hesitation. The desire as she scans my lips. The same longing vibrating through both of us. My fingers tense, wanting to reach for her, but her expression clouds. She turns over to face the wheel well, dousing the heat fastquick. I want to grab her and spin her around and demand that she look at me, but I already know everything I need to know. She feels it and wishes she didn't.

Round and round we go.

I try to give her my pillow, which she refuses along with the camp blanket. She finally allows me to give her my jacket, which she rolls up and shoves under her head. Her back is stiff, her breathing is shallow, and her whole vibe is closed off. I double up the pillow under my head and rest my arm on the wheel well as the exhaustion of the last several weeks settles in over my body.

Before drifting off entirely, I whisper into the cabin, "Thanks for finding me. This is way more comfortable than the ground."

Scout shifts, the air edged and uncertain. "It's safer, too," she responds softly before going quiet.

Moisture intrudes my tired eyes, and I wipe it away, hoping that she doesn't hear the hitch in my breathing. I blow out a deep breath, then let the sleep take me.

Scout

In my dream, I'm holding Evie in that big fluffy bed of hers, and it's as amazing and soft and erotic as I'd hoped. I'm the big spoon, one leg hooked over hers possessively, encircling her as I run my hands up her hips and ribs and along the sides of her breasts. My face is buried in her neck and hair, and she smells so good, like amber and coconut. She moves beneath me, moaning.

I've had this dream more times than I can count, and god, I don't want to wake up. I'm running my hands down a pair of hips so luscious that my brain is shorting out. Case in point, I can actually smell the amber-and-coconut fragrance, and I can feel her moving beneath me, even though I can see the tiny veins and bright yellow-orange of the sun through my closed eyelids.

I register a faint tickle on my face and blink several times. It's hair, which is confusing.

Until it's not.

My body is plastered to Evie's, my face is buried in her sweat-slicked neck and hair, my leg hiked over her hip, and my hand is currently caressing her left tit. She's snoring softly as she adjusts her posture, her ass moving against my belly and thighs.

Fuuuuuuck me. I move my hand (I'm not a perv, I swear!) but linger to smell her hair and just... god, her body against mine. Her skin is perfection, soft to the touch, almost velvety in its plushness. I'm forever staving off some kind of dry patch or toe fungus, but she's... sigh. So. Fucking. Girly. Everyfuckingwhere. And she's got the sweetest pussy.

Really, really regretting that last thought. I swear that I'm not a perv. I'm just slowly being driven insane by a bisexual. You know what it's like.

I've clearly rabbit-trailed because when I refocus, she's shifted, and round, darkly fringed honey-colored eyes are silently looking up at me.

Shit.

"I-I woke up like this. I wasn't trying anything." *I'm not a deviant, really, I'm just desperately in love with you, and it is freaking me right the fuck out.*

I freeze in place, and I can't tell if it's the *l* word that flashed through my head or the look in her eyes. I silently prepare for anger, a biting wisecrack, *something*, but her honey-dipped curiosity has me spellbound.

Neither of us moves to break the hold, and she's not said a thing to me, and we've been in this position nearly a whole minute. Holding her like this feels like home and abject terror in equal measure. I'm too lovesick to tear myself away, and I'm too terrified to bring her closer.

She blinks first, nuzzling into the meeting of my neck and shoulder as she inhales my scent. She then kisses my jaw and shifts back toward the wheel well, like she knows that I need a moment to process and she wants me to know that she's not mad. I press myself against her one last time, then roll away from her and practically throw myself out of the Jeep.

Nothing to see here. Nothing. To see. Here.

Except for the fact that my skin is a live wire, and it's taking everything I have to not jump into the back of my Jeep and make her mine. *God, she is just so fucking soft.*

Evie

Y'all.

She was *totally* spooning me. I mean, I practically suctioned myself against the wall of that Jeep so she would see that I respected her and was willing to give her space, but... ha.

HA.

That subconscious of hers has a pair of brass ones, I tell you what.

I just wish this didn't hurt so much.

26

SCOUT

*I*nhaling a ragged breath, I face my side of the Jeep and take stock of my body. While my knee is purple as hell, I can still move pretty well. Looking over my shoulder—because I am a masochist—I realize that Evie had practically molded herself to the sidewall, giving me as much space as humanly possible, and I still managed to end up right against her body. Holding her like my life depended on it.

And I'm starting to wonder if maybe it does.

I take several cleansing breaths, wrangling my self-control, then climb out and walk toward some low-slung buildings, hoping they have facilities here. It's not running away from the rumpled temptation in the back of my Jeep. I just really need to pee.

And wow.

I finally have a chance to see where we are in the light of morning, and this place is ruggedly beautiful, typical of the hill country landscape. I can see why she might want to stay here. She'd mentioned something about a spring-fed pool. I do my sinful business, then hobble over to the pool and lower myself in, fully clothed. The bracing water is a sharp difference from the warmer temperature outside. I'm almost dizzy from the shock of frigid water, but I soak for several minutes, enjoying the sunrise flaming the early-morning sky as I stretch my battered knee, wishing Evie were here to enjoy the magenta-and-orange sky with me.

Wanting her here starts up the old, sputtering projector of why wanting her at all is the worst, most terrible idea, and those thoughts are starting to seem very analog and tired next to what is real, in technicolor, and here for the taking. Seriously, when did I become the high-maintenance one? I know that if I just go back to that Jeep and make her mine, she would miraculously let me and keep the teasing to a minimum. I shake my head, trying to figure out how I'd blown past the usual steps and fallen—*hard*—for a woman with lavender hair.

In the end, it's not all that hard to just let that woman love me.

Decision fucking made, I make my way back to the Jeep. The cold water and my jangled and still slightly hungover nerves have me shivering so hard that a wave of nausea hits my stomach. Evie is propped up on her elbows, and her look warms my core, releasing some of the unease in my belly.

"Hey," she says softly, her hair still a sexy tangle from sleep, one eye more closed than the other. She's not wearing a stitch of makeup, and she looks like a co-ed. Her beautiful honey eyes shine in the morning light, and my heart thumps in my chest, the memory of her skin against mine tightening my belly and waking up the parts of me that I refuse to ignore any longer. She looks so warm and cozy that I ache with the desire to press my body against hers, and the black interior of the Jeep looks like a magical cave, built for the two of us. *Don't freak out*, I beg myself, *it's just Evie*. She quirks her eyebrow at me. "You feel all right?"

"What do you mean?" I ask, almost breathless as I hold on to the side of the Jeep so that I don't accidentally take a running leap at her.

"You look exhausted, like you've been working too hard," she states, glossing over the mauling I gave her this morning.

I'm here about to pour my heart out, and she's saying I look like shit. It's perfect, really, and I make a scoffing sound. To be fair, I am going to need some coffee after this; I'm so tired that I can barely stand.

"How's your knee?" she asks, biting that plush bottom lip of hers in concern.

"Um, fine." I gesture dismissively. Seriously, my entire body is numb in her presence. "Better, actually, after I took a dip in the spring."

"Oh, you went in? Isn't it cool that it's the same temperature now as in the winter?" She smiles sleepily, rubbing her eyes. Seeing me shiver, she takes off the camp blanket and stretches it out to me. A bit of creamy tattooed skin peeks out between her shirt and pants, and I realize that she's not wearing a bra as I surround myself in the amber-and-coconut scent that she's embedded in this fabric. I look up and her eyes shift down and away from mine. They seem almost sad, and I'm gutted that I'm the one who put that sadness there.

"Yep, pretty cool. I need a few minutes to dry up, and then I'll be ready to head back." I nod to myself, trying to strengthen my resolve.

"Sounds good. I don't know if you're following me, but I'm going stop by that baguette place on Bee Caves for a quick nosh before heading in," she says, shifting up to a seated position.

Damn.

I forgot that we couldn't ride back together. I don't want to have this big, emotional conversation and then get into two separate vehicles. But I also don't want to wait until we get back into the city. As I contemplate a romantic declaration vs a declaration near a soft surface, I notice the chill of the morning beginning to have its way with her nipples, and I swallow. Hard. "Okay," I respond, my voice cracking.

Her mouth curves up, but she only nods and then quietly goes about folding up her things and packing her car. I should say something now, but I notice that her trunk is held closed with actual bailing wire and silently add that to my mental checklist. While I'm standing here, I decide that her whole car probably needs a mechanic to give it a once-over.

Hrn.

Sorry. Might have dazed off for a second there.

Fuck, I really do need some coffee, even though the thought of coffee is making me feel kind of pukey. God, I've got it so bad for this girl. Her eyes land on my skin, dragging my focus back to the present. Her eyebrows stitch together, concern blooming in her expression. "Baby, what's going on?"

I smile dreamily at being called baby, and I suspect that she doesn't realize that she used the endearment. "What do you mean?"

"Seriously, Scout—you don't look so good. You're almost... gray."

Fucking chemo aftershocks. I get to feeling a little queasy if I overdo it physically, and I'm guessing that the cold dip along with the realization that I might actually, kinda, sorta, maybe be in love with a woman who purposefully dyes her hair the color of an Easter egg has done a number on my system. "Just really exhausted, traipsing all over the Texas hill country looking for my cook." I hitch up my mouth when I say that last part.

Woah. I really don't feel so hot.

She raises her eyebrow and opens her mouth to retort, but closes it again as her hand goes to my head. "You're sweating. Are you getting too hot out here?"

I shake my head, and hoo, buddy, am I... woozy. "No, Evie, I..." Another, stronger wave of nausea hits me, and I put my hand and knee down at the same time to avoid falling outright. I end up on all fours, bile making a hasty and undignified exit from my open mouth.

Fuck. I'm so goddamned *dizzy*. Reminds me of those rounds of AFIB during my chemo sessions, which were scary but temporary. At least I thought they were temporary, but I'd never had this much trouble breathing before. It slowly dawns on me that I might be in some kind of trouble. I look up at Evie, my beautiful girl who doesn't realize she's my girl yet, trying to remember the name of the thing she can use to ask for help. Okay, she found it in that big bag of hers and is hitting the buttons.

Good girl.

Phone. That's what it is.

This is so weird. I'm on my back now, and the bright blues and greens are starting to look really fucking fadey. Like someone is pushing down on the dimmer switch.

27

EVIE

The ride in the ambulance was terrifying. They shocked her twice before her rhythm evened out, and I don't think I'll ever be able to forget the look of her boneless body jerking from the electric current. It wasn't quite enough, though, to erase the shock of seeing Scout's bare chest. The two dark strips of keloid tissue in the place of her breasts confirmed what my hands felt as I knelt in the dirt beside her, compressing her chest, doing the work of a heart that wouldn't.

Seems about right.

We arrived at the hospital in Lakeway quickly, and they had her out of the back in seconds, then started *running* with her to the ICU. By the time I'd climbed down, they'd disappeared behind the doors, and now I have no clue what is going on. My arms are Jell-O, my heart is hammering in my chest, and I'm a sweaty, dirt-stained mess, but they won't tell me anything. The intake nurse looks at me with sympathetic eyes but firmly directs me to the lounge. I slump into a moderately comfortable chair and stare out the window, unable and unwilling to think about what could have happened.

Out of the corner of my eye, I see Carla blow in through the front doors. Oh *hell* no.

"What are you doing here?" I ask, getting up into her face.

"Me? What are *you* doing here?" she asks imperiously.

"I was with her when it happened."

"What, exactly, happened?"

I pause, taking in her demeanor. Yeah, no. "Not on your life, Forrester."

A nasty little smile snakes across her lips. "I'm here because I'm her emergency contact, so they're going to tell me, regardless. I still have medical power of attorney, and I can have them do—*or not*—whatever I want."

The implication hangs in the air between us, and an icy chill works its way up my spine. I begin to put my hands out in surrender, terrified and prepared to beg her not to hurt Scout.

Ignoring my distressed look, she plows forward. "And how well do you think she'll recover this time when she's barely recovered from chemo and all those extra rounds of radiation?"

The hospital goes silent, or at least all I can hear is white noise. She says it for the shock value, but instead it's as if she's found the button marked "Evie's Shame Spiral" and decided to lean on it with all of her might.

Even when I'd started suspecting cancer after the Carla thing, I'd still assumed that Scout just looked much skinnier in real life, and now I feel like a monumental fool. The fear under the confidence. How she shuts down at any sign of vulnerability. Why she won't be with me, even though we are a four-alarm chemical fire. It's all coming together so quickly, I…

My sweet, sweet Scout.

An arrested squeal of protest leaves the back of my throat, but no actual words form. I want desperately to stop the tears from spilling, if only to deny Carla the satisfaction. But I can't. I'm gutted and ridiculous, a fool who'd let her illusions of grandeur get the better of her. Scout didn't tell me, and it's pretty clear that she was never going to trust me. More heart-shaped confetti flies by.

"That's a lie, and you know it, Carla," snipes Roly, who strolls up to us with a thick envelope in hand. "She rescinded your power of attorney when she caught you fucking the help. I've got the HCPOA now, and you can see your way to the sidewalk."

I have never been happier to see that man in my life.

"Well, they called me," she replies, haughty factor stuck on high.

Roly rolls onto his tiptoes and puts a finger in her face. "The only reason you know anything is that this is the same hospital group where she had her chemo sessions. They fucked up, and I'm about to unfuck it. Again, I invite you to leave before I have your tired and rejected ass physically removed from the premises."

Realizing he'd talked about Scout's chemo sessions, Roly's eyes widen and slide over to mine as he grimaces. I shake my head and gesture to my chest: *I know*. His eyes search my exhausted face and hunched body, and I am massively impressed that this kind, sensitive man is holding his own against Carla. Take that, you ruthless entrée of tits and ass.

"Hmph," Carla says, crossing her arms. "We'll see about that."

"Yes, we will. Carolina and Hector are on their way and we will sort this out—do you *really* want to be here when they arrive?" Roly retorts, giving her gay brow like it's life. "Here's a hint: *you don't*."

Carla flips her unfairly gorgeous hair over her shoulder, gives another little *hmph*, and storms out of the hospital entrance. Crossing the doorway, she tosses out, "You better hope it doesn't come back, because if that titless wonder goes, I'll be in charge of this little operation, and I have some family members in need of a job."

The doors close behind her perfectly formed ass, and I practically fall into Roly's sturdy arms, weak with relief. Roly puts his hand on my back. "Hey now, don't you listen to her. She's trying to upset you because she knows how Scout feels about you."

I snort, snottily. "How does Carla Forrester know how Scout feels about me and I still have no clue?"

He smiles, taking my hand. "Oh, honey. She cares for you so much. Carla had her wrapped around the axel for so long that it's taking her a minute to figure it out. But she will. I promise."

He circles me in a hug, and the terrible anxiety of the day bleeds out of me. "Thanks, Roly. And, not for nothing, but it was extremely satisfying to watch you show her who's the big bitch on campus."

"You know it, girl," he says with a sly smile. The smile fades quickly, and he takes on a more serious look. "What happened, Evie?"

I look around, making sure that Carla is well and truly gone. "She might have had a heart attack, but they can't tell me anything because I'm not family."

"Do you know where they have her?"

"She's still in the ICU," I say, pointing to the marked doors, just as a medical team rushes past us. Roly and I hold on to each other as they race through the doors without stopping.

28

EVIE

Three hours later, I am surrounded by Scout's entire family —mother, father, brother, and sister. An exhausted-looking doctor walks through the ICU doors and comes over to us in the waiting room. We collectively hold our breath as he takes his place in front of us.

After verifying that we are Scout's family, he takes off his scrub cap, nodding to himself. "She's a fighter, I'll give her that."

We all exhale in relief, and then her mom and dad and siblings start peppering the man with questions.

Seeing the angst, and the fact that he is seriously outnumbered, the good doctor holds up his hands. "First and foremost, you should know that this was not a heart attack. It was ventricular fibrillation—are you familiar with what that is?"

Carolina, Scout's mom, holds up her hand and points to her husband. "When he had his heart attack, it triggered VF. That's what almost killed him. How can you be sure this wasn't a heart attack?"

The doctor nods his head as he listens intently to Carolina. "A heart attack is caused by blockage, and that's what set off your husband's VF. In this case, Scout's VF set off cardiac arrest. Hers is an electrical problem, not a plumbing problem."

While the doctor's words are kind and instructive, Carolina is falling apart at the enormity of it all. The older, experienced surgeon puts his hand on her shoulder, and some of the tense stiffness gives way to tears. "Thankfully, it can be managed by adjusting her medication and working with her to reduce both stress and the training-camp workouts she's been subjecting herself to. We'll get her the meds; your job is to get her to sit down every once in a while."

I want to throw up, I'm so relieved. Scout doesn't know it yet, but I'm about to be an entire pain in her ass. Scanning the lot of us, the doctor lowers his tone, asking, "Who was the person who came in with her?"

Still shaking, I timidly raise my hand.

"Were you also the person who was with her when she lost consciousness?"

My lip quivers, and I nod. His face is serious, all planes and angles. "Her heart had effectively stopped."

I nod again, tears pouring down my cheeks. "N-no pulse," I whisper, and her mother gasps.

"No pulse and you were with her, alone, doing CPR until the ambulance came," he says, warmth again seeping into his face and voice.

I nod once more, my chest caving in. "Some of the people from the campsite helped."

"You are the only reason they had anything to work with when they got to you. She didn't have a pulse, but you kept the circulation going, and she had a shockable rhythm."

Suddenly I have four pairs of arms holding me as her family surrounds me in the biggest bear hug. I find a shoulder—I think maybe it's her sister's—and let out a strangled sob. We stand like that for several minutes, even as the doctor continues to explain the various procedures and drugs that were used to save her life. I memorize all of them. I memorize the name of every technician, nurse, doctor, and maintenance person in this ICU. They will never pay for another slice of pizza if I have anything to say about it.

In the end, he reiterates, "With medication and a reduction in stress and work, we should see her back to 100 percent in short order. She's lucky that she's strong, and that she had the right person with her when it happened."

I am so, so grateful that I got to be her right person. Her family is holding me tight, laying kisses on my head and cheeks, and there is a ball of grief in my chest that I will save till later. Because I still have my Scout. Even if she isn't mine.

Her mother pulls away. "I want to be with my daughter. Where is she?"

"She's in recovery at the moment and will be ready to receive visitors in a little over an hour. I'll have the ICU nurse come find you when it's time."

Once he leaves the waiting area, her mother turns to me. "I'm so sorry. I'm not sure I ever caught your name."

"Evelyn. My friends call me Evie."

Her mother gives me the once-over. "And what does Sophia call you?"

I smile a little. "I've finally worn her down. She calls me Evie."

Her family all look at each other, noting its significance. Her father, Hector, steps forward, putting his long arms around me again. "Evie, thank you for saving my daughter's life."

"Oh," I say, stubbing my toe on the tiled hospital linoleum. "I'm sure the EMTs, doctors, and nurses are the ones who saved her life. I just didn't let her die in the interim."

"And we will never forget it."

Scout

Holy Jesus, I feel like three-day-old shit. Rubbing my eyes, I see my mom hovering over me, expectant.

"Moms. What the *hell* happened to me?" The last thing I remember is gritty dirt making its way under my collar as I stared up at the bluest sky and Evie's spectacular cleavage. I remember thinking that it was a good way to go, while regretting not getting to tell her how much she means to me.

I don't share that with my mom.

"You had ventricular fibrillation, baby."

"Is it like the AFIB from my radiation?"

"Yes, *mija*. But a little worse."

"Did they crack me open?" I ask, reaching up to my tender ribs. God, did someone take a bat to me?

"No, *mija*," she answers, sniffling and pulling out her rosary beads. One of these days she's gonna wear those things down to nothing. "Your ribs hurt because Evie did CPR on you. She saved your *life*."

Evie. My mom knows about Evie.

"So, I'm going to be okay?"

"Yes, Scout." My father's deep timbre fills the room, and I look up and find him and then my sibs, Nick and Jules.

"Everyone is here? Where's Evie?" I ask, trying to not sound panicked. She must be a mess, and I have no idea what she knows.

Nick speaks up, his expression stern. "She's on the phone with her dad, trying to get his cardiologist buddy on the line. You're okay, but you'll need strict follow-up."

"She's talking to her dad?"

"Yeah, looked like a sensitive conversation."

I run my fingers through my flop, and the scrape of grit and dirt is loud in my ears. I itch at the grime behind my ears and down my neck and wonder exactly how close I came to dying. "They had a fight a few weeks ago and haven't spoken much since. Wait, is it still Sunday?"

Jules nods as she walks in from the bathroom with a wet, wrung-out washcloth in her hands. What a fucking day it has been, and I wonder if this bone-deep exhaustion will ever go away.

My mom takes the washcloth from Jules and first dabs away at the dried bile at the corner of my mouth, then wipes the dirt from my neck with the rough, hospital-grade terry cloth swishing loudly between my skin and hospital gown. "What did they fight about?"

"It's a pretty delicate subject; I'm not sure that I'm supposed to know as much as I do," I say, not answering my mother.

I bite my upper lip as Jules hands our mother a dry washcloth, and she narrows her eyes as she brushes the offending debris from my back, ass, and legs. I know better than to protest because she would do it anyway, and also it's keeping her mind occupied, potentially thwarting the follow-up questions I know are on the tip of her tongue.

Evie saves me again, derailing my mom's line of questioning by simply walking into the room. Evie sees me and stops, placing her hand on her heart. Her chin wobbles a bit, and her eyes go shiny. "*Scout.*"

Fuck. She knows.

She knows everything.

My parents turn their heads like puppies when they hear the way she says my name, and realization shadows, then brightens their expressions. I've been puttering around for months with my reasons and my denials, and one word from her and they know.

They just know.

God, how much time have I wasted?

Evie walks over and softly takes my hand, kissing me on my cheek before she touches her forehead to mine. I close my eyes and her tears pling on my eyelashes. If I didn't feel like an elephant had been stomping around on my ribs, I would have pulled her to me right then and there and kissed her with everything I have inside of me.

Instead, I go for humor. "I just didn't want you to quit."

Her laugh is rueful as she stands up, her soft hand still in mine. Her eyes are a bit gimlet-y, but she hitches a smile and retorts, "Yeah, but you only get to use this the one time. Next time I'm leaving your dramatic ass in the parking lot."

Jules snorts. "Oh sister, I like her very much. And she's not a bitch like Carla."

"Language, Jules!" Moms pleads. "We don't want Evie to think that we're a bunch of unrefined hooligans."

Evie raises her brows and points to me. "Too late, Mrs. Martinez. Too. Late."

"Evie, I told you to call me Carolina," my mother insists,

pronouncing it "cah-rho-leen-a" instead of anglicizing it the way she does for most people. She looks at me, and the meaning is clear. In my family, the way you say someone's name says everything, and the way you let others say your name is even more important.

Evie's presence, and my family's acceptance of her, unwinds the tightly spun coil in my chest that I've been walking around with for longer than I'd like to admit. She and I have so much to discuss, but sleep is pulling me under, and I know that she'd want me to rest. I circle the rough pad of my thumb on the velvet skin of her hand and let the overwhelming exhaustion take over, my last thoughts trying to figure out how to tell her that I love, I love, I love her.

God, she even has me quoting *Pride and Prejudice*.

I am so fucked. Ask me if I care.

29

EVIE

I adore Scout's family; they are so kind and funny. I'm guessing that this health scare and my knowledge of her breast cancer have pushed Scout even further away from me, and I try not to be too sad about that. At least I still have her in my life.

With Scout down for the night, we walk to the hospital entrance, intending to figure out what to do about food, which none of us have had all day long.

"Evie."

I turn at the sound of my father's worried voice.

"Dad!" I run over and he picks me up in a big, warm hug. Tears fill my eyes. I'd missed his hugs.

"Is she okay?" he asks, pulling away slightly.

"She will be. Here—this is her family I was telling you about. Her dad, Hector. Mom, Carolina. Sister, Jules. And brother, Nick."

My father's smile warms the room. "Hello. I'm so glad to meet you, though I'm sorry for the circumstances." He shakes everyone's hands, and I notice the huge Whataburger bag in his hand.

"Dad, what is this?" I ask, leaning over to look into the bag, which smells like heaven and fried things.

"Oh, I'm sure y'all haven't had anything good to eat in a hot minute, so I got a bunch of burgers for everyone, and Spence and Jake are coming in with the teas."

As he says this, my twin brothers enter the hospital, each carrying drink carriers loaded with the bucket-sized Whataburger cups. We quickly take over the coffee table in the waiting room, and everyone sits around, tucking into the meal. I demolish the burger and fries and look around to see that I'm in good company. We all silently work our way through the comforting meal, and I crack a smile when Carolina lets fly the cutest burp ever.

Hector looks at his phone and sighs. "I should have made hotel arrangements. I didn't even think about that until now."

My father shakes his head. "Already taken care of. My buddy manages the Hampton Inn right up the road; I got a couple of rooms for y'all."

I look at my father incredulously. "Dad..."

He lowers his head, red touching the edges of his ears. "She's important to you, Evie. I've always liked her as a boss, but this is different."

"And y'all are...?" I ask quietly, looking between Jake and my father.

"Working it out," says my father, his voice low. "You said that your mother would pray for understanding, and so that's what I am doing. I make no promises, save for the fact that I love you both and want you to be happy."

I tear up for about the millionth time today and feel something akin to hope for the first time in a while. Scout's family is quiet, letting us have this intimate moment together, but I catch her mother's kind eyes. She holds up her rosary beads and kisses them, bowing her head. She's praying for us, too.

30

EVIE

I walk into the Cavern of Doom on Monday, exhausted and hating that I had to leave Scout behind, but she's in good hands and will be back home by Tuesday or Wednesday. I make my way over to the cube, only to find it empty. Rolling my eyes, I walk into Chet's office.

"Really, Chet? Where's my stuff? I'm not Milton; you can't keep pushing me around."

"Just check your office."

I walk over, expecting that he's thrown my shit all over the tiles, just to make my life a misery. I'm surprised to see the space free of tiles and set up with a slightly newer laptop and two large monitors.

Oh, my dog.

No, seriously. There, on my chair, is my sweet little schnauzer-poodle mix, Cosette. She looks well-fed if a bit matted, and her head pops up when she hears me walk into the office.

"Cosette! *Mon cher*! Come to Mommy!" I say in my ridiculous puppy voice. She flies off the chair and jumps into my arms. She's a little smelly, but she's my smelly monster, and I will be getting her groomed today.

"Who are you and what happened to Chet?" I ask, walking back into his room with Cosette in my arms. I'm thrilled nearly to tears about getting my fluffiness back, but I'm wondering what it's going to cost me.

"Your girlfriend came in on Saturday and threatened me if I didn't give you your office and your dog back. Not that I wanted to keep that spoiled brat anyway—her fur is a fucking nightmare. But going forward I've decided that lesbians are exempt from the 'you can't hit a woman' rule. If she tries to start shit again, I'll be ready for her."

I roll my eyes so hard it's a wonder they don't end up in the back of my head. Chet is five kinds of stupid, but a fighter he is not. And Scout would *so* kick his butt.

I *knew* she'd contacted him directly. She would've had to have been very worried to come here, and I can't believe she remembered my puppernator—I'd only mentioned her once, like, weeks ago.

And I might feel some kind of way about that.

"Wait, Chet—were *you* working on a *Saturday*? I thought you didn't do that."

He shifts uncomfortably on his chair. "When you're the boss, you have to be willing to work when everyone else is working, too."

Okay, this is some alien abduction bullshit. "No, seriously, who are you, and what did you do with Chet?"

"I'm being responsible, Evie. You might want to give it a try."

"If you're so damned responsible, why don't you give me back my money and let me out of this ridiculous contract?"

Again with the uncomfortable shifting in his chair.

"You sitting on a cactus?"

"No."

"Then why are you so shifty all of a sudden? Temporary burst of conscience?"

"No. Legally that money was mine as well. So you can call it theft all you like, but be careful. Slander and libel are still suable offenses."

"Wow, Chet. I almost don't see your lawyer's hand up your butt, moving the levers around. That's a neat trick."

"Do you think you can get back to work?"

"Fine," I say, shifting Cosette to my other hip and heading to my office.

Before I walk in, I notice that the file room door is slightly cracked open. I back up and verify that Chet is focused on his computer and Itsy is on her break. It's not wrong for me to go in there. It's not sneaking around. And they left the door open. I can help myself to my own files, right?

Quietly, I open the door and my mouth falls open with it. This room used to be filled to the brim with file cabinets, so many that it could be difficult to navigate. Cosette licks my chin, also perplexed by this turn of events. Now, there are only a handful of file drawers in the room, and the rest of the space is filled with the tiles that occupied my office. I can hear Itsy walking in the front door, so I leave the door slightly ajar, just as I found it, and quietly slip into my office.

What in the world happened to those files?

31

SCOUT

I've been in the hospital for two days, and the doctors think they should be able to release me tomorrow morning. Thank fuck.

Evie visited me last night, and I don't know how she did it—it's a two-hour round trip, and once she got there I could only hold on for a few minutes before drifting off, my fingers tangled with hers.

Thing is, I'm feeling better now, and my family has *questions*.

"So, why were you at a camping ground with Evie, Scout?"

"She got upset and quit, and I followed her to make sure she was okay."

"What was she upset about?"

"She has too many jobs and is considering online school to complete her MBA, and can't quit her other day job."

Lies, all lies.

"What were she and her dad really fighting about last week?"

"Doesn't matter."

My mom takes a wrung-out washcloth and begins the daily sponge bath, which isn't at all humiliating, considering that I'm forty-one years old.

Standing up straight, wiping her hands, she pins me with a look, which I avoid.

"Were they fighting about you?"

"No."

Kind of.

"Because I see the way you look at her."

"I'm not looking at her any kind of way, Moms. Get real."

"Are you sure?"

"I'm positive, Moms. Just drop it."

"Fine."

"Thank you."

"It's just they've both taken such good care of us, I want to be able to help. Tell me why they were fighting."

Ugh. "It's not my story to tell. And you shouldn't interfere."

"'Not my story to tell,' huh? The only time you've ever used that phrase with me is when you didn't want to tell me that my best friend's grandson is gay. Is Evie gay?"

"Moms, really, it's not my story to tell."

"So she *is* gay. Is that why she and her dad fought?"

I pinch my eyebrow and shake my head. "Moms, you really need to stop."

Ignoring me entirely, my mom takes a turn around the room. "I mean, he's clearly trying, but.... she's in her midthirties. How is it possible that she's only just now coming out to her dad?"

"Moms, we really need to stay out of that family's business." I look to my dad for some support, and he shrugs, moving out of my mom's path. Traitor.

"That dark-haired brother of hers clearly is or was a closet case, he's got such a careful way about him. But Evie, she's not careful like that. She's open, she shares. How could she have possibly kept this from her dad this entire time?"

Jules and Nick look at each other and shoot me a pitying look. I shake my head and lower my chin to my chest. They know as well as I do what's coming in 3, 2, 1…

Her eyebrows shoot up as the truth dawns on her. "*No.*"

I put my head in both hands and tilt it left and right. Why are so many people in my life human lie detectors?

"*Sophia Lucia Martinez.*" My mother's hand is at her hip and her lips are pursed and her eyes are in full-on mom-glare.

I shrug, sheepish. "Sherlock Mom strikes again."

Crossing herself, she hisses, "Have you *not* learned your lesson?"

I raise my hands in defeat. "Moms… *fuck*. I might be a lost cause." Something sharp breaks loose from my heart as the words leave my lips.

"*Language.*"

"Moms, I'm in the hospital!" I roll my eyes and dramatically let my head drop to my pillow.

She stabs her finger heavenward. "God can hear you everywhere."

Groaning, I cover my eyes with a hand that is porcupined with an IV. "She's not Carla, Moms. If I know anything, I know that. In the end, Carla was just a shitty person."

My mother absentmindedly clutches her rosary, worrying the beads as my father chuckles, "You know what they call a lesbian who falls for bisexuals, right?"

I'm mid-eye roll when a soft voice provides the punchline.

"A masochist."

I move my hand from my eyes as Evie enters the room with a fragile smile and a fluffy, white dog nose sticking out from her purse. My father's laugh booms as her expressive eyes find mine, then drop to the floor. I wonder how much she heard.

"Martinez family, is it possible for me to have a moment alone with Scout?"

Her words sound vulnerable, but my family hops to like she's their commanding officer, and in thirty seconds they are gone without a trace.

Traitors, every last one of them.

I mean, yeah, I love her, or whatever, but it's not like they know that. All I'm saying is a little support would've been nice.

Ah, well. Now's as good a time as any to rip off the Band-Aid. "Evie, I—"

"I need you to be quiet, Scout," she interrupts, her voice soft and steady, her eyes glued to my hands. "And I need you to listen."

I nod my head and wait for her to light into me.

Instead, she takes the dog out of her purse and pops it up onto the bed. Just a guess, but I can't imagine that Chet had the dog groomed into a perfectly round ball of fluff with a purple bow and glitter-pink toenails.

Still, the pup comes right up to me and gives me a lick on my nose, then nuzzles along my ribs, warming me in the chilly hospital room. "First of all, thank you for getting me my Cosette back. She's my sweet girl, and I love her, and it means a lot to have her to come home to."

I nod as I pet the softest dog known to man. Evie's dog *would* be this soft. Finally, she looks me in the eye.

"But here's the thing we're not going to do. We are not going to pretend that our problem is that I'm your employee or that I wear too much makeup or that I've slept with men. Because that's a dirty lie, and you know it. The real problem is that you're afraid. I don't know exactly what Carla did to you, but I would never hurt you. And I mean, I know that you're a big, tough lesbian and that you've got this whole I'll-take-care-of-everything, moderately Dom way about you, but nothing about her screamed supportive or kind. And even big, tough lesbians need to be held every once in a while."

She's not wrong. Cosette, the little ball of fluff, licks my jaw in agreement.

"And on top of everything, your body is trying to kill you before I can even have a shot, and that is *not* fair. So you need to quit. You need to stop messing around, you know, and just... let this happen."

She nods to herself, like she's made her point and done what she came here to do, then glares at me with a challenge in her eyes.

"Are you quite done?" I ask, finally letting the grin take over my face.

Anger tips her eyebrows, and her hands find those stunning hips of hers. I smile even broader.

"That was a really great speech and all, but right before I threw up and passed out, I was going to tell you that I'm fucking crazy about you, and that as soon as the doctor clears me, I am going to take you to my bed and not let you out of it for at least three days." Of course, just the thought of it did nearly kill me, so I might need to work my way up to that.

Her mouth drops open to the cutest little o, and then she snarls adorably and snatches the pillow from behind my head. "I am going to *flipping* kill you right now," she says, pushing the pillow onto my face while Cosette continues to lick my jaw. "No jury in this country would convict me, you... you *withholding... jackass.*"

Laughing, I snatch the pillow back from her, wincing as I put it behind my head. Her eyes go wide, and she brings her hand to my face again. "Oh my dog, Scout—did I hurt you?"

I chuckle, earning a sexy glare from her sleep-deprived eyes. "You goof. I love you so much."

I grimace at the admission, not really meaning to drop the love bomb from my hospital bed, but watching her face morph from teasing to understanding to pure emotion is a memory I will take with me to my grave. She picks up Cosette and pets her, almost as if she needs comfort. Answering her unasked question, I nod my head. "Yes, really."

Tears leak from those gorgeous eyes and her nose gets all red and stuffy. Laughing at herself, she lightly punches my arm, and Cosette nips at her. "I can't believe you let me say all of that. *Jerk.*"

I shrug, mocking her. "If I can't laugh at your expense, then this relationship will never work."

"*You* are a jackalope," she says, chuckling while lowering her lips to mine, hijacking my brain with her earthy amber-and-coconut scent. After a few careful, deep kisses, she rests her forehead on mine, still sniffling from the emotions running between us. I notice that she doesn't say the words back to me. I know that she's there with me, but needs some time to trust me.

We are interrupted by my family, who, shocker, make no mention of the tears in Evie's eyes or the red lipstick on my face. My mother looks back and forth between the two of us and smiles. We sit in relative quiet until visiting hours are over, and she quietly slips away.

32

SCOUT

*I*t's been exactly a month since Evie saved my life, unquit her job, and moved her three sad trash bags plus the adorable Cosette back into her brother's apartment. It's also been a month of having my mother live with me during my recovery, participating in the world's most aggravatingly sedate physical therapy, and dog-napping Cosette as frequently as I can get away with.

What?

Dogs are excellent therapy pals.

I would personally be further along, but my heart doc and Jonathan ganged up on me, saying that attempting to go back to my regular running schedule of seventy-five to eighty miles a week was a nonstarter. I attempted to go around this, but my mother found my exercise app and called a family intervention when she saw that I'd gone on a ten-mile run two weeks out from nearly biting it. Seeing my father snot-cry from worry about my workout routine was enough to give me pause.

My mother has taught him well.

So, I'm pretty much back to normal, save for the fact that Evie hasn't allowed for more than a chaste kiss on the cheek and I've replaced my regular twelve- to fourteen-mile runs with tactical breathing, yoga, and a three-mile-a-day limit. Adam, Jake, and Spence make it a point to come over during the day a couple of times a week to catch up on the latest sports gossip and to take my eighty-inch flat-screen for a spin when any of our teams are playing. I've promised to stick to the hike and bike trails right by the Levee, taking the ball of floof with me to prevent me from going an unreasonable distance, and my family and doctors have, for the most part, managed to crawl out of my ass.

All of which is to say that I'm physically strong, emotionally nurtured, and more sexually frustrated than I've ever been in my entire life. I did get a boob graze in yesterday, and my one thriving business hasn't tanked, so I'm counting that as a win.

We celebrate the one-month anniversary of my body's failure to kill me with a carne guisada picnic at the Levee. My dad's mollejas on the grill are to die for, and my mom brought her tres leches cake, which has Evie groaning with every spoonful. Those satisfied little sounds alone would have me reaching for her, but the rockabilly look that she's been avoiding for a month is out in full force today. I'm pretty sure that she's trying to torture me with winged eyeliner and cherry-red lipstick.

"Baby, I might stick around for this cake alone," she says, planting yet another kiss on my cheek as she walks by with Cosette on a bedazzled leash.

"Um, no," I say, grabbing her arm and pulling her down to straddle me on the picnic bench. "I've been cleared by the doctor, and you are not going to kiss me on the cheek ever a-fucking-gain." To punctuate the not terribly discreet point I'm trying to make, I slide my hands along her jawline into her hair and pull her in for a long, intense kiss.

I release her to the sound of laughter, and Evie's blush is beautiful. Her honey-amber eyes look around the picnic table to see our families' reactions, and they are clapping and happy. The Martinezes are big on embarrassing displays of PDA, if my mother and father's track record is any indication.

"So, y'all have really only been together since the hospital?" Jules asks.

"Yeah, but she's been ignoring her feelings for me for a while, so long enough," Evie cracks, still straddling my lap as she holds the floof's leash in one hand while twirling my silver lock of hair in her other.

Nick gives me a rare smile and asks, "How long have you liked her?"

"Who are you asking?" I say, nudging him. Troublemaker.

"Both of you."

I sigh. Evie is going to love this. Rolling my eyes, I reply, "Since she ran into my U-Haul."

Evie's eyes grow big, and her smile is off the charts. I swear, if I didn't have a reputation to maintain with her father and siblings, who are also present, I would shoo everyone away and pull her down onto this picnic table and wipe that self-satisfied smile right off her gorgeous lips. I look at her with my eyebrow raised. "Your turn, Evie."

She blushes deeply. And bites her lip.

"Spill."

Looking down at her lap, she covers her eyes and grins, completely self-conscious. "Fine." Taking a deep breath, she turns to my brother and answers, "Since she was a Lady Longhorn."

"Pigtails or long braid?" he asks, continuing to tease her in the way that has become familiar over this last month.

"Oh, I've got the answer to this," Spence pipes up, wiggling his phone in the air.

"*Spence...*" Evie warns, her eyes narrowing.

Spence eyes me and I grab her around the waist, pinning her down as he passes the phone to me out of the range of Evie's shorter arms. It's open to a photo app under a folder simply named "Family."

The very first pic is the scan of an old photo. Evie is twelve or thirteen, wearing pigtails and a massively oversized UT basketball jersey with the number 19 on it. My number. I swipe to the left, and in the next picture, also an old scan, her back is facing the camera, and her two long, orange-red braids frame the name on the back of the jersey. Martinez.

The next one shows Evie at a UT basketball game, wearing the same jersey, and she's about sixteen years old with chunky highlights in her hair. I recognize the scoreboard—it was my last college game. She has her hand out, and I'm giving her a high five on my way back to the locker room. Her face is beet red, and her eyes are completely lit up.

The last photo is the one that rocks my world. I'm in my Stars jersey, and she's about twenty years old, hair blonde and done up like Gwen Stefani, still wearing her old UT jersey, now filled out. I've got my arm around her, posing for one of the millions of fan pictures I've taken in my professional career, a long braid over my shoulder. But I'm not the most interesting thing about the photo. While I'm looking dead on at the camera, Evie is looking up at me, longing in her eyes, her mouth slightly open.

Her blush creeps up from her neck into her face. "I'm an OG Scout fan. Pigtails all the way. Though, to be fair, I am a huge fan of the current do." Her look makes my heart speed up, steady and strong in my chest.

"Okay, okay, enough flirting," my mom says, blushing. "It's time for us to pack up and for Sophia to get her *rest*," she says, eyeballing Evie.

Jules snorts. "Really, Moms? Flirting is a perfectly healthy activity, and the last time we all went to the Riverwalk, you and Dad *flirted* so much that the manager of the restaurant asked you two to take it outside."

My father grins, proud of himself. "Oh, *hija*. True love cannot be denied."

He's right, of course, and I don't intend to be denied a minute longer.

Shifting Evie to the side, I stand up and clap my hands together. "All right, ladies and gentlemen. I appreciate you coming here, I appreciate everything each and every one of you has done to make my recovery possible, and now I must ask you to leave. As a wise man once said, you don't have to go home, but you can't stay here."

Everyone laughs, and I'm heartened to see that Jake has put his forehead on his father's shoulder, and both are laughing so hard that they are shaking. Mom gives a little *hmph* and makes to begin putting things away with Suzi's help, but she's smiling to herself as she does so.

It takes about thirty minutes for everyone to leave, and Evie puts her hand in mine as her brother and sister-in-law set their sleeping kids in their car seats. I take Cosette's leash, then lean down and whisper in Evie's ear, "Are my mom and dad out of the parking lot yet?"

She looks around me and nods her head. "They just turned down the streeee!!!" Her sentence ends in a squeal as I pick her up and put her over my shoulder in a fireman carry.

"Oh!" she exclaims breathlessly. "Oh myyyyyy."

I slap her ass, noticing that my large hands look almost normal-sized against her generous curves. Huh. Kind of a perfect fit.

I let us into my place, which is quickly becoming our place, and unleash Cosette, who jumps against my leg, wanting to be a part of the game. Sorry, fluffernutter, it's grown-up time. "Cosette—kennel up!" I command, and Evie's perfect, sweet dog immediately drops down, trots over to her open kennel, turns around four times, and starts playing with her chew toy. With my reduced schedule, I've taken it upon myself to keep that bowed and primped babygirl groomed in the style to which she has become accustomed. In honor of my party, her bow is green and her nails are black glitter, and it is all very becoming.

Once Cosette is out of harm's way, I smile and let Evie slide down my body with my hand on her ass to control her descent. She purrs, "That was... that was very nice—unh." I cut her short with a kiss as I close the door behind her, pinning her up against it. I grab her hips and explore her mouth with my tongue. She lets out a needy sound that quickly disintegrates into a moan as I trail kisses down her jaw and throat. "*Scout.*"

My name in her mouth has never sounded so sexy, and I will break every fucking rule I'd made over this last, terrible year to make her say it again and again and again. Panting, I pull up at her shirt, fumbling at the knot as she unbuttons it from the top and I strip her of it. I pause to admire her gorgeous tits in a bra that is 0.5 seconds away from being ripped off her body. I'm not gentle as I reach around to unclasp the thing that is between me and those pale rose nipples, then stop to check in.

"Hey. Are you okay with this?"

She flushes under my gaze and smiles, looking a bit cheeky. "Are you kidding me right now?"

I try to maintain a serious look, but that beautiful face causes me to break. And then heat, because her fevered eyes are telling me a story. I look at her lips for a long beat, then run my thumb across her already smeared lipstick. She leans into my touch, and I crash down on her lips as I press my body into hers.

She meets my fervor, leaning into my kisses, pushing me backward until the backs of my legs meet the couch. I sit down, pulling her down into a straddle with me, her hips pinning me to the sinking surface. I suck hard on the pebbled nipple through the lace of her bra, and her core heats up against me. I remove her bra with practiced hands, then return to the red, abused nipple and anoint it with soft kisses. She sighs and arches at the stinging sweetness, and I send my hip up, flipping her down against the couch, kissing her strongly, tickling my fingers along her ribs while she runs her hands through my flop of hair, twirling the white streak in her tapered fingers. I can feel her skin turn to gooseflesh under my palm, and we kiss like this for a while, hungry for each other as our hands get bolder. Frustrated by the intervening fabric, I stand her up and undo her jeans as she kicks off her shoes.

Still kissing, I push her back down to the couch, her shoulders splayed against the soft material. "You have lesbian flowers tattooed all over your body," I say, tracing the erotic petals and vines that swirl along her torso and curve under her breasts.

"I know what I like," she responds, softly fucking me with her eyes.

Growling, I crush her again with my kisses, and she moans when my thumb slips under her panties. I roughly part her labia, dipping into her wetness before circling her swollen, needy clit. She arches up against me, increasing the pressure. "Scout," she gasps, undulating her hips. Within seconds she begins to tense, so ready for me, and I stop, ignoring her colorful protestations.

"You are so beautiful," I whisper hoarsely, and she shoots me a look that ignites every nerve ending. I slide the underwear down and off her body, ready to hook her legs over my shoulders, but I am stopped short by the sight of her fully naked body, with her lavender hair, pale skin, and... "Ginger?" I say, nearly croaking on the word. She blushes and nods. It was dark the last time I visited these parts, and I am so glad that I get to see her in the daylight. I push my fingers through her copper curls, awed by the beautiful color combination of lavender and Irish red.

I lean in to kiss her and be scorched all over again by those hungry, molten eyes. I kneel and maneuver between her thighs, running my hands up and down them, watching her writhe against the white suede, silently begging me to take her. Slowly, I hook her legs over my shoulders, one at a time, bringing her to my lips. Her deep breaths have become soft panting, and she is losing her mind. Grabbing her ass with both hands, I run one long lick up her pussy, dimly aware of the tattooed vines that curve along her thighs, another detail I missed in the dark. She moans loudly as I plunge my tongue into her, and she bucks against me, asking for more.

I sense her trying to hold her own weight and pop her in the ass. *Let go.* She struggles against it, and I pop her one more time, raising my brow as I swirl her clit. Softly protesting, she releases the tension in her body, letting me hold her. I growl at the small shift, and everything goes into overdrive. Her breathing is chaotic, and she lets out the sweetest whimper with every lick of my tongue, her body thanking me for finally giving it the thing she's been asking for. She starts to go rigid again, this time with pleasure. She's moaning my name, tumbling off an edge so high I know for a fact that she's never seen the view from up here. I nearly come from the sounds that she's making and from the intense clenching of inner muscles as I lick and kiss her swollen pussy. Another wave of delicate spasms, and she rag dolls, completely spent.

I lower her to the couch, and we breathe in unison for a few moments, the intensity washing over both of us.

"Omigod, omigod," she whispers, shy about looking up at me. I'm not gonna lie—turning this beautiful girl into a heated puddle feels pretty damned good.

And god, does she glow.

I lie down next to her and she wiggles up against me, kissing me, tasting herself off of my lips and tongue and nose. We separate to take a breath and her honey-colored eyes finally find mine, killing me with their intensity. She goes in for softer kisses, the opposite of what I'd given her, and I'm lost in my body with the headiness of it all.

My neck, my jaw, and once more my lips; her soft kisses will be my undoing. We sit there entwined, making out, alternatively looking at each other with curious eyes and kissing so deeply that we're melting into one another. She slips her hand beneath my track pants.

I stop her. "We've, uh… we've been out all day. I need a shower."

She looks into my eyes. "I don't care."

"I do," I say, slowly disentangling from her, then standing to my full height. "I'm going to take a shower."

She groans, impatient. "Can I join you?"

"But you're all done up," I say, running my fingers along her rouged cheeks.

She leans in for more kisses and says against my lips, "Then help me come undone."

Fuck, Evie.

Looking into her eyes, I am again overwhelmed by a free fall of emotion so rare and beautiful that it can only be described as magic.

She stands, naked, and begins to walk up the stairs. Her unruly body is divine, and now that I am lucky enough to see all of it, I realize that her tattoos create the illusion of a bustier, curling around the softest parts of her. I quickly catch up to her, my large hand perfectly fitted to her round ass as we ascend together. At the top of the stairs, I wrap my arms around her and begin walking her toward the master bedroom and then into my bathroom.

Evie

I don't even know how I'm fucking walking right now.

Her tongue was in my… My knees her over her… Her face was… God, she's so strong.

Right now, she has her hand on my ass and is guiding me into a huge walk-in shower.

I step in ahead of her to start the water, and she looks at me with an expression close to wonder in her eyes. I place my hand on her chest. Her heart is *pounding*.

I eye her tank top, fingering the edge of it, and she looks briefly uncertain. I don't think many people have seen these scars, and I immediately feel protective of them. I'd seen them only briefly in the ambulance after the EMTs had cut off her shirt, but I'd averted my gaze out of respect for her privacy. That was then. Now, she pushes my hand away and pulls the top over her head, revealing two jagged, knobbly, purpled scars across her chest, and I allow myself to fully look at her.

My eyes mist over. That must have hurt so badly.

She sees my reaction, and her hand reaches for my face. "No, no, no. No sad eyes. You just had a stunning orgasm, so sad eyes are not allowed."

I nod, gulping down the residual emotion while pushing down the waistband of her pants. They fall to the shower floor, and I step back for a moment to admire her lean, strong build and her gorgeous, tawny skin. While still not up to her basketball weight, her sheer power is intoxicating. Her legs curve up into a muscular ass and down into narrow calves like wired cantilevers. My eyes shift to her body again, and I realize for the first time that she has an actual six-pack.

Looking down at my body, with its pale skin, round belly, and full thighs, then over to hers, I gesture to the ridiculous abs. "What the hell, Scout? What am I supposed to do with all of that?"

Grinning like a devil, Scout responds, scorching me with a look up and down my body as she does, "I ask myself that same question every time I see you."

We wrap our arms around one another, and I kiss her scars, her heart fluttering under my sensitive lips. Still linked, we stand under the hot water, my skin turning pink and hers a burnished red. I quickly scrub off the rest of my makeup, then soap up a washcloth, swirling the sudsy terry cloth over her skin, using care and delicacy, my own body tightening as I draw out the pleasured sighs that rumble from within her chest.

The large surfaces done, I soap up my hands and begin easing the suds into her more sensitive crevices. I hesitate, then run my fingers through the dark thatch of hair on her pubic bone, dipping finally into her center. The minor slick between her soft lips makes me feel like I'm ten feet tall because I made her wet.

"What's that smile about?" she asks, toying with my nipples as I rinse her body.

I grin up at her like a loon and blush at the newness of it all, knowing that my overblown sense of grandeur is likely due to my noob status and not any real accomplishment. I let my hand drift downward and finger her some more, spreading the thin silkiness along the length of her want. She lets out another little pant, then nudges me. "You didn't answer my question."

Red is the color of my embarrassment, and she laughs, running her fingers up the length of my neck. "Tell me."

Rolling my eyes, I let out an agonized groan and then pull my fingers away, swirling my thumb around their honey-dipped tips. Shyly, I look up at her through my eyelashes while wiggling my fingers at her. "I made a lesbian wet. I mean, you obviously have no problem making me drip like a faucet, but that I could get you even a little wet feels... good."

Her laugh is rich and deep and not too much at my expense. "Baby, you've been making me wet for a while now, which in itself is miraculous given what breast cancer treatment does to a body. Don't go comparing." As she says this, she kisses my palm, then holds my fingers up to my lips. I inhale her scent, bloomed by the steamy shower, and tentatively flick out my tongue. My eyes fly open as I taste salt and sweet and almost... metallic. Like a salty-sweet penny. I giggle a little at this discovery, then look into her eyes as I slowly lick each finger.

"You like that?" she asks, her eyes dark with curiosity and maybe concern.

I blush and nod, almost too shy to answer. Her face shadows again with lust, and suddenly she has me pinned against the wall, pushing herself into me as the cold tiles send me into her, kissing me so forcefully I would rather faint than pull away for a teaspoon of oxygen.

Her own breath ragged, she pulls away and whispers roughly in my ear between blistering kisses on my neck and shoulders, "This... this blush of yours is the sexiest damned thing I've ever seen in my life."

...Aaaaand I'm back to feeling ten feet tall again. I AM THE QUEEN OF GIRLSEX. I CAN BRING DOWN TOWERING AMAZONS WITH THE FLUSH OF MY CHEEKS. Scout's six or seven inches taller than me, but I push her off balance and turn her toward the wall, spreading her legs, rough and sweet. I resoap my fingers for extra lubrication and dip them into the cleft of her ass, stroking the delicate nerve endings. She flinches as I brush along the puckered bud, though she does not pull away.

"You're so cute and sexy when you try to go all baby dom on me," she pants, breathing hard as my fingers enter once again into her slick, "and I'm happy to let you, but don't forget who the big dyke is, okay, *mamas*?"

I smile to myself. "Never. I'd never forget that," I say as I continue to soap her up, working her up until she begins to tense and moan with pleasure. She lets out a soft exhale when I switch the handheld showerhead to massage and rinse her off. I adjust the water down a few degrees and swish the pulsing water over her sensitive skin.

"You are trying to kill me, aren't you?" she accuses, shivering.

"Delayed gratification can be quite pleasurable. You taught me that," I say, a wicked gleam in my eye.

She grabs me by my shoulders and pushes me out of the shower, laughing and cursing under her breath. We dry ourselves in her luxurious towels, and she pulls me into her bedroom.

I yank my hand from hers and forcefully push her down into a sit on the bed, using my knees to part her thighs. Her body is so long that, even sitting on the bed, she's nearly my height. Her eyes are searching mine, and I know that she's looking for any residual hesitation. She won't find any. I wrap my arms around her and kiss her deeply, slipping my tongue into her mouth as I fist the hair on the back of her head. She pulls me in close, and we kiss harder, my nipples pressing against her rough scars, the friction feeding the fire. I pull away and kneel in front of her, smiling. Her strong, wiry, long-limbed body looks royal as she sits in her easy athleticism. The delicate hairs on her arms are raised, and the big vein in her neck pulses. She stays upright, her eyes boring into my skin, watching my every move, and I let her.

I dip down and smile against her pussy. She grunts, delicately pushing on the back of my head. I smile even wider, then take a beginner's lick, tasting her wetness. I groan when the pennied sweetness hits my tongue, and I begin to lick the most sensitive parts of her, every single sensation a revelation. I look up and her eyes are black with desire. I dip down deeper, my tongue finding her brownish-pink bud nestled in at the top of her labia, and she sighs in pleasure. Her breath catches as I close my lips around it and suck lightly, tracing my tongue in a circle. Her dark thighs tighten, and she leans forward, palming the back of my head, silently asking for more suction, more pressure. I respond by opening my mouth and taking more of her in, more suction, more pressured licking, and her entire body shudders with pleasure.

Seeing how close she is, I change tack and begin to thumb her clit while dipping my tongue into her hot center. "Evie," she breathes out, clutching my hair. "Lube." I rise and make my way to the bedside table she's inarticulately pointing and groaning at, and find (angel chorus) a veritable buffet of lube. I opt for the plain one but make note of the mint-flavored tingle gel for later. I squirt a small amount of lube on my fingertips and rub them together until it's warm.

Properly lubed, my thumb slips back and forth over her clit as my tongue does the rest, dipping into her over and over again, until she leans back and lets the sensation take over. She bucks her hips, begging for more, more. I change again and tease her, ignoring her desperation while keeping time with her hips and hands, lightly—*too lightly*—circling and sucking and penetrating in a long, lazy rhythm. *Fuck*, she says under her breath. I draw it out for a few more moments and then push a heavily slicked finger near her entrance, and she bucks into me, pulling my finger farther into her. I suck and swirl her clit, now with more and more pressure, while I slip a second finger inside of her, separating and undulating both fingers against the soft inner pad. She says my name at a higher pitch, and within moments her muscles begin to clench and spasm. She cries out, lost to the orgasm, and I pulse my tongue on her clit, milking the spasms for a few more moments before sliding my fingers out of her.

I lean forward and lie against her mound, running my hands up and down her calves, listening as both of us breathe in time, slowing down as our hearts find their normal rhythms. Groaning, she leans over and pulls me onto the plush bed, wrapping me up in her long arms. She kisses my neck and murmurs about the wetness of my pussy as she dips her fingers in and out of me, swirling and pushing on my clit. I stretch like a cat against her, heightening the senses as a quick orgasm ripples out over me, my nerve endings happy and satisfied.

She continues to caress me, running her nails over my skin, my nipples. Delicious. "I have to ask," she says, her voice husky and dark. "You've really never done that before?"

I smile and wiggle my butt against her crotch. "No."

"Are you sure about that?"

"All those years of Xena fan fiction seem to have paid off. Well, that and I have a really good imagination."

Her jaw tightens. "What else have you imagined?"

"Everything," I answer, breathless against her skin. "I want everything."

Scout

We spend the rest of the evening touching and kissing and exploring each other's bodies, keeping the conversation intimate and familiar. She delights in finding out the things that turn me on, and I can see her mentally filing away my preferences for use later on. She was sad to find out that I have no sensation on my chest at all but vowed to map out my body to find alternative erogenous zones.

I'd forgotten how fun it was to be new and excited about this whole new way of feeling good. When we talk about her turn-ons, I'm not surprised to find that she's adventurous in a try-anything-once kind of way, though I'm pretty sure she's holding back. I am a little shocked and kinda disappointed to find that, when it comes to toys, and especially strap-ons, she's a bit more reticent.

"But... you've had an actual dick inside of you," I say, not understanding. Carla loved it when I used the strap-on. Not that I care what that selfish bitch likes anymore.

"Put it to you this way," Evie responds, recapturing my attention as she traces her finger along the grooved edges of my stomach, "if I were a vegetarian, I would *not* subject myself to tofurky when there are so many delicious fruits and vegetables out there. Why bother with fake meat?"

I laugh at her reasoning, then tease, "You bisexuals are a complicated group."

Her bottom lip pouts out, and I give her my sternest look, the one I use in tough business negotiations. Her eyes haze over and she bites that bottom lip, her chest blossoming.

I crack first, smiling at her adorable, sensual faces.

She rolls her eyes. "I'd say I can't believe you'd be scared of a lil' ol' bisexual, but, having scrapped with Carla a couple of times now, I kind of understand."

I sit up in bed, rubbing my jaw. "With everything going on this month, I haven't really talked to you much about the details."

Quietly, she says, "She's not a good person, Scout. When she visited the store that one time, I saw her with a guy, and they were definitely *together* together, and there was no earthly reason for him to be there with her. She either wanted you to see them together or wanted me to tell you about it."

I nodded, absolutely sure that she was on the money. "You know, things weren't great before my diagnosis. But I'd kind of forgotten that she was bi, so when I caught them—"

"You *caught* them?"

"They didn't see me, but... yeah."

"*Dang.*"

"So... when I caught them, I was completely unprepared. Made it hurt worse, somehow. Like maybe I was never actually enough for her, and she had to go back to men. That she left me for a man. So, her coming into the store with him was—"

"Salt in the wound," she finishes. "While you were trying to get back on your feet." Her angry pout is both a little scary and sexy as hell.

I shrug, distracted by what I'd like to do with those lips. "In her mind, we're square because I hurt her. She looks at the way I'm putting my life back together, and it's a complete rejection of the life she wanted us to have. I shredded my bank account—seven million dollars in assets to get away from her. I've started over here in Austin. And it's terrifying because I'm nowhere near operating in the black, but at least it's on my terms. And *that* pisses her off more than anything—that I would rather hemorrhage money than stay with her."

I blow out a big breath, relieved to finally say that out loud.

"I didn't know," she says softly.

"No one does, except Kimberly. And now you."

"*Scout.* You know that's not true, though, right? She didn't leave you because you couldn't give her what a man could."

I shake my head, the insecurities pushing against my rib cage. "I *don't* know that."

"Y'all don't even sound like you were a good fit. Well, that, and because she's a manipulative, emotionally vampiric *bitch*."

She balls her hands into fists as she says this, and her anger over my mistreatment is... making me horny as hell. I imagine her tightening a strap over those hips of hers and...

"Scout?"

Growling, I push her down on the bed and grab both of her hands, pinning them up above her head. Her eyes fly open at the change, and she looks like a dangerous animal. She pulls against my grip, and I tighten it. She begins to pant, her hooded eyes flashing with need.

Damn.

She moans, pulling at my grip on her wrists. "Shhhhh," I say, stretching her arms up even farther as I lean down to capture her rising nipple in my teeth. She swallows the cry that threatens to break free, so beautifully submissive. Her wide eyes latch on to mine, and I gaze into hers, letting an evil smile creep up into my lips. She shivers and her mouth opens, just a little.

"You like this?"

Her blush reaches from her hairline down to her nipples, and it's… so adorable. Biting her lip, she nods.

With her wrists still captured in my hand, I push her down against the bed, smothering her body with mine, using my knees between her legs to widen them apart. I attack her neck as I grind against her, sucking and biting at the tender skin, a part of me longing to see the marks there tomorrow. She stretches and tilts her face up, trying to go harder, trying increase the urgency. I lean back until she submits and lets me control the timing. She moans in fake protest, but that pitches up to pleasure when I trail kisses down her neck, into her collarbone.

Wanting to touch her, I let go of her wrists and run my hands over her body as I lean in and kiss her more slowly, exploring her mouth with my tongue, controlling the pace.

I make a fist and brush the knuckles along her silky underwear. She lifts her hips while I lower mine, lying on her body, angling to catch my own clit with the trapped fist. Soon we find a rhythm, with her thrusting up, and me thrusting down, our eyes locked. Watching her pleasured face, and seeing her tilt her head back, mouth slightly parted, breathing heavy as she comes is so sexy that I immediately follow her.

"I'd never done it like that before."

"I wanted to watch you come."

She blushes, but I know she likes the idea of me watching her. "It's even better with a strap."

She goes from blush to scarlet in half a second. "Okay, fine. I... I might try your tofurky dick."

I don't think I've ever laughed so hard in bed with a naked woman. At some point we put on pjs and call Cosette to join us in bed. I'd been so busy imagining how many things could go wrong with us that I didn't stop to think about the things that could be so right. Like this moment right here. She still hasn't said the words to me, but I can feel them on her like a living thing, waiting to bubble up.

Going serious for a moment, I lean forward and whisper against her ear, "I'll never *not* take care of you. You can trust me."

33

EVIE

*A*fter the day and evening (and early morning) we had, I don't want to remind the boss lady that it's time to go to work, but... it *is* time to go to work, and we should probably get a move on. Jake comes by to pick up the floof since she likes following him around the complex as he fixes up things.

It feels nice to get ready and ride over to the pizza shop together. I cheat and use preraised, frozen dough to make up for the time we spent screwing like teenagers, and it comes out pretty well, if I do say so myself. The 10:30 crowd likes my apple and goat cheese with bacon creation, and it goes on the board as the special of the day. By 10:55 the shop is empty, and the first preorder isn't set to walk through the door for another ten minutes, so I walk behind the pizza oven and lean sensuously up against the wall, trying to catch Scout's eye.

"Evie," she asks, her brow raised, "why are you standing like that? Does your back hurt?" She walks over, putting her big man hands all over my shoulders and back, looking for something wrong. I draw in a ragged breath as her fingers glance across my collarbone.

"Wait." She steps back. "Are you getting turned on right now?" I inhale and nod, my eyes heavy-lidded and my nipples hard. "Is this you trying to seduce me?" she asks, laughing. "You looked like you were having a stroke." I pout and push her away from me, walking toward the counter. She blocks my way with her long, muscled arm and pushes me back against the wall, her hands by my head and her knee between my thighs. She leans in, her lips brushing my ear, scorching the sensitive skin, her voice velvet and low. "Baby, if you want to seduce me, you only ever need crook your little finger and I will come running."

Looking around, she sees my step stool, the one I use to get the cans of tomato paste from the tippy top of the shelving and sets it against the wall beside me. "Step up," she says roughly.

I comply, and we are now relatively the same height. Bracing her hands, she straddles the step stool, crushing into me, flattening me against the wall as she finds my lips with deep, hungry kisses. One forearm on the wall, she threads her hand up my skirt, pausing briefly to finger the pooling desire. She spreads my slick on her palm, which she then pushes onto my clit, shifting her wrist to give my entire pussy this heated, broad-spectrum pressure. She pushes aside one leg to make more room for her hand and pushes me back into the wall. I come fast and hard against her, reveling in the brute force.

As she cups her hand to her nose, inhaling my sex, the bell above the door rings. She smiles roguishly and steps over to the handwashing station, leaving me to pull myself together and step up to the counter, face flushed, lips swollen, and hair thoroughly sexed.

Scout

I wash her slick from my hands, smiling like I just fucked the prom queen. Which I kinda did. My smile is short-lived, however, as Tennessee Woodley comes sauntering up to the counter. I notice that she has a similar smile and her cute wife walking in right behind her with flushed cheeks and reddened lips.

"Hey there, Scout. How are you today?"

SCOUT AND THE LAVENDER GIRL

"Fan-fucking-tastic, Tennessee. Penelope—you look absolutely radiant."

"Thanks, Scout. Ten was telling me that your girl does a killer pizza with peaches on it."

The memory of that night—at least the first part—makes my neck heat up a little. "Yeah... that was deemed too damned sexy for our customers. We don't offer it anymore."

"Bullshit," Evie says, walking up behind me. "Peaches are still in season." Turning to Penelope, she asks, "Would you like the sample I gave to Ten? The one with the rosemary oil?"

I growl at her under my breath. "Uh-uh. We don't give out samples like that anymore."

Tennessee and Penelope look at each other and come back at us with a pair of shit-eating grins. "You sure about that?" Tennessee asks cockily.

"Absolutely. And absolutely not," I say, pointing directly at Tennessee as Evie slices up the peaches in the back. Hip-checking me, she places two peach slices on a small plate and drizzles them for her audience. Thankfully, she leaves the fruit on the plate and hands it over to Penelope to taste.

"Smart woman," I say, growling at her.

They each take a slice and eat it, moaning their appreciation. Tennessee eyes Evie while licking the juice from Penelope's fingertips.

"You're pushing it, Woodley."

"Mmmm. My apologies, old friend. Maybe next time."

I pull Evie behind me and shake my head. "Not. Going. To happen."

Tennessee smiles a little too broadly but nods and begins to lead Penelope out of the store. Something clicks as she does, and I call out after her. "Woodley, wait!"

She turns around, her eyes questioning me. I grab someone else's pizza from the oven and box it, despite Evie's objections. Running over to Tennessee and Penelope, I hand her the boxed pizza. Leaning in so that Evie doesn't hear me, I ask, "Your dad... he goes by Woody, doesn't he?"

Tennessee's friendly expression falls, and the set of her jaw indicates that she does not like this subject matter one bit. "He does. Why do you ask?"

"Thought he looked familiar. He's been hanging out with Evie's ex-husband."

"He's a crook and a homophobic asshole," she says, pointing to a long scar on her hairline. "Kicked me out when I was fifteen. Not a good guy. Tell her to be careful around him."

I puff out air through my nose and nod. "Okay, good to know. Sorry about what he did. Truly. You're okay… when you're not trying to corrupt my girl."

"I'll take that as a compliment," she says, gesturing with the box of pizza as she and Penelope make their way out of the store.

I turn back to Evie, who has her hands on her hips. "Hmph," she declares. "You know, those two still haven't ever paid for a pizza."

Smiling as I file away the information Tennessee gave me, I grab her by the waist. "Why buy the pizza when you're giving away the peach slices for free?"

She spins on me, laughing. "You're so cute when you're jealous—I love you."

Her eyes go wide at the admission and I swear, I could get used to my heart beating in my chest without wanting to throw up. I'd made her unsure about her feelings with my stupidity, and hearing her say that for the first time is… well, damn if that isn't doing something foolish to my tear ducts.

34

EVIE

While Scout had been recovering over the last month, I'd had more and more opportunities to check out the Kavanaugh file room. They only have files on current clients, and there's nothing untoward in any of them. I've opened every directory on their network and know for a fact that they haven't decided to up and digitize everything. Or if they have, it certainly isn't on their server, and I've all but run out of time.

More than that, Chet hasn't tried to come on to me since that first time. His attitude has been... interesting. This whole time I'd been wondering if this was a sick attempt to either get me back or get back at me. But his face looks resigned. And stressed-out. Like, maybe he's just trying to get through these weeks, too.

I'm down to the last week or so of work here, and I go into the file room to grab the Schultz file. Chet is outside the door, waiting for me, his face red.

"What are you doing?"

I turn around, the Schultz file in my hand. "Checking out the lighting receipt for Mrs. Schultz. She didn't like the first set of lights that she ordered, and I need to get this taken care of—her Fourth of July party is coming up quick."

Looking around at the stacked tiles, he shuffles and puts his hands in his pockets. "I don't want you in this room. It's for Kavanaugh employees only."

"Dude. I'm a Kavanaugh employee against my will. I don't want your files. I mean, clearly you've had a bit of a shredding party, but I'm just trying to do my damned job."

He shakes his head. "I didn't shred the files. We scanned everything over twelve months old."

I decide to let the lie stand. It's not like I have any evidence, and I don't necessarily want to admit that I've accessed the VPN and know that he doesn't have anything.

Huh.

He doesn't have anything.

He doesn't have anything.

I begin to put a few things together in my head and remember Scout wondering how they'd stayed in business. Scout's portfolio businesses run as they want to… unless she has something different to say about it.

Hmmm.

"You didn't want me here, did you, Chet?" I ask lightly, pulling him in with my gaze.

"You know I want you here," he says, letting the heat into his eyes. "And you owed me a completed project."

"Yeah… but you know that you screwed me over with the money," I say, ignoring his protestant look. "You at least have enough of a conscience to want to avoid me. Having me here isn't your idea."

He flits his eyes over to his mother's office, but I'm not buying it. I'll pretend that I do, and she might be happy with the arrangement, but this isn't her idea. She doesn't have the forethought.

Chet pushes himself off the doorframe and stands over me, a little too closely. "Is that what you think?" he asks, twirling a lock of my hair through his tattooed fingers.

I roll my eyes and pluck my hair from his fingers.

"Oh come on, baby. You used to get so hot for me. And the things you did with my dick, that you allowed me to do to you? No way this woman is satisfying you."

"I'm more than satisfied," I say easily. *Because I can still feel her breath on my neck from when she finger-fucked me over morning coffee.*

Rather than let him hurt himself coming up with a retort, I turn my back on him and go back to my office.

Scout

Evie is rapping on my door like she wants to break it down. I open it, Cosette tucked into my arm like a football, and we're both wondering what's flown up her gorgeous ass. She's wearing regular office clothes and minimal makeup, but she is *beaming*.

"I think I know why they insisted on me completing the contract," she says, pushing her way inside, gathering the fluffy one in her arms. "I think—" She stops midsentence, looking at me. "What are you wearing?"

"A suit. Surely, you've seen a suit before," I say, hitching up a grin.

Her eyes rove up and down my body, and I know she wants to touch me. Her hands are doing the exact same clenching and unclenching that mine are.

"I wanted to take you on a date."

Evie's shine fills the room, and her smile is amazing. "Really?"

"Yes, baby. Really. I want to take you out on the town, show you off." *And then take off your clothes and do terrible things to you.*

Focus, Scout. I look down to check my cufflinks, trying and failing to break the enchantment she has over me in close quarters. "So, why are they insisting on completing the contract, if not to screw you over?"

She does a little head shake, sets down Cosette, then draws herself up to full height. "They no longer have a ruling percentage of ownership."

Huh.

"A new investor," I say, the truth of it dawning on me. She nods, her whole body animated. I pull Evie into my townhouse and push her toward my office. "No time to waste. We need to make a call."

Evie

Scout asks me to ring up Ten Woodley while she looks up public records online. I'm pretty sure she'd like for me to pretend that that particularly hot piece of polyamory doesn't exist, so I know she means business.

Ten's voice is like rough silk on the line. "Evie, I'm surprised to hear from you. Finally given up on pining for that jock?"

"Still here," Scout mutters, her face a razor blade. The effect is ruined by the fact that she is also snuggling with a schnoodle in her lap, but I'll never tell.

"*Ladies*," I say, setting Cosette down so that I can take her place on Scout's lap. "There's enough of me to go around."

"No, there's not," growls Scout.

"*Fine*, not that it matters because this is a business call." I undo Scout's tie and pull it from her starched collar.

A soft chuckle filters through the line. "Not my fault you didn't tell me we were on speakerphone."

"So stipulated, counselor," I say, kissing the bulging vein in Scout's forehead. I can't force myself to be sorry about her jealousy, it's just too delicious. I loop the fabric around my neck and start a Windsor knot with my brand-new tie. "We have a question in your field of expertise."

"Happy to help in any way I can," she croons, her voice low and sexy.

Scout shakes her head at me, grinning. "Hey, Tennessee, I mentioned seeing Woody at the Kavanaugh place the other day. Is he an investor?"

"No, *I'm* an investor. *He's* a crook."

I mouth *stalker* at Scout and turn to the phone. "Wait, Ten—your dad is that creepy, busted-leather version of Donald Sutherland that's been hanging around Kavanaugh?"

"Yeah. Please tell me that you're being careful around him."

"Pursed his nuts on the first day, and he's pretty much ignored me since."

"Good woman."

Well, darn. "So, is he the reason Chet came after me? And why *decades'* worth of files went away overnight?"

"Yep, and that is straight out of the Woody Woodley playbook. Do whatever it takes to prevent a lawsuit, shred the rest, then sell to the first sucker that walks through the door." Ten snorts and continues, "But he's no fan of my *degenerate lifestyle*, which is too fucking rich, and we haven't spoken for years. I'm sorry that you're caught up in this, sweetie."

"No worries, I'm out in a few days."

"Tell me—has he been visiting a lot?"

I nod. "More so recently."

"Hmmm," Tennessee considers. "That means that a sale is imminent, and / or that he's losing money."

"Probably both, if I know the Kavanaughs."

"I'm going put in a notice to the city's council for ethical business and report him to the Better Business Bureau again. Nothing'll come of it, but at least it documents the concern."

Scout nods and takes up the conversation. "Hey, Tennessee, does Woody have holdings in San Antonio? I'm still trying to figure out where I know him from."

"You're still with that investment group, right?"

"Yeah."

"Thought so. He's got shared holdings with them. It's why I never joined."

Scout shakes her head, unhappy with that turn of events. "I'll let Tricia know we don't want anything to do with him."

"Agreed."

"Thanks, Tennessee."

"No problem, Scout. Hey, Evie?"

"Yeah, Ten?"

"Take care of that one, will ya? She's kinda grumpy, but she's good people"

A warm blush creeps up my neck. "Will do." Always, if she'll let me.

"Good woman. Penny and I will stop by the shop next week."

"I'll have your peaches ready for you," I say, laughing as Scout grumbles and hangs up the phone.

35

SCOUT

Well, I did not see *that* coming.

Retrieving the violently crumpled piece of paper, I flatten it out on my desktop, reading it again, in case I missed anything.

Dear Sophia,

Thank you for alerting me to the issues that you noted with Calvin Woodley and Associates (CWA). However, given that there have been no convictions and no indictments against Mr. Woodley or his company, it is within our rights and for the benefit of our organization that we continue our partnership with CWA. We will, however, keep an eye out for any untoward behavior.

Given your misgivings about continuing a business partnership with Mr. Woodley, and given the recent dissolution of your relationship with Ms. Forrester, All-Star Investment Capital (ASIC) would like to instead offer disinvestment without the usual penalty, in order to give you the funds and space to heal properly. While ASIC has not and will not force a separation, we have come to believe that it is in your best interest to simplify your holdings.

K.C. LITTLETON

Sincerely,
Tricia Louis, CEO
All-Star Investment Capital

TL;DR? I'm on my own.

36

EVIE

I'm no Einstein, but I know an upset lesbian when I see one. Scout's eyes have had storm clouds brewing in them for at least two days now, and she's been standoffish. If I've done something wrong or annoying or just too straight for words (her lingo), then I'd rather know about it up front. So, once again I go to knock on the Sapphic door to see what lies within.

I'm dressed to the nines—I know the rockabilly look gets her superhot, so I do my lavender hair like Gwen Stefani with a victory roll in front and pin curls cascading down my back, and I wear a bodice-hugging floral halter top with a full skirt and super-high heels. I check my lipstick—cherry red—in my Pusheen pocket mirror and make sure that my winged eyeliner is on point as I walk down the sidewalk. She swings open the door as I reach it and pulls me in, her hands rough around my soft arms.

Damn.

I do love it when she comes to the door hot and sweaty.

Wordlessly, she shuts the door and pushes me up against it, pinning me down with a molten hot kiss. Her hands are everywhere: on my waist, on my ass, on my tits.

"You're not wearing a bra," she says, breathing hard as she palms the soft material.

I shake my head, then wipe the red from her lips and sigh. "I've missed you."

"Shut up and take off that dress," she orders, her hawkish eyes searing me with a look. "But leave the heels on."

Why, yes. I *do* like a take-charge lover.

Caressing her furrowed brow and sharpened jaw, I smile and hum, then slide the side zipper down my rib cage. No sooner than the *zsush* of the zipper halts, she bats away my hands and rips the dress up over my head. I slide the crinoline down to my feet with a satisfying and crinkly *woosh*, then step out of it, now only wearing red pinup panties and matching patent leather heels. She inhales sharply, her eyes roving up and down my body, and she puts her rough hands on my hips, sliding the panties down, all the way to the floor. Holding her patent leather gaze, I quietly step out of those as well. Her eyes look up to the stairs, an order. I make it a point to pause and admire her dark energy before walking up the stairs, lazily swinging my hips, my sky-high stilts making sharp sounds on the polished wood.

Halfway up, I hear a growling "Stop" come from her lips. I comply and turn around, hand on my hip, waiting for her next order.

Her eyes are smoldering, following the lines of my tattoos as she sets my body on fire. "Sit down."

Biting down on my lower lip, I comply, pinning my knees together as I rest my heels on the step below me. The cool, slick wood against my ass sends chills up my spine, making my nipples peak and harden.

"Spread for me," she says, her voice gravelly and demanding.

I lock eyes with her and slowly part my legs, letting my feet glide across the wood until both click on the edge, finding the width of the staircase.

"Lean back."

I melt into the stairs, letting my head rest on one of the stairs above me as I arch my back, displaying myself to her. I reach out and hold on to the wrought iron balusters on either side of me, open and exposed. She's a few steps below me, and I can't see what she is doing from this angle. She doesn't move or make a sound for several seconds. I lift my head and find her eyes devouring my body with a ferocity that boils my blood and causes a thumping pulse at my core. It's the hottest goddamned thing I've ever seen.

"Lean *back*," she demands, her voice like whiskey. I let out a steadying breath and rest my head on the step again.

Several seconds pass.

I inhale sharply at her hot breath on my thighs, then softsoftsoft kisses, up and down my legs. Her strong hands spread my thighs even farther apart, then move to my nipples, pinching and rolling them as her tongue finds my core and begins to lick me from bottom to top, rough and demanding. The pain and pleasure intensify until I shiver at the thought of stopping one for fear of stopping the other.

"*Scout.*" My voice is strangled.

She groans at the sound of her name and fills me with her thumb, grasping at my clit with her middle and pointer fingers, rolling them in tempo. Far too quickly she removes her thumb and a whine works its way up my throat, begging for more.

"Shhh," she chastises as she traces her thumb down my seam, trailing it to my ass, plunging it into me. I gasp at the pressure and stretching pain. Her middle and pointer fingers now slip into my pussy, and she begins to roll her fingers against the thumb through the shared wall. Satisfied that I like this repositioning, she lowers her mouth to me and begins ministering to my swollen clit.

I move my hand down to her head and she pulls away from me completely. I whimper *please*, but she shakes her head. "No hands."

Cursing her in my head, I grasp the railings. Once she's happy with my compliance, and she attacks me again, pushing her fingers and thumb so far into me, sucking me with such pressure that my eyes roll in the back of my head.

"Ungh. Scout. I'm—"

The orgasm ripping through me renders me mute, and only strangled breath sounds punctuate the air. She pulls back on the pressure, drawing out my orgasm with a gentle tongue while feathering slippery fingers across my nipples. I tense and come again, more softly this time.

My body melts farther into the stairs, and I am high, fucked stupid on her tongue and fingers.

"Stay here," she orders, her eyes lapping me up as she steps around me and up the stairs. "Don't move a muscle."

I thrill at the roughness in her voice and obey, if only because I am a skeleton-less pile of goo at this point. I grip the balusters a bit harder as the AC kicks on and cools the wetness between my legs and on my nipples. I hear her walk into her bedroom, then the bathroom and turn on the shower.

"Mmmm, that's my good girl."

I jump at the sound of her voice and continue to stare at the ceiling, chilly and horny at the same time.

"Wanted to make sure I can trust you to stay where you're told," she laughs, and walks back into the bathroom.

Several minutes pass, and I start to wonder if she's actually showering or if she's still looking at me, spread-eagled on her stairs. Moments later, I hear the water turn off and feel her presence at the top of the staircase.

"You really are the best kitten, ever, aren't you?" she asks, her voice velvet.

Scout

Fuck. Me. Sideways.

I'm not even sure why I went all soft-dom on her, but I've been confused and livid ever since I got that damned letter, and I've been staying to myself a lot so that my shitty mood doesn't affect everyone else. Then she shows up with her pinup girl look that I *know* she knows I like, smelling of coconut, and... I don't even give a shit about the board anymore. Even the shower couldn't temper the fire in my belly. Looking down, I see her big, beautiful amber-honey eyes looking up at me with want, her undulating body all round tits and curved hips and luscious belly and parted thighs.

Holy hell.

I was so rushed that I didn't even bother with a towel. Droplets of water plink on the staircase around her, body runoff from one freshly washed lesbian. She opens her mouth, catching a drop or two. My breath catches, and her lips lift in a knowing smile as she fucks me with those honey eyes.

"You may get up now and come to the bedroom," I say, my voice and countenance more stern than I feel. Because what I feel is weak in the knees.

She does as asked and slides her legs together, rising slowly, giving me a glorious view of her womanly figure and gorgeous skin art before turning to face me. My heart catches when I realize that she's in towering heels and I've dripped water down the slick wooden stairs, but she takes a brief moment to solidify her stance, then continues to the top of the stairs, each heel strike a sharp rapport that vibrates deep in my chest. She is naked and flushed, but her satisfied look gives way to something more. Her eyes rake my dark muscles, glinting with water, and the small purse of her lips and tightening of her jaw indicate that she wants her turn.

She follows me to my room, where I have her stand near the foot of the bed, facing away from it. I kiss her deeply, then put both of my hands to her delicate shoulders and push her down to her knees. The carpeting is plush, but I know that it digs a little, and her butt is resting on the edge of her sharp heels as her shoulder blades rest against the bed. She looks up from her supplicant position, and her arousal and desire to please is unmistakable. My pussy is level with her mouth.

Looking down, I grab her by the hair and pull her face into my center. "Lick."

She scorches me with a look before opening her mouth and parting my folds with her pink tongue. Her eyes flick up to mine when she tastes my wetness, a knowing smile playing at the corner of her mouth. She knows exactly how much she turns me on. Softly, she flicks my half-hidden clit, rousing it out of hiding, working it into a swollen button with broad, easy strokes. I put my hands on the bed behind her, widening my stance around her shoulders, forcing her to lean back and rest her head on the edge of the mattress. I ride her face as I slowly give her more of my weight. She pushes her tongue along the length of my pussy, dipping into me as she uses her nose to keep pressure on my clit. Her inhalations become more and more ragged as I grind against her, and she ever so lightly grazes my swollen clit with her teeth, eliciting a deep, dark groan. I am quickly coming apart, and I'm the one who's supposed to be in charge. Narrowing her focus on my clit, she sucks and licks at the same time, continuing until my body feels like it was doused in kerosene and I am the fire. I grind and ride her willing, devil mouth, and her eyes never leave mine. I hold out, pulling back before my climax, giving her room to breathe before pushing myself against her, edging myself again and again. The look in her eyes is sex and trust, and it twists my insides until I'm shouting in climax, clenching so hard that my knees give way, and I lose my balance to the orgasm. I slump down, straddling her thighs and resting my head on the bed behind her.

God.

Damn.

She pulls my shattered hull against her soft, warm body, kissing me, sharing my arousal and orgasm. I know without looking that her eyes show heat and love in equal measure.

"Fuck, you are so good at that," I say, pooling into the crook of her neck, still not willing to come up for air.

I feel her jaw shift, no doubt spreading her lips into a full-tilt smile.

"Thank you, Madam Scout. Now, tell me—what has you so wound up?"

37

SCOUT

*G*uess I didn't hide my foul mood as well as I thought. I groan and flop down beside her, our bare asses on the high-density carpet.

"I warned the board about Calvin Woodley, and they have invited me to disinvest," I say, using the stiff financial terminology.

"Disinvest?" she asks, sitting up a little straighter. "As in, here's some cash, now get the heck out?"

I nod. "It'd be a pretty significant amount of cash, plus the pizza shop, the consulting firm, and the printer. The entire portfolio, of which I get a share, is doing fantastic."

"Do you think he had them do it?"

"Don't think so; he would have made me pay the penalty and would have forced it to go through the court system, just to make it ugly."

"So, they know, but they don't care."

"Basically."

She turns to me. "And... the pizza shop?"

I nod my head. "All mine. You cook, I'll take care of the business, easy-peasy."

From her pursed lips and the cock of her head, I can tell that I have said something entirely wrong. "What?"

"Uh... what about these last few months make you think that I want to just be the cook?"

"But... cooking is your passion."

She shrugs. "Don't get me wrong, I enjoy the hell out of coming up with new things to do to a pizza, but my passion has always been the business. I mean, when Kimberly asked for my help with the restaurant that she'd opened with *the* Scout Martinez, I was worried about an oversaturated market, but completely ignored my instincts because it meant I had a chance to maybe get a glimpse of my laminated lesbian."

I wrinkle my nose at the phrase. "Laminated lesbian?"

Evie smiles mischievously and straddles me, hooking her legs back so that the bottoms of her now-bare feet land flush against the sides of my calves, her breasts are mashed up against my chest, and her hands are gripping my shoulders. She gives me a deliriously delicious kiss, then places butterfly kisses along my jaw, stopping just shy of my ear. "My list only ever had one name on it," she whispers softly. "Number 19. Laminated."

My eyes go wide, and my mouth kinda just hangs there. Well, shit. I think about the pictures that Spence showed me. That look in her eyes. Somewhere along the way, I'd lost the sense of what it was to be the object of someone's desire. That my cut-up, bony mortal coil could only ever be accepted, not actively desired. Pride swells in my chest, and I whisper against her lips, "Damn skippy."

She lets out a beautiful laugh, and I can feel its reverberations throughout her hedonistic body, her breasts and belly and thighs shimmering joyfully against me. I allow myself to get lost in her for a moment. Or ten. Or infinity. I have no idea.

Eventually, my brain reroutes to the topic at hand. "So... the thing about redirecting the cash flow around the oven, and reaching out to the ladies at Bluebonnet..."

"Was a helluva a lot of fun," she replies, looking me in the eye as she undulates against me.

I sit there, bare-assed on the carpet, my hands on her hips, looking past her shoulder in a near-fugue state for several minutes. To her credit, she lets me.

"So," I ask, turning my attention to her profoundly kind eyes, "what do you think I should do?"

Her eyebrow arches dramatically, and a small smirk quirks up her lips. "Now that's the question you should have been asking the whole time."

Her confidence is contagious. "Well?"

"Hold off on expansion until you're fully disinvested and I'm fully disentangled, then begin to consider expanding Bluebonnet's offices. If the pizza continues to have two-hour wait times, then get a good strategic location in East Austin, then the lake."

"Not downtown?"

"Too expensive and the market is flooded."

"Then why East Austin and the lake?"

"Roly lives in East Austin, and there's a lot of really cool neighborhoods where this could fit in nicely. And the lake because, well, it's the lake. You can charge more, you can get away with a brunch menu on the weekends, and we could put in a full bar. There's a couple of properties that foreclosed with the flooding—not that I want to work in a flood plain, but we might find a couple of good deals."

"You wanna do both at once?"

"Oh god, no. East first, get them coming out the door like right here, then the lake. I mean, that's where you're building your house, right?"

Uhhh...

"Scout?"

"I'd stopped the project before they began because too many of these projects were losing money at the beginning."

"Wait," Evie says with mocking round eyes. "Are you telling me that you're not my sugar daddy?"

"Nah, I can still take you out for a nice steak dinner," I tease, "but I didn't want to tie up any more liquid capital than was totally necessary."

She nods, understanding the importance of that at this juncture in the business. Gorgeous and smart as all get-out. She is *not* going to be putting on any clothes anytime this evening.

"So, what is it that you want to do?"

"What do you mean?"

"Do you want the other businesses?"

"They're interesting and good for the portfolio. I figure we'll eventually publish a pizza recipe book for you, and the lawyers at the oil and gas firm are helpful with the paperwork."

"Okay, but what's your passion?"

"Aside from your sweet ass?"

"Obviously."

"I really like real estate and development."

"Like the Levee, or are you thinking large-scale neighborhoods?"

"I prefer urban development. So, yes, the Levee. Definitely a mixed-use development. And mixed-income developments. I really like creating community."

She rounds her eyes and purses her lips, and a performative, dramatic slow blink plays out on her eyelids.

"What?"

"So… why don't you take the damned money and do the thing you've liked doing the whole time."

"Build a kick-ass condo community in the heart of Austin?"

"Yeah," she says, nodding slowly and emphatically, her hair, undone from sex, bouncing. "And wouldn't it be neat to build your own construction company? And wouldn't it be great if you happened to know a couple of trustworthy, connected guys that would help you get it off the ground?"

Woah. I mean, yes, that sounds awesome. But, wow. That's a lot of her family, all up in my chili.

"Consultants," she says.

"Huh?" I ask, still reeling.

"We'd be your consultants. The Koenig Consulting firm, if you will. We don't have to be all up in your business. We can perforate it so that you can make a clean getaway if you need to," she says, twisting her mouth so as not to smile. Or laugh.

"Am I that transparent?"

"You do look a little horrified."

"I'm sorry, I…"

"No need to explain. No need to rush into making the same mistake twice. We keep our money separate. Church and state."

She extends her hand across her naked tits, and we shake on our first official business deal together.

"I do have one bit of free consultative advice, if you're up for it," she says, her face going serious for a moment.

"The board?"

She nods emphatically, her hair skimming her breasts. "They no longer have your best interests at heart, baby. Make no mistake, if you don't take what they're offering now, you'll still be out within the year, and maybe with less money than you started with."

I take a deep breath, the thought of striking out on my own overwhelming.

"You're not on your own."

"How do you always know what I'm thinking?"

A warm emotion creeps into her honey-colored eyes, and she shrugs. "I know you, Scout."

I lean over and gently kiss her on the lips. "Thank you for the consultation. And I know you're right. It's just a hard pill to swallow."

She smiles under my approval. "It'll be a little tight while we transition, but there's a pretty great opportunity to making a lot of money for ourselves and not be beholden to anyone else."

I nod, knowing she's right. Her confidence is giving me confidence. And a good idea. "You know, the board will probably pay you a pretty penny to stay on as a consultant for the San Antonio restaurants on the books," I offer, knowing that she wouldn't want me to help her out financially.

She shakes her head.

"Why not?"

K.C. LITTLETON

"I wouldn't want a fee, baby. I'd want a percentage."

God, she is so fucking sexy.

I say so, then drag her up onto the bed and make love to her until we pass out.

38

EVIE

At the moment, Scout's construction company is just a website. But a kick-ass website, if I do say so myself. And, since Scout has recognized my brilliant business mind, she is fully on board with my two-part, grow-and-get-revenge business model.

Step one: Secure a rich, sensitive client with a penchant for bragging to her neighbors, and make darn sure to write change fees into the contract. Which is why Scout and I are at the Schultzes' Fourth of July party wearing tacky Hawaiian prints and fake leis.

Scout leans over and whispers in my ear, her many-ringed fingers tickling up the bare back of my dress, "Okay, three things. One, we should have had her hire Jules' catering company because this food and these decorations are sad. Two, your tits look awesome in a halter top, and I can't wait to get this dress off of you. And three, I think we might be the token gays at this party."

"One, agreed. B. Stop it, you know how badly I blush when you do that, and finally..." I say, looking around, "you are probably right."

Just as Scout nips the outer edge of my ear, I see Mrs. Schultz making her way over to us and push her a safe distance away. "Evie! I'm so glad you came! Look at how beautiful this pool house is!"

"It is beautiful, Mrs. Schultz. Rogelio does some good work. It's why he's our first new hire."

"Wait, what? You're not with Kavanaugh anymore? We have designs on a whole new deck! How do I find you?"

"I'm hoping you'll consider M&K Construction Partners," I say, placing my shiny new business card in the palm of her hand.

She looks over the card, her eyes widening. "You're the business manager?"

"Yes, ma'am. We have highly qualified consultants on the payroll, but the buck stops with me on every project."

"And you don't plan on going anywhere else?"

"No, ma'am, this is where I make my stand," I say, looking over at my devastatingly handsome date.

Part B: Introduce Carla to the delights and perils of Chet, and let nature take its course.

"I don't know why I have to be here for this," Chet grumps, leaning against the receptionist's desk at Bluebonnet, slouched in his patented Instagram pose. I'm not sure if he's still trying to get to me somehow, or if douche-bro posturing has somehow morphed at the DNA level and now he can't help himself.

"There was an overcharge in our shared account, and there was an extra $476 dollars that technically belong to you," I say, waving a cashier's check in front of him. "Unless you don't want it."

He snatches the check from me, a little too quickly for someone who's about to pay off his debts. Though, if the new, tricked-out Harley sitting in the front of the office is any indication, he's probably racked up a bit more debt in anticipation of his windfall. Shocker.

The door swings open again, and I can tell by the violence of it that Carla has arrived, right on time, and she immediately gets up into Scout's face. "What the fuck is this? You're threatening to sue me? For $500 dollars? What kind of bullshit is this?"

Scout steps aside as Samantha walks up to the desk and puts her hands in front of her, an apology. "My bad. There was an issue with escrow, and some confusion about who owes who what."

"Ha," says Chet. "So, instead of her owing you $500, you owe me $500? That's rich. Y'all really know how to run a business, don't you? I'm guessing you'll both be out on the street in six months."

Carla's eyeballs sweep Chet from the top of his gorgeous blond hair to the bottom of his sexy biker books, and he nails her with his Facebook smile. "Can you believe these yahoos?" he asks, his eyes dragging down the length of her body and back up again.

Carla rolls her eyes. "I can't believe I ever thought she was a good businesswoman. Complete amateurs."

"Tell you what," says Chet, tilting his cashier's check at Carla, "let me buy you a drink with their stupidity and we can compare notes."

Carla sweeps a look at Scout, then at me, and smirks. "Perfect."

And then they walk out of the door like—I kid you not—a Hollywood movie ending.

Scout looks at me incredulously. "Did that just happen?"

I snort and dissolve into a bowl of giggles. "Yes. Yes, it did."

Snarling, she drags me into her arms. "You are an evil genius, and I am so glad that you are on my side."

39

EVIE

Mrs. Schultz has, shockingly enough, changed her mind about decking out the pool and has already started calling me about her daughter's engagement gift—a condo in Scout's first downtown development. Thankfully, this is my last day at Kavanaugh Construction, and soon I'll be able to spend all day with that wackadoo sweetheart. I saunter in twenty minutes late, which feels fan-freaking-tastic.

I pick up an envelope from my desk, and it looks much like the envelope that brought me to this place. With more than a little trepidation, I slide my letter opener through the tightly sealed flap and angle it up carefully with a slight rip-rip, rip-rip. My hands shaking, I pull out a familiar-looking piece of perforated, watermarked, and signed paper.

$25,000. Half of my savings back to me.

I've never held a check so big in my entire life.

So glad I made him give me a cashier's check.

Inhaling deeply, I kiss my pointer and middle fingers and point them to the god of dropped ceiling tiles.

Mother.

Humper.

I am free.

There are a few things I want to close out (because I can't help myself), and I do want to stay for the lunch that Itsy has planned in my honor, but I am out of there after that. I might just go get myself a mani-pedi and have someone else do my nails for a change.

And Goldie is about to get a set of sweet rims.

Honestly, I was so focused on my save/spend list that I hadn't even heard the front door open or the sharp clack of five-inch heels walking in my direction. Folding the envelope carefully, like a precious object, I put it in one of the million side pockets in my purse and vow to deposit a couple thou in my bank account and the rest in my college savings account.

"What's that dopey smile all about? Last I checked, you didn't have all that much to smile about, what with your seven jobs and my leftovers."

Carla. Effing. Forrester. Right outside my office.

"Hey there, stalker. Can't you just hound me at the pizza shop? Do you have to come to my place of work?"

Her smile, in all its red-lipped glory, is as sexy as it is sinister. "Oh, you mean *my* place of work?"

Wait. What.

"Why would you work at a construction company?" I ask, entirely confused.

"Why would I work, period?" she sniffs. "I'm about to own this place. And my first act as the owner will be to fire your ass, so you might want to start packing now because payback is a bitch."

Y'all.

Mngh.

I was just going for her everlasting sexual disappointment. I wasn't planning on tanking her bank account.

See also: I am an evil genius who can't be stopped.

She looks so smug and happy with herself that... I say again, *mngh*. It's going to be a real shame what this business is going to do to her portfolio. Leaving out the fact that Woody and the Kavanaughs had clearly shredded their salacious past and given me what was very likely their last $25,000 from the Schultz contract, I am pretty sure that Chet's next big project up over in Manor was already under water. And it's none of my nevermind, but I'm also pretty sure the taxes that are due next week will go unpaid.

Ugh.

Look, don't judge me.

I can only do evil part-time.

"You know what, Carla? Save your breath. And save your money—you do *not* want to buy this place. Just… trust me on that."

Her arched eyebrow—which, frankly, needs tweezing—and imperious sniff tell me that she has no intention of following my well-meaning advice.

"No, seriously. You need to walk away."

"You're adorable," she says, patting the top of my head.

Alrighty then.

Full-time evil it is.

I roll my eyes as Chet strolls up to her. "Ms. Forrester," he says, surreptitiously-ish eyeing her cleavage.

"Mr. Kavanaugh," she says, running a perfectly manicured red-lacquer nail along his collar. "This soon-to-be ex-employee doesn't think I should go into business with you."

He shrugs his broad, manly shoulders with a laugh and lets his hypnotic eyes wander freely down her ridiculously hot body. "Well, if you want to believe my ex-wife, go ahead."

Giggling to herself, Carla looks me with her curled scarlet lip and scornful sex eyes and responds, "I don't think so. In fact, if you fire her right now, I'll even pay the asking price."

Holding her gaze, Chet smiles that panty-dropper smile of his and says without ceremony, "Evie, leave now." I sigh as they walk toward the kitchen. So beautiful. So dumb.

Swallowing a self-satisfied smirk, I close the unsaved email asking for a payment extension from the lumberyard and press the power button on the Kavanaugh computer. Reaching into the drawer, I remove the lid on my shrimp pasta and place it under some files, taking with me the lunch bag and my giant purse.

Passing them as I walk out of the office, I cough into my fist to choke down the cackle that desperately wants to climb up my throat, my eyes red and teary from the effort. Carla juts out her chin and smiles a full-toothed grin, like the sexy saber-toothed cat that she is. I don't look at Chet because I know that he's shitting a brick hoping that I won't say anything about this already being my last day.

Oh, *honey*.

If that bitch wants to pay full price for your clitphobic ass and your shitty accounting skills, she can go right on ahead with that.

Passing Itsy, I murmur an apology for having to leave before the lunch and make it out the door, across the caliche parking lot, and into my precious Goldie before losing my ever-lovin' mind. I am laughing so hard that I feel drunk in the middle of the morning. Gathering myself, I fire up Goldie, crank up the radio, and sing at the top of my lungs all the way home.

Every. Thing. Every damned thing I'd been through this last year, and these last two months specifically, was worth knowing that Carla was going to be broke and unsatisfied and that Chet was going to be broke and screwed over before he figured out what that smell is in my old office.

Wait till she finds out that he hates giving oral.

Speaking of which...

Scout

"Honey, I'm hoooommmmeeee!" rings throughout my condo, and I make my way to the top of the stairs, looking down on my brilliant, radiant girlfriend.

"You're back early," I smirk, making my way down the stairs. A few new toys, including a high-end strap came in the mail today, and I am about to blow her fucking mind.

She rakes me with a gaze and pushes out a pouty lip. "I got *fired*, baby."

"On your last day?"

She nods, biting her lip. "Carla stopped by to work out a deal to buy Kavanaugh, and I tried to warn her, but she just... wouldn't listen."

I snort, wholly impressed by my sexy, curvy, not-quite-evil genius lover. I fake a concerned look. "Awwww. But did you get paid?"

Sticking her tongue out to the side, she plunges her perfectly manicured paw into the unfathomable depths of her purse and pulls out a check, waving it in the air. "You bet your sweet butt I did!"

"God, I love you." I reach her and pull her in close for a kiss and a grope.

"I love you, too," she murmurs against my lips as I unbutton the top of her work slacks with one hand while pulling up her blouse with the other.

"Fuck it," I growl, shredding her shirt with my hands, buttons flying everywhere. "I hate it when you wear business casual." Her laugh is a shot of adrenaline, and I roughly spin her to face the door, then pin her to it with one hand while unhooking her bra and pushing her slacks down to her ankles with the other. She shimmies out of her bra and steps out of her pants and underwear.

Still wearing her heels.

God. Damn.

Coyly looking back over her shoulder, she says in a sotto voice, "Come on, baby. Fuck me against this door, and then let's go build a fucking empire."

Yeah, baby. Let's.

EPILOGUE

EVIE

Y'all didn't think I was going to leave you hanging, did you?

I'm standing here, facing the door, waiting for Scout to grab… something—she wouldn't say what—and I'm wondering why I didn't just tell her to put me over her shoulder and take me to bed. I mean, I was feeling sexy with the heels-and-sex-up-against-the-door combo, but now that I'm cooling my heels waiting for her, I'm not so sure. Should I take a shower? What if she wants to rim me?

Oh, fuck, I really want her to rim me.

I'm about 0.5 seconds from turning around and telling her to meet me in the shower when suddenly there is six foot two inches of powerful, sexy lesbian pressed up against my body. How the hell did she make it back down the stairs without me knowing? She's pushing her hips into my ass, and her pants are undone, the teeth of the zipper bite-burring along the sensitized skin. I expect the feel of her soft Tomboy X underwear but am met with the tickling of pubic hair and something… rubberized, and flat against her skin.

I make to turn around, wanting to see what kind of sexy, strappy underwear she's got going on, and perhaps to suggest a more comfortable venue when she spins me back to the door, pressing my hands against the cool, solid surface. "Stay right there, kitten. You wanna be fucked up against the door? You're gonna get fucked up against the door."

"Yes, ma'am," I say, half-jokingly, half-dead-fucking-serious. I love it when she tells me what to do in bed (or, you know, against a door), and I have a feeling that she's finally well enough to show me what she's really got.

"Mmmm," she rumbles in my ear. "That's a good kitten."

Fuck. I whimper with need. "Please, baby. I'm so ready. Please." Dirty promises and dirtier words fall out of my mouth, urging her on. She's reduced me to babbling and curse words, and I'm not mad about it. Seconds later she snakes her hand between my thighs, forcing them wider apart until she's dip-painting my throbbing core with long, devious fingers as she nibbles along my ear and jawline. Filth pours out of my mouth, begging her to go harder, to stop fucking around, to give me more. She's moving around behind me as she fingers me, and stretching, rubberized noises echo through the living room. I want desperately to turn around and see what she's doing back there.

"More, doll?" she growls, palming the back of my head, forcing me once again to face the door.

Leaning my forehead against the door, I huff out, "Yes. For the love of Christmas, more, Scout. *Now.*"

The sharp snick of a plastic lid startles me. "Scout, I'm literally fucking dripping. I don't need any more lube. Just put your hands on me. *Please.*"

She bites at my shoulder, grinning into the skin there. "You'll probably want some lube for this," she says, thrusting something cool and rubbery along my pussy, slowly dragging it out between my thighs.

Holy fuck, you guys.

"Is that a…" I start.

"Mmmhmmm," she responds, rolling her hips, continuing to pull the fake dick along my already tingling nethers.

I'm a heady combination of intimidated and turned on as I imagine her powerful body rocking into me. "*Fuuuuck me.*"

"I plan on it." I don't see her predatory smile, but I know it's there.

I whimper as she pulls away, my breath catching as the wet, slurpy sounds of a dildo being properly and generously lubed up filters through my sex-obsessed ears. Scout grabs my hips to tilt my ass up and back, and I groan when the large, round head of the dildo parts my lips.

Leaning forward, she whispers in my ear, "You ready, baby? Want my fingers first?"

"No. Fuck me, Scout. Please. Ple—" A high-pitch bark flies out of my mouth when she pushes the head of the dildo into me. Fuck, that stretches so good. Fuck. *Fuck.*

Oh god. Her hips roll against and away from me, and she's still wearing her jeans, and something about fucking me with her clothes on just feels dirty in the best way possible. At some point, her T-shirt comes off and she drapes herself across my naked back, her ridged scars setting off goose pimples along the electrified skin as she sucks at the juncture of my neck and shoulder, swirling the cool silver of her ringed thumbs around my swollen and peaked nipples. Holy fuck, my brain has gone on walkabout, and her rolling thrusts are hitting my usually uncooperative G-spot in a way that is making me wobble on my five-inch heels.

One of her hands rounds my belly and snakes between my thighs. I widen my stance even farther and am rewarded with the same rings-and-thumb action on my clit as I am being chaotically, rhythmically stretched by a dildo attached to a machine of a human being. I might actually be panting at this point, but I could give a fuck about my dignity.

Moment of honesty: I didn't want strap play when Scout first brought it up because I was 99 percent sure that it wouldn't compare with dick play, and I didn't want that hanging out there between us, you know? Like, let's focus on the amazing chemistry we have and not try to recreate some hetero fantasy, m'kay?

Well, I was right, kinda. This in no way compares to the dick play of the past. I had clearly been playing with boys when what I needed—what I really *fucking* needed—was to play with dykes. Strike that; there's only one dyke I want to play with, for as long as she'll let me. Forever, if possible.

As that little lightbulb moment flits past, I am brought back to the reality of the orgasm building, not from the outside, not from my spine or my thighs or even my clit, but from the inside. The rest of my body gives way to the heaviness building in my core until Scout's devil thumb flicks at my clit like a hammer striking flint in a room full of gasoline. My body is a conflagration, and I clench—hard—against the soft-firm phallus, the lush texture throwing my body into chaos. Suddenly, I'm wondering if it's possible to orgasm up to the tips of my ears as my toes clench and my knees lose all sense of structure.

Slumping against Scout drives her farther into me, dragging out yet-and-still another glittering, ravaging detonation. Pretty sure I semi blacked out because the next thing I know, my back is supported by suede and I am looking up into Scout's worried eyes.

"Baby? Are you okay?" She's kneeling on the couch, rubbing my arms, concern knitting her eyebrows, the dildo heavy and wet against my belly.

I reach up to her square jaw and skate my fingers along it, chuckling.

"Are you laughing at me?"

I laugh harder. "No. But I might be drunk, or high. Can I be high on strap-on sex? Is that a thing?"

I grin when her grin breaks across her face and pride swells her chest. "Looks like it."

"I need a snuggle and a cigarette, and some ass play after that. Seriously, Scout, what *the fuck* did you do to me?"

Her grin spreads even wider, and now it's my turn to be slightly insecure. "What? Are you laughing at *me* now?"

She shakes her head, running her large, warm hands over my body. "No, baby. I just really like foul-mouthed Evie, who only comes out when I've well and truly fucked her."

I blush. "If you are going to be some sort of supernatural sex creature with toys, then I can't be held responsible for the things that come out of my mouth."

She nods, pride running through her bright smile. "Mmmm. New plan: turn you into my own personal sailor."

"Your personal sailor, huh? So… you don't want me to start cursing in general? Like a certain dyke I happen to like a whole lot?"

She growls and pulls me closer. "No fucking way. That potty mouth is mine and mine alone."

I hum to myself. "Yes, it is."

We roll over a bit, and I snuggle into her shoulder as she wraps her long limbs around me like a protective cocoon. "Love you, babe," she whispers into my ear. "And this is just the beginning. With those fools in our rear view, our time is all ours now, and we can start building that empire tomorrow."

"Love you, too, baby. You make me feel so safe," I whisper, snuggling more deeply into her embrace. "But I have a very important question."

"Ask me anything."

I pluck at her waistband, trying to decide if I want to make her eyes roll to the back of her head here or on the bed upstairs. "Don't you own a property in Hawaii?"

She smiles against my hair and pulls me in a bit closer. "Yes, in Kailua."

"Then I submit, as your consultant and business partner, that we pack in a couple of weeks of sun and sand before we begin planning for world domination."

"Evie, baby, you always have the best ideas."

THANK YOU

Thank you for reading Scout and the Lavender Girl!

If you would like to read about the Martinez and Koenig families' newest venture, a gym for combat vets, check out my male-male series, Wrecked, under my main pen name, **Kelly Fox**.

Nick and Elijah's story, *Sanctuary*, will be available on January 31st. Jake and Jean-Pierre's book, *Surrender*, will be released at the end of February 2020. Roly's love story, *Stillness*, will be released at the end of March 2020.

ACKNOWLEDGMENTS

Special thanks go to my beta readers for helping me make Scout less of an asshole, and to my friends who read early versions of this story and helped to point me in the right direction.

Thanks also to Sandra, whose kind edits and words of encouragement helped me to keep going with this whole writing thing.

ABOUT THE AUTHOR

Hi there! I write contemporary gay romance under the pen name Kelly Fox, and contemporary wlw and paranormal romance under K.C. Littleton. I also curse way too much, drink exactly the right amount of red wine, and sleep far too little. I'm also lucky enough to live in Central Texas with my wife and three dogs (and usually a foster dog or two), where the astonishing diversity of humans and landscapes and tattoo shops serve as my muse.

If you enjoy what you've read, reviews on Amazon and Goodreads, along with word-of-mouth (er, Facebook) are so appreciated, and are incredibly helpful ways to support my work.

For the latest info on new releases and access to free short stories, check out my website:

https://www.authorkellyfox.com

Paranormal Bisexual Romance as K.C. Littleton

Violet Crown

Violence and bloodshed should not be the foundation for a relationship.

Dr. Hedy Villarreal is a 40-something criminal psychologist with a foul mouth and a dead wife, and recently, life has taken a turn for the weird. One minute she's living on a beach in South Texas; the next she's discovering that there's a black ops unit operating out of her family's property deep in the Texas Hill Country. Oh, and her new best friend is a muscle-bound woman with fangs and hair that rattles.

When Hedy agrees to use her skills to profile and recruit mercenaries for this not-quite-legal enterprise, she wasn't counting on ex-Navy SEAL Edison Fitzwallace. Their first interview ends in a shouting match, and their second ends with her covered in someone else's blood. It's not an auspicious beginning, but she soon learns that he would sacrifice everything to keep her safe.

Including the truth.

Coming Soon from Kelly Fox

Wrecked: Sanctuary

(Nick and Elijah; January 2020)

Wrecked: Surrender

(Jake and Jean-Pierre; February 2020)

Wrecked: Stillness

(Roly and Heath; March 2020)

Want to know what projects I have coming up? Check out my Facebook reader group The Fox Den for giveaways, first-look cover reveals, and more, and follow me on Amazon to be notified of new releases by email.